"Go home, Bo, and leave my kid alone."

"Sorry, I can't do that."

She was halfway through the door and she quickly swung back. "What?"

"I promised Luci I would play with her."

"No!" Becky walked out onto the porch, and her blue eyes were doing their usual thing, sending daggers his way. "Stay away from my daughter."

"Why does it make you so nervous that I'm talking to Luci?"

"It doesn't." She brushed a flyaway strand of hair behind her ear, belying that statement.

"Who's Luci's father?"

He thought the question would spike her blood pressure, but she was very calm, staring at him with cool eyes. "And that concerns you how?"

"It doesn't."

"Good, we're clear on that. Now please stay away from my daughter."

He strolled across the street and knew he wasn't going to do as she'd asked. His interest was piqued. What was Becky hiding?

Dear Reader,

How many times have you said *I'm sorry*? A lot, right? How many times have you meant it? Probably not so many. I grew up with three brothers and we fought all the time. My mom would make us say *I'm sorry*, but we never meant it.

Bo Goodnight and Becky Tullous fell in love in high school and Bo promised her forever, but he bailed on her and joined the army. When he comes home, he repeatedly tells her how sorry he is and he can't understand why she can't forgive him. It was simple: she doesn't feel his *I'm sorry* in her heart, and until that happens, she can't forgive him. As kids we're taught to say the words, but as adults the words have no meaning unless the other person feels them in his or her heart.

Bo and Becky are now older and back home at the same time reliving old memories. But will that be enough to guarantee a happy ending for them?

With love and thanks,

Linda

PS: You can email me at Lw1508@aol.com, send me a message on Facebook.com/authorlindawarren, find me on Twitter, @texauthor, write me at PO Box 5182, Bryan, TX 77805 or visit my website at lindawarren.net. Your mail and thoughts are deeply appreciated.

HEARTWARMING

A Christmas Proposal

—

Linda Warren

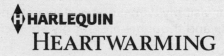

HARLEQUIN
HEARTWARMING

⒣ HARLEQUIN®
HEARTWARMING™

ISBN-13: 978-1-335-88998-0

A Christmas Proposal

Copyright © 2020 by Linda Warren

Recycling programs
for this product may
not exist in your area.

This edition published by arrangement with Harlequin Books S.A.

For questions and comments about the quality of this book,
please contact us at CustomerService@Harlequin.com.

Harlequin Enterprises ULC
22 Adelaide St. West, 40th Floor
Toronto, Ontario M5H 4E3, Canada
www.Harlequin.com

Printed in U.S.A.

Two-time RITA® Award–nominated author **Linda Warren** has written over forty books for Harlequin. A native Texan, she's a member of Romance Writers of America and the RWA West Houston chapter. Drawing upon her years of growing up on a ranch, she writes about some of her favorite things: Western-style romance, cowboys and country life. She married her high school sweetheart and they live on a lake in central Texas. He fishes and she writes. Works perfect.

Books by Linda Warren

Harlequin Heartwarming

Texas Rebels

A Child's Gift
To Save a Child

Harlequin Western Romance

Texas Rebels

Texas Rebels: Egan
Texas Rebels: Falcon
Texas Rebels: Quincy
Texas Rebels: Jude
Texas Rebels: Phoenix
Texas Rebels: Paxton
Texas Rebels: Elias

Visit the Author Profile page
at Harlequin.com for more titles.

To Christi Hendricks—for all the book signings through the years.

CHAPTER ONE

"LOAD UP. WE have a situation." Lieutenant Nancy Haskins's voice boomed through the intercom system.

SWAT officer Beauregard Goodnight grabbed his ballistic helmet, goggles and scoped sniper rifle, and crawled into the SWAT Hummer with his teammates. The lieutenant slid into the passenger seat and Theodore Kopenski, better known as Speed because he had a thing for racing cars, took the driver's seat. Six officers sat in the back ready to face the dark underbelly of Austin's society.

"Listen up." His boss's strong voice echoed in the Hummer. This was the first time Bo had reported directly to a woman, and the lieutenant was strong, confident and didn't take crap from anyone. She could bust a man's chops just as hard as their male commander. "We have a fifteen-year-old pregnant girl and a sixteen-year-old boy holed up in a house in East Austin. A neighbor called and said she heard screaming and went to check to see if anything was wrong. The boy said they were just horsing around. She continued to hear screaming and went back over. He told her to mind her own business. She called the cops and the boy told them that nothing was wrong. They called us for a better assessment since the girl is pregnant. The girl's name is Melissa Tate and the boy is Bradley Taylor. Need information, Patel."

Kyle Patel was the geek on the squad, in charge of all technology and robotics. There wasn't anything he couldn't find on a computer. He always sat behind the lieutenant to give her the information she needed.

His hands flew across the keyboard. Isaiah Williams, otherwise known as Preacher, asked everyone to bow their heads. Preacher was about six foot four and weighed 260 pounds, and no one ever objected when he asked them to pray. He did the same thing every time they left the station and also when they returned. He was the negotiator on the squad and was known for his ability to con a con.

Caden James sat next to Preacher. His family owned a large ranch outside of Austin and in his younger days he'd been a bronc rider. Almost every day there was one woman or another waiting for him. He was the ladies' man of the group and was often teased about it. Because he was a diehard cowboy, when the combat boots came off, the cowboy boots went on. He was a bomb and explosives expert.

Across from him was Cordero Cruz. He was the shortest man on the team and what he missed in height he made up for in speed. If they needed someone to get in and out quickly, they always called on Cruz. He could scale a building faster than anyone. He had an unflappable personality and was always smiling, except when they were on a scene. He was the team's medical tech.

Bo sat on the end across from Malachi Hutchinson, known as Hutch. He was a firearms expert and a sniper, as was Bo. They worked in tandem and some days it was hard for Bo to fit into that mode, but he'd slowly learned to trust and to work as part of a group. His life depended on it, as did that of every member of the team.

"Cruz, James, give me a hand." Patel was speaking and Bo listened closely. "Information on Taylor was easy to find on Facebook.

He's a junior in high school and is scheduled to graduate early. He's an honor student and has a Harvard scholarship waiting. He lives with his mother, Tina, who rents the house from Frost Realty. The lease is up June 1. At that time Taylor is supposed to join his mother in Dallas. She moved there to be with a guy she met on the internet.

"Melissa Tate's life is written all over media accounts and lived with her grandmother due to the fact that her parents moved to California six months ago for her father's job. She's also an honor student and as soon as the school year ends, which is a week away, she's supposed to join her parents in California. There is no information that Melissa is pregnant.

"Got quick responses from the school and the grandmother and neither is aware of a pregnancy. The grandmother said Melissa left two days ago to stay with her boyfriend to study. The mother is supposed to be there, according to the grandma. I've messaged Taylor's mother on Facebook and she's finally answered. She's unaware of any pregnancy with the girlfriend. She says the neighbor is just nosy. I've asked her to call her son and get him to open the door."

"Hold on," the lieutenant said. "We're almost there and hopefully the young man has complied."

Bo stared down at his combat boots, perfectly shined without a speck of dust on them, mentally preparing himself for the scene ahead.

In Afghanistan, dealing with the enemy had become routine. He'd been a soldier fighting in a war and it was his duty. Back home in the States, it wasn't so easy. Thank God he hadn't had to kill anyone. He'd shot a man in the arm and another in the leg to avoid taking a life. He had honed his skills overseas and today he could place a bullet just about anywhere he wanted to. That wasn't bragging. It was a skill he'd learned to stay alive. And to save lives.

If the boy was holding the girl against her will, they would have to go in. He would do his job to save the girl. When on a job, by sheer force of willpower, he didn't sweat, nor did his hands get clammy and neither did they shake. He went into his own zone in his head, one he could control.

He sat on the end in the Hummer. That was his thing, and everyone knew it. He had to be the first one out to assess the situation. Of course, that was probably news to the lieutenant, but the guys knew.

"Taylor's mother said he's not answering his phone," Patel announced.

The Hummer swerved in behind two cop cars. Speed had lived up to his name. They were in a mostly rental area in a run-down neighborhood. Brightly colored houses dotted the street and people gathered around, wanting to know what was going on.

"Stand ready for orders!" the lieutenant shouted. She stopped a minute to speak to the cops. The bright May sunshine sparkled with light and freshness in the early morning as a dog barked and murmurs echoed. The team stood ready. "Secure the perimeter!" the lieutenant shouted again. "Goodnight, stay with me."

He hated it when she singled him out like a rank rookie, but he stood by her side as she fired questions at the cops.

"How long has the couple been in there?"

"We've been here about thirty minutes and Mrs. Gonzales—" he pointed to the woman standing behind him "—heard the girl scream about an hour and a half ago. The girl came to the window to show she was okay and told an officer they were just fooling around. We called SWAT before we broke down the door for no reason. We didn't want to look like idiots."

"All clear in back," James said into his shoulder mic. "There's a back door, but all the blinds are drawn and there's no way to see inside without breaking a window."

"Stand ready," the lieutenant replied, walking to the front door. They all wore Kevlar protective vests and panels, and she stood slightly to the side in case someone started shooting. With her right hand she banged on the door. "This is Lieutenant Haskins with SWAT. Could you please come to the door?"

"We haven't done anything wrong!" the boy shouted back.

"There's a pregnant girl in there and we have to know that she's okay."

"She is. She just wants everyone to leave us alone."

The lieutenant walked back to where Bo and the cops were standing. "There's a small glass window in the front door. Has anyone looked inside?"

"We don't have anyone tall enough," a cop replied. "It's, like, two inches by two inches and about six inches from the top of the door. It's weird. We can't understand why someone would put a piece of glass there. There's about a ten-inch step up into the house, which puts the little pane out of our reach. Mrs. Gonzales was going to get a chair we could stand on when you arrived."

"You're tall, Goodnight. See if you can get a look through that small pane."

"Yes, ma'am."

He bounded toward the door. Grass scraped against his combat boots and the wind blew a disposable cup into his path. His boot crushed it; his focus never wavered. In a sweeping glance he took in the perimeter. Grass and weeds grew onto the sidewalk and into the flower beds. Someone hadn't tended to the yard in a long time. It looked as if no one lived there. As opposed to the yellow house next door, which had blooming flowers reaching for the sunshine in a yard that was neatly maintained.

He went up the steps and stood on his tiptoes to get a glance through the little window. At six foot two he still had to strain to see. Once he did, tension gripped his body and without a second thought he jammed his shoulder against the door to pop it open.

He leaped over the coffee table to get to the girl on the couch giving birth. Blood had soaked into the cushions and dripped onto the carpet. Her knees were drawn up and the baby was almost out. That's what Bo had seen—a blue baby with the umbilical cord around its neck. Time was crucial for the baby. He fell down beside the couch and reached for the pocket knife on his duty belt to cut the cord. The baby slid into his waiting hands.

"What's wrong? What's wrong?" the boy asked. "It wasn't supposed to be like this. What's wrong?"

Bo didn't have time to deal with the boy. The baby wasn't breathing. He jerked off his gloves, stuck his finger into her mouth and cleaned out the mucus. The baby still wasn't breathing. He had to do CPR. He placed two fingers near the center of her breastbone and did compressions and then tilted her tiny head and covered her nose and mouth and blew. He had to be careful because her bones were very delicate. He repeated the procedure.

"Come on, little angel. Come on." Her eyes were closed and her blood-covered blue body was limp. "Come on, little angel. Give me a breath. One little breath." He heard a whimper and stopped compressions. He waited. "Breathe, little angel."

The baby turned her head toward the sound and Bo placed his hand over her tiny chest. Her heart began to thud against his palm. "Yes!" He grabbed a blanket that was on the end table and wrapped it around the baby and his hand, making sure to keep her warm. If he removed his hand, he was afraid she would stop breathing.

"The ambulance is here," the lieutenant said, and Bo hadn't even realized the whole team stood in the room, watching. Cruz and Preacher were attending to the girl.

Cruz stood and nodded, meaning the girl was gone.

"What?" the boy asked, and then the meaning became clear to him, too. He shook his head. "No. She's just tired. She's been in labor all night. She's just tired. No!"

Preacher put his arm around the boy and Bo walked out of the room with the baby cradled in his right arm.

"Goodnight," the lieutenant called. "The paramedics will take care of the baby."

"No, ma'am. I'm not taking my hand off the baby's chest. I'm going to the hospital with her."

"Goodnight—"

He walked out the door even though he knew he would catch flak for it, but he wasn't letting go of the baby, even if it cost him his job. The paramedic tried to take her and Bo said again, "I'm afraid if I remove my hand, her heart will stop."

In the back of the ambulance, the paramedic placed a warming blanket around the baby then used a warm wipe to remove blood from the baby's face and clean the gook from her eyes. He was on the phone to the hospital, giving a status report.

"Her heart rate is low. An officer has a hand on her chest and doesn't want to remove it in case her heart stops. Okay. Got it." He turned to Bo and Bo prayed they had time to make it to the hospital. "The doctor says okay. Push it," he said to the driver, and they zoomed through traffic and red lights, the siren blaring all the way.

The ambulance came to a screeching halt at the ER entrance. Bo got out, ran into the emergency room and carefully laid the baby on a gurney with his hand still on her chest. He blinked at the bright lights and realized he still had his helmet on.

Three nurses and a doctor were in the

room. The doctor came around to where Bo stood. "Officer, you can remove your hand now."

"Her heart started beating again when I placed my hand on her chest and I'm afraid to remove it."

The doctor reached under the blanket and placed his hand over Bo's. "I got it."

Bo slowly removed his hand and stepped back. "I'll be outside. Would you please let me know how she's doing?"

"Yes," the doctor replied. "We'll be taking her to pediatric ICU, but someone will let you know. Thank you, officer."

Bo walked out of the room, gave a long sigh, removed his helmet and came face-to-face with the woman he'd loved most of his life. Rebecca Tullous. Her blue eyes opened wide as she saw his blood-soaked grayish-green SWAT uniform.

She rushed forward. "Bo, are you okay?" At the worry in her eyes he knew she still loved him, but getting her to admit that would be like pulling out his own teeth with his fingers. Becky was never going to love him again. And it was his fault.

"Yeah, I'm fine. I just brought in a newly

delivered baby and I'm waiting to see if she's going to be okay."

Becky was as beautiful as the first day he'd met her. Blue eyes and long blond hair were always a trigger for him, but there was also something different about Becky. She was sweet, kind and loving, and touched a part of his heart that had just been waiting for someone to love. At seventeen years of age, he'd fallen in love for the first and only time in his life.

When they met, her father had just moved them from Dallas to Horseshoe and she wasn't happy. She missed her friends and wanted to go back. Bo had offered to show her around the school and introduce her to people. From that moment forward they'd been an item, boyfriend-girlfriend and later much more. He'd never wanted to be away from her. But then the devil had heaped a whole lot of misery on him and he'd done what every teenager would do in that situation. He ran.

"Oh." She stepped away from him quickly as she realized how close she was. "I was just waiting for Dr. Eames." Dr. Janet Eames was a gynecologist and head of a women's center connected with the hospital. Becky was her physician's assistant and a breast cancer advocate, since her mother had died from breast cancer.

"I—I have to go. Hope the baby's okay."

As she turned away, he couldn't resist. "Bec, could we talk?" For almost eighteen years he'd been asking her that question and always gotten the same answer. It wasn't going to be any different today, but he kept trying. He should get points for that.

At a glance he could see the worry replaced by a blazing fury, and it was directed straight at him. "No, we have nothing to talk about. We've talked it to death and for me it's over. It's time you realized that."

As he watched her sashay down the hall, a white medical jacket over her scrubs, he knew she was right. He'd burned his bridges with Becky, but he'd walk through hell to get back to her.

With a deep sigh he swung around to face another angry woman—his lieutenant. His teammates stood behind her. This just wasn't his day. He'd disobeyed a direct order and from the look on her face she was ready to tear a strip off of him a mile wide. But he'd do it all over again for that little girl.

Almost four years later...

"GOODNIGHT, MY OFFICE!" Lieutenant Haskins's voice blasted through the intercom as Bo pulled a black T-shirt over his head. He'd just finished his shift and was ready to go home and sleep a few hours before he returned. His teammates stopped what they were doing and looked at him.

"What did you do now, Sarge?" Cruz asked. Bo was now leader of the team under the lieutenant and the commander.

"I'm sure one of you did something wrong," he replied in a good-natured way. "And I'm supposed to explain your actions."

"I'll pray for your soul," Preacher said as he picked up his carryall and headed for the door. Everyone laughed. Bo made his way to the lieutenant's office.

He walked in and stood at attention with his hands behind his back, waiting for her to speak. She took her time writing in a file. In her forties, her brown hair was cut in a short, no-fuss style. On her left hand was a gold wedding band, no frills for the lieutenant.

She was as straitlaced as they came and held everyone accountable for their actions. Blue blood ran in her family—her dad was a cop, her brother was a cop and her husband was head of Vice. She closed the file and raised her head. Displeasure emanated from her cool green eyes. *Nope.* This wasn't about the team. It was about him personally.

"As of today you are on a one-week vacation."

"Excuse me?"

"You heard me, Goodnight."

"May I ask why?"

"It has come to my attention and the commander's that you haven't had a day off in two months. You've been taking other cops' shifts. You took Beal's duties on the night shift twice, each for four days. That meant you were working twenty-four hours around the clock and that is unacceptable. From now on, your shifts will be monitored by me."

"Come on, Lieutenant, I was just helping some guys out. There are a lot of family things like weddings, births and deaths. The guys like to be there for those."

The lieutenant got to her feet, her eyes as cool as metal. "That is not your concern. They can ask for time off when these things happen. I didn't expect this from you, Goodnight. You're a sergeant now and second in command under me. You have to be mentally focused and physically fit to control a scene, and a sleep-deprived sergeant cannot do that."

"I beg to differ." The moment the words left his mouth he knew they were the wrong words.

"Are you bucking for two weeks off?"

He squared his shoulders. "No, ma'am."

"I don't want to see you at the station until next Monday and then we'll have this conversation all over again. Maybe I'll be in a better mood and maybe you'll be more receptive to listening."

"Yes, ma'am."

"You're dismissed."

He swung out the door, angry, and took a couple of deep breaths to steady himself. She didn't understand that he needed to work. Work was his life. If he wasn't working, he was thinking and that was pure torture. As long as he was active, the past stayed in his rearview mirror. And now...

The guys waited for him. They were a team and knew each other's strengths and weaknesses. When they had accomplished some amazing task, they called themselves the magnificent seven. That was on a good day. On a bad day they stood like disobedient soldiers being dressed down by a woman who always seemed to be stronger than they were. And today she'd hit him where it hurt.

"What's up?" Hutch asked.

He grabbed his carryall and threw it over his shoulder. "I was given a week's vacation for taking other guys' shifts."

"Oh." James got to his feet with a frown. They all knew he liked to work and that time off wasn't his thing. "Take it like a man, Sarge. That's all you can do."

"Yeah. See you guys in a week."

Bo headed for his truck in a bad mood. He sat there, looking out at the scenery. It was late September and the heat of summer held on with a fierce grip, but fall had nudged its way into the scenery and atmosphere. The green grass wasn't so green anymore and the leaves on the trees were just waiting for a gust of wind to set them free. The Texas sky was an umbrella of beautiful blue.

As a cop he'd been just about everywhere in Austin from the Colorado River to Barton Springs to the Hill Country to Lake Travis to Lake Austin to the University of Texas and everywhere in between, especially Sixth Street with the music and the bars. That's where he'd made most of his arrests. His favorite place was the state capital. From where he was parked he could see the Goddess of Liberty atop the capital building.

When he was nine, he and his best friend Cole had gone on a school field trip to the capital. There was so much history in the building to see, but he and Cole were fixated on the portrait of Davy Crockett, who died at the Alamo, and his coonskin cap. They each wanted one just like it. Standing in the rotunda, arm in arm, staring up at the Texas Star, they were Texas proud.

But today he wasn't interested in seeing any of Austin. What did a guy do when there was nowhere to go and nothing to do? He went home.

CHAPTER TWO

Bo TURNED OFF Highway 77 and headed for Horseshoe, a little town that seemed to be in the middle of nowhere, southeast of Austin yet closer to Temple. No sights to see here. Nothing but hardworking people. The limestone courthouse took pride of place on the town square; the sheriff's office was connected with a walkway. Quaint and innovative shops surrounded it. Some had been there from the beginning, like the bakery and the diner.

Crepe myrtles dressed up the place and around July they would be in full bloom, giving the courthouse a spiffy look for the Fourth celebration. He'd missed it for the last several years. Coming home was never easy.

Tall, gnarled oaks shaded the square and two old men sat on a bench talking as the American and Texas flags flapped high in the sky. He was home.

Bo's best friend Cole was now the chief investigator for the DA and worked as a deputy when needed. Bo wanted to stop in and see him but, figuring he would be busy, thought better of it and turned off Main to Liberty Street where his mother lived.

As much as he liked his hometown it always blindsided him with bad memories. Sad, painful memories. He'd been five when his dad left them for the first time. His mom, Ava, worked at the grocery store and couldn't support them on her own so they'd had to move in with Grandma and Grandpa Goodnight. He liked it on the farm and he liked the outdoors. Bo worshipped the ground his grandpa walked on and he'd been happy.

But three years later Mason Goodnight had returned, apologized and asked Ava for forgiveness. And she'd taken him back. They'd moved into a tiny apartment where Bo and his younger sister Kelsey had to share a room. All Bo had wanted was to go back to his grandparents, but his mother wouldn't let him. She wanted him to try and forgive his father. Bo did his best and life settled down.

Two years later his dad left with a woman he'd met at Rowdy's beer joint. That had lasted about a year, and then he'd returned with more excuses and Bo's mother had taken him back once again. Bo couldn't understand how his mother could do that and there was no forgiveness left in Bo.

His dad had gotten a job at a car dealership in Temple and they'd bought a three-bedroom brick house on Liberty Street. His mom had said that his daddy had changed and Bo really wanted to believe that. So, once again, life had settled down. His dad came home every night and they were a family. But Bo never lost those doubts.

One day he'd thrown up in school and the teacher wanted to call his mom to come get him, but he'd told her that his mom was working and couldn't get off. After calling Ava and making sure it was okay, the teacher took him home on her break.

His dad's truck had been out in front of the house and Bo had thought that was strange. But then he'd thought that maybe his father had gotten off work early. When he'd opened the door and heard moaning, it occurred to him that his dad might be home sick, too.

He'd gone to his parents' bedroom and stood frozen in the doorway. Two naked people were in the bed and the woman wasn't his mother. The woman noticed him, and she and his father started scrambling for the covers. Bo had wanted to run out of the house, but instead he went to his bedroom and got the shotgun his grandfather had given him.

He'd charged back into the room and pointed the gun at his father's bare chest. "Get out!" he'd shouted.

"Son…"

The woman darted past him, half-dressed. "I didn't sign up for this, babe."

"Get out!" Bo screamed once again, his finger on the trigger. His body had been shaking and sweat broke out on his forehead.

His dad had grabbed his shirt and followed the woman. When Bo heard the truck start, he walked into the living room, sat on the sofa and placed the shotgun across his legs. He was still sitting there when his mother came home.

He'd told her what had happened and she was devastated. They held each other that day and his mother had cried on his shoulder for what happened and what had been done to Bo. He'd wanted to cry, too, but he was almost twelve years old and too old for that.

His mom allowed his dad back into the house to get his things and they hadn't seen him again until Bo's grandfather passed away when Bo was sixteen. His dad had come to the funeral. It had been hard, losing his grandfather and having to deal with his dad at the same time.

Mason had always been his mother's favorite, though. He was gifted musically, and played guitar and piano, and that was how he was making a living, working in different bands. When that didn't pay the bills, he'd get a regular job.

At the funeral Mason had played the organ and sung, at his mother's request. He had done a beautiful rendition of "Amazing Grace," even Bo had had to admit that. Mason left soon after and neither Bo's mom, Bo nor Kelsey had spoken to him. Bo had hoped that was the end of his father disrupting their lives.

But when Bo graduated from high school, his father came for the ceremony. Bo had seen his mom talking to him. That blew Bo's mind. He just couldn't stay in Horseshoe if his mom was going to take his dad back once again. That wasn't something he could handle. He and Cole talked, as they had so many times, and decided to join the army to get away from their dysfunctional families.

Bo had one problem, though. He was in love with Becky, the girl who lived across the street. They had made plans, like getting married and having a family of their own. But she would understand. He just knew it.

He'd been wrong.

She was furious with him for taking the easy way out of a family problem. She told him to face his dad and talk to him like a man instead of running. But back then running was all that was on his mind, because deep down he was afraid he might really hurt the man who had given him life.

Becky had said, "If you go, that will be the end of us. I won't be waiting for you."

He'd tried to cajole her into taking back what she'd said. She wouldn't. But he hadn't worried because they loved each other and she would forgive him. That thought lasted in his head until a year later when he got the news that she'd married someone else. Then he knew she'd meant it.

Memories. Good ol' memories were waiting for him right here in Horseshoe, Texas, on Liberty Street. As he neared the house he saw his mother's car in the garage and a truck pulled up behind it. He didn't recognize the truck. He parked at the curb and went in through the garage door.

His mom was talking to someone and the

answering voice lit a fuse that burned Bo all the way to his soul. He knew that voice. His dad was here. He marched into the room, the fire burning deeper into his chest.

He pointed a finger at his father. "Get out!"

"Bo, I didn't know you were coming home," his mother said, wiping her hands down her jeans in a nervous gesture.

"Obviously. How long has he been coming here?"

"Bo, really? This anger is out of place after all these years."

"I'll leave, Ava," Mason said in a smooth, lyrical voice and Bo looked at his father for the first time in a long time. His dark hair, likely dyed, was down to his shoulders and a bandanna was tied around his head. From the full beard, worn jeans, sneakers and brightly colored shirt, Bo knew his father was in a band again. People said Bo looked like him and he supposed they were right. Same dark hair and eyes, but Bo didn't see any resemblance beyond that.

His mother stepped closer. "Bo, this is my house and I'm speaking to your father. That's it."

"For the record, this is not your house. It's mine. I've worked since I was fifteen years old to help you pay the mortgage because—" he flung a hand at his father "—he bailed on you. He bailed on his family and he is not welcome here."

His father walked out, but Bo followed him, as did his mother.

"Bo, stop this," his mother ordered.

"I didn't come here to argue, son."

"Don't call me *son*." The word infuriated Bo. The rage inside him ballooned and he couldn't seem to control it. How dare Mason come back after all these years?

His father turned to face him on the front lawn. "I am your father whether you want to admit it or not."

"You're not my father in any meaning of the word."

"I made mistakes…"

"Oh, please, I don't want to hear your mistakes, excuses or lies. My mom falls for them, but I don't." Bo pointed to the house. "This house is in my name and you are not welcome here ever again. Do you understand what I mean?"

"What's going on here?"

Bo swung around to face Becky and he suddenly realized he was standing in the front yard yelling. The flame died inside him and he took a long breath.

Why was Becky here? She lived in Austin. Whenever he did come home they always seemed to miss each other, which suited them both.

"I could hear y'all yelling from inside my dad's house and it's upsetting my daughter. Please consider others when you want to act like two-year-olds."

"I'm sorry, Becky," his mother said. "But there will be no more yelling, will there?" She looked straight at Bo.

His father got in his truck and drove away, and the weight on Bo's shoulders pressed down a little deeper and made him realize that someday soon he would have to deal with his feelings about his father.

He turned to face Becky and her angry blue eyes. He was so tired of her anger. It was so different than the love he used to see in her. "I'm sorry if I disturbed your daughter."

In shorts and a sleeveless top, she reminded him of a time when he'd crawl through her window just to spend time with her, and when he was the most important person in her life. Now she had a child who wasn't his. That was hard to take on top of everything else. He'd destroyed the one thing that was good about him—Becky's love.

"Thank you." She strolled back across the street without another word, and Bo and his mother walked into the house.

"How could you?" his mother asked.

"That's my question," he shot back. She wasn't going to make him feel guilty. He had every right to be angry, but maybe not to the extent that he was.

"Why bring up the house? Do you want me to move out? Yes, you paid for it. I couldn't have made it without you. Throwing it in my face is very rude and that's not like you."

She took a breath. "And for the record, Mason didn't come here for money or asking for a place to stay. He's in a band and they're doing very well. They're playing in Austin, Temple, Killeen and a lot of other small towns. He stopped by to see how I was doing and asked about his kids. And, yes, you are one of his kids, and I can talk to whoever I please."

Bo sank onto the sofa and leaned his head back against the cushions, wondering if this day could get much worse. "I was way out of line, but he does that to me and I can't help it."

"Why? You have a good job as a sergeant on a SWAT team. You're in control of your life. Mason has never been. He smokes too much, drinks too much and parties too much. He wakes up in a new world every day and I'm so happy you're not like him. You're my responsible, stubborn son and I'm so proud of you."

Oh, man. She was driving the last nail into his coffin of guilt. "Sometimes I'm not so in control, like today. I'm sorry for mentioning the house. The reason I put the house in my name was because I didn't want *him* coming back here and you letting him in. It gave me some control. You're notorious for falling for all his lies. That's fact. That's truth. But this house is yours. I have my own place."

Ava sat in a chair across from him and he raised his head to look at her. With green eyes and blond hair, she didn't look more than forty, but she'd turned fifty-three two months ago.

Her whole life had been a struggle. Her parents had been killed in an accident and she had moved to Horseshoe to live with her older sister. That's how she'd met Mason and they married right out of high school. They traveled with a band and lived out of suitcases until Bo started school, and then they stayed in a little apartment his dad had rented in town. Bo didn't remember much about that time, but it couldn't have been easy for his mother with two small children. He just wanted her life to be easy. She deserved it.

"I'm sorry my temper got the best of me."

"You know, we never really talked about this. We just dealt with it the best way we could. But today, I want to talk about all the bad stuff." Her hair was in a short bob and she brushed it back behind her ears. He noted that it was now streaked with a little gray. She was getting older. He just didn't want to see it.

"That first love is powerful, so powerful that it's something you'll never forget and you'll never feel again. When I met your dad in school, he was always singing with his guitar, girls all around him. Once he looked at me my heart just filled with love, kind of like he wrapped my heart in velvet. It was warm, so warm that I've never felt anything like it again.

"After a while, I needed that warmth. I craved it. Every time your father came back my heart filled with that warmth and I wanted him back in my life. I needed him.

But the day I came home and my little boy was sitting on the couch with a shotgun across his lap, all that warmth I had inside for him turned cold. Icy cold. As I held my trembling boy I knew I would never feel that warmth again." She paused and looked at him. "I will never take your father back again and I haven't been with him since then. I don't love him anymore."

"But he came back when I graduated."

"And he left soon after. He asked to come back, but I said no. I told him then that I didn't love him anymore."

Bo frowned. "Why didn't you tell me this at the time?"

"I did, but you didn't believe me, remember?"

He remembered and a chill ran through him. He hadn't believed her back then. Why? he asked himself now. Why was he so hell-bent on leaving everything he loved?

"Oh, man." He ran his hands up his face as so much of the past became clear. Everything was his fault. How did he go back and change things? Could he go back and make Becky love him again?

The truth was…he couldn't. He stood, walked over to the window and looked out at the Tullous house. He was beginning to see this week's vacation as something good. Maybe now that they were in familiar surroundings he could get her to listen to him. But there was the kid. He had no idea who the father was, as Becky had divorced her husband a long time ago. It had been eighteen years since high school. Was there a way back? He honestly didn't know, but if he was known for anything, it was his tenacity. He strolled across the street.

CHAPTER THREE

"WHAT. HAPPEN?" Becky's bright-eyed baby girl asked.

"Just two guys arguing. Nothing to worry about." Unless you're a member of the Goodnight family, and they weren't.

"Like. You. And. Grand. Pa."

Becky leaned down and said, "Say it in a complete sentence, baby."

"No. No. No! I. Can't! You. Don't. Love. Me!" Luci ran to the sofa and buried her face in a pillow, crying.

Becky had to restrain herself from comforting her daughter. It was hard. Her child had been a preemie and had some developmental delays. They'd made so much progress, and she was catching up with other children her age in so many ways, except for her speech. She paused after each word and some days it was nerve-racking, but Becky wasn't giving up on her daughter. She just didn't have the strength to force her.

Her dad, Craig, stood in the kitchen, watching her. With his brown hair, blue eyes and friendly face, she'd always thought her dad was super-cool and handsome. He'd been her hero until… She cleared her throat and looked away. Even though he was in his fifties he was still worrying about her.

"Don't say it." She reached for a cup in the cabinet and filled it with coffee.

"Luci needs to talk correctly. She does so in the therapist's office and you need to make her talk the same way at home. I know it hurts you when she cries and says you don't love her, but you have to be the adult. You have to do it, Rebecca."

She sat at the kitchen table with her coffee, feeling maxed out. The pediatrician and pediatric therapist were saying the same thing, and yet when Luci cried, Becky always caved. It just broke her heart to watch her child struggle and Becky was hoping against hope that Luci would start talking correctly on her own.

She didn't want Luci to be bullied when she went to school next year. She glanced to where her daughter lay with a pillow over her head. Purr, the cat, sat on top of the pillow. Becky immediately got to her feet, not wanting her baby to be smothered. Pink, the basset hound, licked Luci's face beneath the pillow and she giggled. Everything was fine—except it wasn't.

Her dad sat across from her. "What was all the yelling about?"

"Mason is back."

"Ava's ex-husband?"

"The one and only. Bo was kicking him out. Hence all the yelling."

"Was Ava upset?"

Her dad had had an accident about four years earlier and had been in critical condition for a while. Becky didn't know what she would've done if it hadn't been for Ava, who had looked out for her dad and brought him food while Becky was at work. They'd gotten close, and so had her dad and Ava. But they never talked about Bo. That subject was off-limits.

"I suppose, but I didn't ask since Bo was there and quite angry."

"He has every right to be and I hope Ava refuses to see Mason."

Becky looked at her dad. "Oh, you're on Ava's side."

"She deserves better than that louse."

"I agree, but it's none of our business." She opened her laptop to update some charts.

"Really, Rebecca? You came home for the weekend and you're going to work?" He glanced to where Luci lay. "You need to deal with Luci and you need to talk to Bo."

"Talk to Bo? Whatever for?"

"You need to talk about the past and tell him how you really feel. You need to air everything out, even if it hurts, that's the only way you can heal. That's the only way you can go forward."

"Dad, I'm over Bo Goodnight and I don't need to talk to him."

Her dad got to his feet with a scowl on his face. "You were stubborn as a kid and you were stubborn as a teenager and you're more stubborn as an adult." Having had his say, he marched to the French doors and out into the backyard.

Becky stared after him. What had gotten into her father? He was usually very supportive, but obviously he was upset about something. She still wasn't talking to Bo. The past was best left in the past, along with the heartache and pain.

She leaned back in the chair and allowed herself to think about Bo. He'd done very well for himself, but then, he liked living life on the edge. It suited him. Every day he did his job his way, regardless of the consequences. He'd always lived like that, a daredevil, a foolish, impulsive, inconsiderate daredevil. That's what made him so appealing. That's what she had loved about him at one time.

She wasn't a teenager anymore and his dark good looks didn't move her like before. Oh, she was lying. When she had confronted him in the yard, she'd wanted to reach out and touch those hard muscles in his shoulders, to feel those strong arms around her. He wasn't a lanky teenager anymore. He'd filled out nicely. Her pulse leaped at the thought and she knew without a doubt she couldn't talk to Bo ever again. He was her weakness—that was her secret. Bo would never be a part of her life again.

Bo STROLLED ACROSS the street into enemy territory. A little blonde girl, pigtails tied with pink ribbons, sat on the porch. She wore pink shorts and a top that had balloons on it, and there were even pink shoelaces on her sneakers. The little girl liked pink. An orange tabby curled around her and a brown-and-white basset hound lay beside her. A frown marred her pretty face.

He squatted in front of her. "What's your name?"

"Luci."

"And who are these guys?" He pointed to the cat and the dog.

"Pink. And. Purr."

"Why are you frowning?"

"My. Mommy. Mad. At. Me."

Why is she pausing after each word?

"Why?" He didn't know a lot about kids, but this one was as different as he'd ever seen and he didn't want to upset her.

"I. Can't. Talk. Right."

He could see it was a real effort to get the words out and he wasn't sure what to say.

"Nobody. Likes. Me."

"I like you."

"You. Do?" Her blue eyes lit up as bright as stars.

"You betcha. I love blue-eyed little girls. And big ones, too."

She giggled. "Can. You. Be. My. Friend?"

"It would be my pleasure." Bo had thought he wouldn't like the kid because of the circumstances of her birth. He wasn't her father. Bo realized at that moment that she was a sweet little girl with problems and in no way would he ever feel any differently about her. He actually wanted to help her.

"Can. You. Play. With. Me?"

"Sure thing."

The door opened and Becky stood there. "Luci, come into the house, please."

Luci got to her feet and obediently went inside.

He stood. "What's up, Bec?"

"Go home, Bo, and leave my kid alone."

"Sorry, I can't do that."

She was halfway through the door and she quickly swung back. "What?"

"I promised Luci I would play with her."

"No!" Becky walked out onto the porch and her blue eyes were doing their usual thing, sending daggers his way. "Stay away from my daughter."

"What's wrong with Luci?" he asked as if she hadn't said anything.

"It's none of your business."

"Bec, I'm going to keep on keeping on. You know me. I never stop until I get answers so you might as well tell me."

Her eyes narrowed. "Will you stay away from Luci if I tell you?"

"Maybe."

"What does that mean? Oh, forget it." She waved a hand at him. "If you want to know, I'll tell you because, like you said, you'll just keep on until you make me angry. Luci was a preemie. She was born six weeks early and she has some developmental delays. That's all."

"Like what?"

"She didn't roll over until she was eight months old and she was a year before she could crawl. It took two years before she could walk, but she has slowly caught up with other kids her age, except for her speech and we're working on that. I'd appreciate it if you would just stay away and not get involved."

"Why does it make you so nervous that I'm talking to Luci?"

"It doesn't." Becky brushed a flyaway strand of hair behind her ear, belying that statement.

Her hair used to be long, and one of his favorite things had been running his fingers through it. Today it was shorter, covering her ears, and tousled. When she worked, she usually wore it up in a knot at the back of her head, professional, prim and proper. But he knew the real Becky, all fire and brimstone with a big dose of heaven.

"Who's Luci's father?"

He thought the question would spike her blood pressure, but she was very calm, staring at him with cool eyes. "And that concerns you how?"

"It doesn't."

"Good, we're clear on that. Now, please stay away from my daughter."

He strolled across the street and knew he wasn't going to do as she'd asked. His interest was piqued. What was Becky hiding and who was Luci's father?

BECKY WENT BACK into the house and straight to the sofa to talk to Luci. She pulled her daughter onto her lap and Luci snuggled against her.

"I. Sorry. Mommy."

She kissed her daughter's forehead. "I love you, no matter what, but we have to work on your speech."

Luci raised her head and frowned.

Becky kissed the frown. She loved this kid with everything she had in her and she never wanted her to feel any pain. "Tomorrow we will start doing some exercises. The therapist says you can do them."

"To-morrow?"

Make her do it now. Make her do it now! But the part of her that protected her daughter couldn't make the leap to mean ol' mommy. "Yes, tomorrow." And hopefully by then Becky would have found a way to do what was best for Luci.

After supper and getting Luci to bed, Becky took a shower and sat in her bedroom trying to face the monumental task before her. Knowing Bo was right across the street made it that much more difficult.

She went to the window and cracked the blind with her finger so she could look at the Goodnight house. Bo's bedroom window faced the street, just as hers did, and when they were teenagers she would blink her bedroom light twice to let him know that her dad was asleep and he could come over.

Her dad had caught them necking in the living room and from then on Bo could only stay until ten o'clock. But Bo had had a job and sometimes he didn't get off until eleven. He worked at the feed store and the hardware store, and bussed tables at the diner to help his mom pay the mortgage.

But when they'd been teenagers there was no stopping them. When Bo got off, he would knock on her window and she would let him in. They'd found their way around the rules. Bo became her whole world. She had to breathe the same air. She had to be with him. It was all about Bo and a fairy-tale life. She'd been young but she'd known she wanted a big family.

They talked and talked about the future and she'd thought Bo wanted the same things, but evidently that had been all in her head. He and his best friend, Cole, started talking about the army and how cool it would be to serve their country. She'd thought it was just talk.

Then Mason came back for Bo's graduation and the next thing she knew Bo and Cole had signed up. That last night she and Bo had made love in his truck by Yaupon Creek. She'd just known she could change his mind. After all, he loved her and she loved him. That should have been enough, but it wasn't.

Sitting in his truck at the curb in front of her house he'd told her that he and Cole were leaving in the morning and he would see her when he was home on leave. He'd made the decision without talking to her and that made her mad. She'd told him then that she wouldn't be waiting for him. He'd tried to cajole her into taking it back, but she wouldn't. She'd been hurt and had jumped out of the truck and run into the house.

The next morning she sat at her window and watched the Goodnight house. She just knew Bo would come over and apologize, and everything would be the same. Ava and Bo had come out of the house, gotten into Bo's truck and driven away. Not once did Bo look back. She'd fallen on the bed and cried, and she cried for many days afterward. She'd finally realized she had to get herself together and live her life alone.

Her dad was president of the bank in Horseshoe and he'd encouraged her to go to college—he would help her pay for it. That first year she'd met Kevin, and for some insane reason she'd married him. It had only lasted a year because she wouldn't sleep with him. She's been so immature and so insecure, and she'd made many bad decisions. She eventually signed up for nursing school and soon realized that what she really wanted to do was to work with breast cancer patients.

Her mother had died from breast cancer. It had made Becky angry that her mother ignored the warning signs of the disease. All it would have taken was a mammogram or self-examination. When the doctors had finally discovered the cancer, it had been too late.

Becky had signed up for the physician's assistant program and was lucky enough to get an internship with Dr. Eames. She'd finally had her dream job and loved it. The scars of her youth had healed and she'd moved on to new friends and a new life. Without Bo. She didn't want him back in her life in any way. He'd hurt her too deeply.

But there was Luci.

If she told Bo about Luci, he would take over and try to control her life. She would never let that happen. Getting over Bo once had been enough. Soon Bo would go back to work and forget about them. He was good at forgetting.

AFTER SUPPER, BO went to his room and pushed the curtains aside to look across the street. Becky's light was on and in his mind he went back to the years he would stand there and wait for the blinks. They'd been teenagers on hormone overload, but he would treasure those years till the day he died. He'd screwed it up and there was no way to go back, so he had to go forward. The first thing he needed to know was—who was Luci's father?

A few years ago Craig had been in a car accident. What month had that been? Early October. Craig had been in bad shape and Becky spent most of her time at the hospital. His mom had offered to sit with Craig so Becky could go home and get some rest. He was visiting Horseshoe and had gone over to tell Becky how sorry he was about her dad. Becky had cried on his shoulder and it was the first time since he'd left for the army that she hadn't pushed him away or told him to leave. One thing led to another, and before they knew it, it was morning and they were tangled in the sheets. But as soon as Becky had opened her eyes she'd started yelling, "Get out. Get out!"

That rang in his head for months and he'd finally had to admit that he and Becky were not getting back together. He pulled his phone out of his pocket and checked dates and then he went to the laptop at his desk. Being a cop, he had access to a lot of information and soon he had Luci's birth certificate in front of him. Mother: Rebecca Diane

Tullous. The father line was blank. Nada. Zip. Nothing on the father.

He sat there for a moment trying to figure it out. Why wasn't Luci's father on record? He reached for his phone again and went over the dates. Luci had been a preemie and the dates would fit. Oh, man! Would Becky do that? Would she keep his daughter from him?

He stood up and glanced out the window again. Was Luci his daughter?

CHAPTER FOUR

WHEN BO GOT up the next morning, his mother had already left for work. He'd heard her moving around earlier, trying to be quiet. But he was a light sleeper. He'd learned that little trick in the army.

He slid out of bed and pulled on his jeans, the smell of coffee urging him forward. After pouring a cup, he leaned against the counter, noticing the note on the refrigerator. He smiled. Oh, how he'd hated those notes when he was a kid. His mom had to be at work before six and since he was the older one he'd been responsible for his sister, who was only two years younger. Being responsible for Kelsey was like having custody of a rattlesnake. One way or another, you were going to get bit.

One thing about his sister—she hadn't liked getting up early, and every school morning it took a dose of courage to deal with her. He'd turn the stereo up to high and she'd put a pillow over her head. He'd drag her out of the bed and she'd curl up on the carpet. He'd put ice in her pajamas and she never budged. The trick that had worked was carrying her to the bathroom, placing her in the tub and turning on the shower. She'd gotten up then, and had come after him with a baseball bat. His smile grew wider.

He credited her aggravating personality to her red hair, which she'd inherited from their grandmother Goodnight. Their grandmother had a firecracker personality and it didn't take much of a spark to set it off. She was one of those eccentric types. If you met her once you never forgot her. And Kelsey had a lot of her qualities.

The note on the refrigerator read, *I'll be home for lunch.* And there was a heart beneath it, like she always put on her notes.

"Really, Mom? I'm not ten and I can fix my own lunch." He ripped the note off and threw it in the garbage can. That was his mom's job, though, looking out for them her whole life.

Considering their turbulent childhood, he and Kelsey turned out pretty good. She'd wanted to go to college and he'd told her he would help and he had. She'd stayed in his apartment for two years, testing his patience every day, while she attended Texas University. Then she got an apartment with a friend. After earning a business degree, she'd worked in the office of a big hospital and today she was the personal assistant to the hospital administrator. Soon she'd probably have his job. If there was one thing they'd inherited from the Goodnights, it was tenacity.

He took his coffee and went outside to sit on the stoop, trying to figure out his next move concerning Becky. Two old rockers his mom had bought at a garage sale and refinished rested on the porch. Flowery cushions daintily tied in place with bows were too fancy for his taste. Large flowerpots full of colorful blooming flowers nestled close. He had no idea what they were, but his mother had a little bit of everything growing around the house. She had always loved flowers. He didn't want to intrude on her decorated space and he felt more comfortable sitting on the step. The Tullous house was dark. No one was up yet.

Who is Luci's father?

The question kept prodding at him—he should just march over there and demand that she tell him the truth. But something held him back. He knew pushing Becky wasn't going to help anything. He couldn't make demands. He didn't have the right, so he had to wait for her to tell him. And that might take just a little more patience than he had.

And he couldn't allow himself to believe Becky would keep the child from him. He knew her better than anyone, and doing something like that just wasn't in her. But then, she'd been angry at him since high school and getting even might appeal to her. Hurting him might appeal to her. Leaving him a broken, lonely man might *really* appeal to her.

He was about to go back into the house when a white Chevrolet truck drove up to the curb. Cole must have heard Bo was home. Gossip in this town spread like poison ivy.

They'd been best friends since first grade and had been through the trenches together with their dysfunctional families. They knew each other in and out, and there weren't many secrets between them, but he'd never told Cole that he and Becky had slept together. That was private, intimate. Cole didn't need to know that.

"What are you doing here so early?" Bo shouted to his friend.

Cole got out and then got his two-and-a-half-year-old daughter, Zoe, out of the car seat in the back. Then he placed Zoe on her feet and she ran up the walk to Bo with a doll in one arm and a sippy cup in her hand. It had taken a long time for her to grow hair but now she had a topknot with a bow on it, which bounced up and down.

He picked her up and sat her on his lap. She kissed his cheek and then winced. She hated his beard.

"Ouchie."

He rubbed it over her face and she giggled, wiggling to get down. She pointed to Cole. "Daddy."

Cole walked more slowly up the walk in his customary khaki pants and a white shirt with a shiny deputy sheriff's badge on his chest. In his boots and Stetson he reminded Bo of a Texas Ranger.

"The sheriff is on vacation and I had to check in at the office. Luckily, everything is quiet in Horseshoe, Texas. And since it's Saturday, I'm letting Grace sleep in. She's still having a little morning sickness."

They were expecting their second child in late January. Cole and Bo had always thought they'd stay bachelors. They had no idea what love was since they hadn't experienced much of it in their families. Love had happened unexpectedly for Cole after rescuing a woman in a winter storm. Bo was stuck in Becky-hell-ville.

Cole eased down beside him on the step. "Bubba passed through here a little while ago and he saw your truck, so I thought I'd check and see what you're doing home. It's such a rare occasion."

Bo told him what had happened in the last twenty-four hours. "I didn't feel like talking to anyone."

"So your dad is back?"

"I don't know. Mom says she's not in love with him anymore and I don't have to worry about her taking him back, but I guess I'll never get rid of that feeling of distrust."

"Your mom seems happy these days and I would hazard a guess she's telling you the truth."

Zoe ran up and down the walk and then into Cole's arms. He picked her up and she wiggled to get down. Over and over they did that.

"Doesn't that drive you crazy?"

Cole frowned. "What? Playing with my kid?"

Bo nodded and knew he could say anything to his friend. "I'd make a terrible father. I'm not patient like you."

"You'll change your mind when you have one of your own."

He looked across the street to Becky's house. "I think Luci's my daughter."

"Whoa. Wait…what?" Cole's mouth fell open and he was at a loss for words, but he quickly recovered. "How could that be? You haven't been with Becky since high school. Or is something going on that you haven't told me?"

"Remember her dad's car accident?"

"Yeah."

"I went over to her house to console her, and one thing led to another and the next thing I know it's morning and she's screaming at me to get out. Ever since then she's avoided me and it's ironic that we're both now home at the same time."

"Becky's home just about every weekend."

"What?"

"Her babysitter is going to be gone for two weeks and Becky's slowly getting Luci into the habit of staying with her grandfather. Craig's going to keep her while Becky works. He's excited about that."

"Are you now the town gossip?"

"It's a small town and I know just about everybody, and if there's anything people love to do, it's to talk. I've met Becky a few times when I've been out patrolling and always stop to talk to her and Luci."

"Did you notice how Luci talks?"

"Yeah. Becky says she has some developmental delays and they're working on them. She's a really sweet kid with big blue eyes and…"

"I know what she looks like," Bo snapped.

There was silence for a moment and even Zoe stopped running up and down the sidewalk.

Bo drew a deep breath. "If she was my kid, I would know, right?"

"You have to talk to Becky. I can't imagine her keeping something like that from you."

"Me, neither, but…there's Luci."

"Why didn't you think about this before now?"

"She wouldn't see me or talk to me, and I had no idea she had a child or had even been pregnant until about two years ago. I tried to wipe that night from my mind, but yesterday I went over to apologize for my behavior when my dad was here and Luci was outside.

Becky was furious that I was talking to her child and told me to stay away from her. I couldn't understand why she didn't want me near the little girl. Then later I got to thinking about it and looked up the dates. Yes, Luci could be my kid. Becky said she was premature and the dates would work."

"If she is, you have to take responsibility and…"

"Don't lecture me, Cole. I know my responsibilities, and I thought if anyone would be on my side, it would be you."

Cole patted him on the back. "I'm always on your side. Take some advice from a man who knows you very well. Be patient. Don't go over there and jump in with both feet demanding things. Be patient and let Becky tell you."

He patted Bo on the back again. "I hope she is your kid. She deserves a good father." Cole got to his feet. "Now I'm going home and fix breakfast for my family."

Bo sat there for a long time after his friend had left. Becky came out of the house and walked to her car, got in and drove away. She was wearing scrubs so that must mean she was going to work. And that meant Luci would be home today with her grandfather.

Bo hurried inside, showered and changed clothes.

All the while a plan formed in his head. He would heed his friend's advice and take this slow. He ate the breakfast his mom had left for him and drank a couple of cups of coffee, watching the clock. By nine o'clock Craig and Luci should be up.

Opening the curtains and blinds in the living room, he took a peep outside. He didn't want to miss Luci. He couldn't wait to see her face again, to search for a resemblance to him. Could Luci really be his child? That sent his nerves blasting through his system, ready to burst forth in a fit of injustice, and it took all his strength to keep himself under control.

Out of the corner of his eye he saw movement and looked closer. Luci was coming out the front door with a ball in her hands. Craig was trying to hold the door open while the cat and the dog came out, too. He was on the phone. Luci sat on the step and turned her head to look back at Craig. Obviously, he was talking to Becky. He went back inside, leaving the door ajar.

Bo didn't waste any time. He strolled

across the street to where Luci was sitting with the ball in her lap. Pink lay beside her.

"Good morning, Luci."

"Bo. You. Come."

He squatted in front of her and couldn't drag his gaze away from her beautiful blue eyes, magnified by her pink-framed glasses. Her eyes were just like Becky's. Blue as a Texas sky and bright as a diamond. She was all Becky and there was no evidence of a dark-haired, dark-eyed man. That didn't mean anything, though.

"Can. We. Play?"

Before he could answer, Craig appeared in the doorway. "Bo, what are you doing here?"

Bo stood. "I have a date with a beautiful young lady."

"What are you talking about?"

"He. Play. With. Me."

Craig frowned. "Does Becky know about this?"

"I didn't ask her. Is that a problem?"

"Well, yes. I have strict orders for Luci's play schedule and you weren't included."

Luci turned to look up at her grandfather. "Please. Nobody. Wants. To. Play. With. Me." Tears simmered in her eyes and a weakening gripped his gut. It was Craig's undoing, too.

"Grandpa plays with you." Craig tried to console her, but it didn't work.

"You. Have. To." A tear rolled down her cheek.

"Okay. Okay, you can play with Bo for a few minutes in the backyard."

A smile split Luci's face and in that moment Bo knew he and Luci had a connection. A special connection, which just had to be biological.

Luci jumped up and ran through the house to the French doors to the backyard. Bo followed more slowly.

"I resent you pushing me into a corner," Craig said in an angry tone, and that blew the cap off Bo's patient stance.

"You don't want to know how hard I can push, Craig."

"What are you talking about?"

"Why doesn't Becky want me anywhere near Luci?"

"You're a grown man and she's a little girl. Luci doesn't even know you and I find it very strange you want to be friends with her. I just have this nagging suspicion that you're up to something."

Bo took a step toward the older man. "Yes, I am up to something. Who's Luci's father?"

Craig's chin jutted out. "You'll have to ask Becky that." He wasn't going to budge. His loyalty was to Becky and that was okay. Bo could wait for the answer.

"Bo." Luci called from the doorway.

Bo gave Craig one last look and went to play with Luci. What he knew about playing with kids he could stuff into a thimble, but they weren't keeping him away from Luci.

Outside, the first thing Bo noticed was the yard. Years ago there had been no flowers anywhere. Today flowers bloomed along the wood fence and around the covered patio, even in late September. Craig must've taken up gardening for a hobby.

"Bo." Luci was impatient.

"Okay, little lady, what do you want to do?"

"Throw. Ball." She handed him the ball. "To. Me."

"I'll throw you the ball and then you throw it back to me?"

"Yeah."

He backed up and threw her the ball. She made no attempt to catch it. It hit her in the chest and she stumbled around and fell on her butt. He rushed forward. Oh, man!

"Are you okay?" Her glasses were lop-sided, but she was smiling.

"Yeah."

He straightened her glasses. "Are you sure?" He was very aware that Craig had come out onto the patio with his coffee, and was watching him closely.

Luci got to her feet. "Yeah. I. Missed. It."

He brushed the grass from her skinny legs. "Okay. We have to have a few lessons first this time."

She rubbed her head. "'Kay."

"Now." He put the ball in front of her. "Pretend you're catching it and put your hands around it." She did as he told her. "That's what you have to do when I throw it to you. Put your hands out and try to catch it."

Over and over they practiced. He'd hand the ball to her and she'd hand it back to him. He backed up a couple of feet and tossed the ball to her. She missed it. She was flushed, but her eyes were bright. She was enjoying herself so he didn't stop.

It didn't take him long to realize she had a problem with coordination. "Keep your eyes on the ball. When you see it coming, grab it with your hands." She missed it the first few times, but they kept at it. On the tenth time she caught it. Her eyes opened wide in shock and she jumped up and down.

"I caught it. I caught it!"

This time Bo was shocked. She'd said the words without pausing. Craig had heard it too and stood up. Bo didn't want to point it out to her and embarrass her. He wanted her to know that he liked her just the way she was.

"Your cheeks are getting red," Craig said to Luci. "It's time to come in, have lunch and take a nap."

To both men's surprise, Luci didn't object. She looked at Bo. "You. Come. Back?"

Craig walked forward and picked up Luci. "Your mommy will be home this afternoon and you're going to the park. Remember?"

"Yeah." She rested her head on Craig's shoulder and they walked toward the house.

"You know the way out, Bo," Craig said over his shoulder.

Bo walked around the house to the gate and across the street to his house. He changed clothes and headed for the gym in Temple. He had to stay in shape. The whole time he was lifting weights he thought about the Luci situation. Craig knew Becky's secret, and if Bo kept pushing he'd get it out of them, but he had to think about Luci's health. He didn't want to do one thing to hinder her progress.

He thought about Becky, too. Why would she keep something like this from him? He didn't deserve that. Yes, he'd been a foolish teenage boy who had run the first chance he had and hadn't thought about her or her feelings. He was older now, more mature. But that maturity seemed to fly out the window whenever his father was around. He had a big problem with that, and as long as he recognized it maybe there was hope for him. But he didn't see any hope for him and Becky.

CHAPTER FIVE

"REBECCA, WHEN ARE you coming home?" Her dad's voice was agitated and Becky knew something was wrong.

"Is Luci okay?" That was her worst fear—that something would happen to her child.

"She's fine. She's taking a nap right now."

"Then what are you upset about?"

"Luci spent the morning with Bo."

"What?" Becky was visiting with a patient in the hospital and she took her phone and went into the hallway. "What are you talking about?"

"Obviously, yesterday he told her he would play with her and she remembered. When he saw her outside, he came over. I told him we had other plans and Luci's eyes filled with tears and I couldn't deny her wish. So he stayed."

"Is he there now?"

"No. I told him Luci needed a nap and he

went back over to Ava's house. I don't know how to handle this. You need to be here."

"Dad, we have a double mastectomy patient who's not doing very well. Her husband walked out and she doesn't think he's coming back. She wants to die and I can't leave her right now. I'm waiting on a therapist and the patient's daughter to get here. But as soon as they arrive I will come home and deal with the situation. When Luci wakes up, take her to the park for a little while and I'll be home by then."

"Why weren't you answering your phone earlier? I called." Her dad's agitated voice was getting stronger and she knew it wasn't right to dump the situation on him. She had to do better. For her child. And for herself.

"I turned my phone off when I was in a meeting and I just turned it back on. I'll take care of the problem when I get home. I'm off tomorrow so you don't have to deal with it."

"I got the impression from Bo that he thinks Luci is his daughter. Is that possible?"

She took a deep breath to calm her shaky nerves. "He's just fishing for answers. He asked me who Luci's father was and I guess he's now testing you." Oh, she wanted to kill

Bo Goodnight. Why couldn't he stay out of her life?

"Why don't you just tell him the truth?"

"Okay, Dad. I have to go. Just take care of Luci and I'll be there as soon as I can."

She'd told her dad she would take care of the situation, but in truth she didn't know how to deal with Bo's interest in Luci. Her dad was right. She had to talk to Bo and bare her soul, and maybe then he would leave her in peace.

IT WAS AFTER two when Bo returned from the gym. He'd texted his mom and told her he wasn't going to be home for lunch so she didn't need to worry about him. His mother's car was in the driveway, though. He glanced toward the Tullous house and noticed Becky's car wasn't there. Or maybe they'd gone to the park, but he didn't think so. The moment Becky found out he'd been visiting with Luci there would be fireworks. He was depending on that. He was good at defusing fireworks.

He went in through the garage, as always. The house was quiet. He found his mom in the living room, sitting in her chair with her feet propped up, sound asleep. His heart ached at the sight. For years she'd worked hard just to put food on the table and keep a roof over their heads. Of course, he had helped, but it had to have been an enormous burden for her. And it just spiked his anger for his father.

When he'd joined the army, he knew his mother couldn't make the mortgage payments without Bo's help. He feared she would lose the house and then she and Kelsey would be homeless. He talked with a guy at the bank and they set up an account so his earnings from the army would go straight into it and the mortgage payments would be deducted from that. At that time, the banker had alerted him that the house was still in Mason Goodnight's name.

From thousands of miles away, he contacted Gabe Garrison, an attorney in Horseshoe. He'd asked if Gabe could take care of it and he'd said he could, but he needed Mason's signature on the papers for it to be legal. Gabe had tracked Mason down and said that Bo's father had signed without a problem. For that, Bo should be grateful, but somehow he couldn't dredge up that emotion concerning his father.

He sat on the sofa and his mother woke up.

"Oh, Bo, you're back," she said in a sleepy voice. "What time is it?"

"After one."

"Oh, my goodness. I have to get back to work." She pushed forward to get up.

He put out a hand to stop her. "Mom, you're the boss. You can come and go as you please."

"I don't want to take advantage."

"Could we talk for a minute?"

She pulled her cell phone out of the smock she was wearing. "I have to call my assistant to let her know."

After speaking to someone, she leaned back in her chair and yawned. It made him wonder if she was getting enough rest.

"You look tired."

"The owner of the store and his entourage are coming next week and we're working a lot of overtime to make sure everything is spick-and-span and up to his standards."

"That store is always clean. I can't see that he would have an issue with anything, so stop worrying."

"It's not just that. We haven't had a raise in over two years and I'm going to bring up the subject. I have two single mothers working and they need more money to support their families. They work very hard and I'm going to see that they get it. I may lose my job over it."

"Go get 'em, Mom. And if you lose your job, I'll take care of you. Don't worry about it. Stand up for what you want."

"I don't need you to take care of me, thank you very much. I can take care of myself. My kids are grown and I want you to live your own lives now." She clapped her hands together. "I'm so very proud of both of you, despite my terrible ineptness as a mother."

"Hey, you're talking about my mother, and neither Kelsey nor I blame you for anything. You gave us all you had so get those thoughts out of your head."

She sat forward. "What did you want to talk about?"

"You're good friends with Craig, right?"

"Sure. After his accident I helped him out while Becky worked and got to know him a little better. We're neighbors, after all."

"Then you would know who Luci's father is."

She frowned that trademark frown she'd worn when he did something wrong. "Why would I know that?"

"Why is it such a secret? Luci has a father. Who is it?"

"Why are you bothering with this? It's only going to cause trouble and it doesn't concern you."

"Again, why is Luci's father such a secret?"

Her phone buzzed, and she glanced at it and pushed it back into her pocket. "Craig and I agreed a long time ago to never discuss our children because we knew I would take your side and he would take Becky's. So it was best if we just left that subject alone and we have. When Craig told me Becky had a baby, I said congratulations. When Becky brought the baby home, I fell in love with her. She's just so sweet. I know her problems will get worked out. Becky just has to be stronger."

He could hear the love in his mother's voice and that made his cop sensors go off. Did she know Luci was his? And was she keeping it from him, like everyone else seemed to be? He couldn't make himself believe that. Maybe his mother saw Bo in Luci. That could be the only explanation. But something else caught his attention.

"What did you mean, Becky has to be stronger?"

She got up and waved a hand. "Oh, nothing. I have to get back to work."

"What did you mean?" he asked in his best cop voice.

His mother shook her head. "Oh, you're so tenacious. I'll tell you, but you promise me you'll leave this alone. This is Becky's problem, not yours or mine or anyone else's."

"What is it?"

"Becky has a problem making Luci do what she's supposed to. Luci cries and says Becky doesn't love her, and Becky doesn't force her. The therapist can get Luci to talk normally in her office, but with Becky, Luci drifts back into the same old pattern. It's become a habit. Luci has to be forced to talk and Becky is struggling with that."

"You mean she's impeding Luci's progress?"

"No, that's not what I meant. What I meant was for you to stay out of it." Her eyes narrowed on his face. "You know, you haven't visited your grandmother in a while, and now that you have some time off you need to do that."

"Oh, Mom, I don't like that place they put

her in." After his grandfather's death, his grandmother, Estelle, had lived on the farm for a while, but she'd lost her driver's license after getting too many tickets and smashing her car into the courthouse. She had to depend on her daughter to take her places. Aunt Lois and his grandmother didn't get along all that well, and the next thing he'd known they were selling the farm and putting his grandmother in a retirement home.

"It's called Enchanted Oaks and it's very nice."

"I know *he* talked her into selling." It always irked him that his father had so much control over his grandmother.

"He did not. Estelle was tired of the isolation and having to ask Lois to take her places. Imogene Cooksley moved to Enchanted Oaks and your grandmother went to visit her. She liked the place and decided on her own that she wanted to be around people. It was her decision, totally. Now be a good grandson and go visit her. She always asks about you."

Bo drew a deep breath and succumbed to the guilt trip. "I'll go tomorrow."

"I'm sure she'll appreciate it."

But would he? Every time he visited his

grandmother she always questioned his marital status. Or the lack of it. He braced himself for another round the next day.

Bo got out of his sweaty gym clothes and took a shower. He dressed in his usual jeans and T-shirt, and walked into the living room.

Sitting on the sofa, he called Hutch. He had to know how things were going at work.

"Hey, Sarge, are you lying on the couch, watching a movie and drinking beer?"

Bo ignored the sarcasm. "How are things going?"

"Fine. We had a convenience store robbery this morning and the guy was holed up in there. We had to go in and take him."

"Anyone get hurt?"

"Of course not. We're professionals and the lieutenant was on the scene."

"Did she call anyone in to take my place?"

"No. We got it covered."

"Yeah. Talk to you later."

Bo stared at his phone, feeling deflated because he wasn't really needed. He ran the team, but he guessed they were doing just fine without him.

A scratching sound caught his attention. Did his mother have a mouse in the house?

If she did, he would be looking for that thing all night. She hated the little critters.

He followed the sound to the front door. To his surprise, Luci stood there with Pink and Purr at her feet.

She raised a hand. "Hi. Bo. Can. You. Play?"

"Does your grandfather know you're here?" He had a sneaking suspicion he didn't. She'd walked across the street on her own.

Luci shrugged. "Don't. Know."

Bo glanced at the Tullous house as the front door opened and Craig came out. "Luci!"

"Uh. Oh."

"I got her, Craig," Bo shouted, and picked up Luci and strolled across the street.

When Bo reached him, Craig grabbed Luci and held her close. "You scared Grandpa."

"I. Sorry," Luci mumbled into Craig's shoulder. "Play. With. Bo."

"Don't you ever do that again."

Bo thought about how lonely it must be not to have anyone to play with, and a mother who worked all the time. He wasn't Luci's age but he was someone other than her mother and grandpa who paid attention to her and didn't bully her about her speech.

And now he would have to be the adult and impart to her how dangerous it was to be out alone and crossing streets.

"Your grandfather is right. You shouldn't be outside by yourself. Do you understand?"

"Sorry. Go. My. Room." She wiggled down and marched toward the hallway.

"Is that usually her punishment?" Bo asked.

"Yes. Sometimes it's five minutes and sometimes it's ten. Right now I feel like locking her in there. I was so scared when I couldn't find her."

"Do you mind if I go talk to her?"

"No. Go ahead. I need my heart rate to subside."

Bo walked down the hall and into a pink-and-white room that was like a cotton-candy dream. A candy-striped comforter highlighted the white furniture and light pink walls. Lace ruffles adorned the pillows and the comforter on the single bed with half rails. Stuffed animals and dolls rested in every nook and cranny. Children's books filled a large shelf. Luci lay on the bed, face-down, whimpering. Purr had crawled up next to her and Pink lay on the rug beside her bed, which just happened to be pink-and-white stripes.

He sat on the bed. "Hey, Luci."

She turned over and scooted to sit beside him. "You. Mad. At. Me?" Her feet barely hung over the bed. She was so tiny, which probably had to do with the developmental delay.

"No. I'm just concerned. You see, I'm kind of like that. I'm a cop and I've worked a lot of jobs. One of those jobs was a liaison to the schools. A liaison is someone who tries to keep kids safe and let children know the dangers of their actions. You know what the number one rule is for kids your age?" He was making this up as he went along to get her attention, to make her realize that what she did was wrong and not to point a finger at her.

She shook her head.

"To never go out alone."

"Oh."

"And to never, ever, cross the street by yourself. That's very dangerous. Cars whiz by here all the time. I would hate for a car to hit Pink."

"No!" she shouted, her eyes big. "I. Not. Do. It. Again."

"Good."

"Are. You. Mad. At. Me?"

He put his arm around her thin shoulders. "I could never be mad at you, angel face."

A smile widened her features and she pushed those pink glasses up her nose and smiled even bigger, if that was possible. This kid was extra special and he knew that deep in his heart he would do anything to keep her safe. He realized that that was a father's job, and if Luci was really his, he'd lost a lot of valuable time. Anger gripped his stomach. He couldn't take it slow. He needed to know, and as soon as Becky showed up he intended to get that answer.

BECKY HURRIED INSIDE. It had been a horrible day. Men were such jerks when it came to women's breasts. Mr. Batson had just disappeared. He couldn't take it that his wife would no longer have breasts. Ms. Batson was a mess and didn't want to live anymore. Finally, her daughter had arrived and gone looking for her father. Becky stayed until the therapist got there and ordered sedation for the night. As Becky was leaving the hospital she saw the daughter and the father going back in, which was good. She was hoping they could work this out. It always took time to adjust to this kind of situation, especially since the woman was only forty-two.

"You're finally home," her dad said from his chair.

She threw her purse on the sofa. "Yes. I'm sorry it took so long, but we had a situation that had to be addressed. Where's Luci?"

"In her room."

"I'll check on her and then we'll talk."

"She's not alone."

Becky swung around. "What?"

"Bo is in there with her."

Becky took a deep breath. "Why is he here?"

Her dad told her a story that gave her chills. "Luci walked across the street on her own?"

"Yes. I was scared to death until Bo brought her back. She knocked on his door. He's in there now, talking to her and hopefully telling her how dangerous that was."

"I don't need him to tell my child anything."

"Well, you should've been here, then. It's the weekend and Luci needs you. I'm sorry that's blunt, but Luci is soaking up Bo's attention because she needs it. She needs to be around children. Things have to change, Rebecca."

"Dad, please, not today."

"When, then?"

"I have to talk to Bo."

"Now there's an idea."

She headed for the hallway, fuming. Why was she angry all the time? It was pulling her down, affecting her actions and her words. And it was all because of Bo. He thought he could come back into her life and take over her child. He was mistaken and she was going to get rid of him one last time.

CHAPTER SIX

BECKY STOPPED OUTSIDE the door when she heard Bo's deep smooth masculine voice, which touched her skin like cashmere, soothing, comfortable and deliciously rich. The baritone made her want to lean her head against the wall and absorb every nuance of his voice into her skin. She hated herself for that reaction. She would never give in to those feelings again. She'd learned her lesson, but her heart was not on her side. It craved his voice.

"You have a lot of stuffed animals and dolls," Bo was saying.

"This. Is. Bear. Soft." In Becky's mind's eye she could see Luci rubbing her face against the stuffed animal.

"What's this one's name?"

He wasn't worming his way into Luci's life. She stepped into the room and Luci ran to her.

"Mom-my."

Becky picked her up and kissed her cheek. "How's my baby?"

"I. Bad."

"We'll talk about it later. Go help Grandpa fix supper. I want to talk to Bo."

Luci ran to the kitchen and Becky faced Bo with steel-like determination. He stood from the bed and his tall frame looked out of place in this pink little girl's room. Dark eyes stared back at her with a heat level that matched hers and she didn't know if there was a way to win against him. It would be better if he wasn't so darn good-looking. With his longish hair and growth of beard he reminded her of Keanu Reeves. And Bo was just as big a daredevil as the characters the actor played.

"You want to talk? Talk. I've been trying to get you to talk for years so this is a momentous occasion."

"Stay away from my daughter."

"Your daughter came looking for me because she's lonely and her mother works on weekends."

"Don't bring up my job. That is none of your concern."

"It is when I see a little girl hurting."

"She's not hurting."

"Then why isn't she talking correctly? That hurts her. She wants to be like other little girls, but her mother is lax in her therapy."

He hit her right where she'd feel it most— in her heart. For a moment she was powerless to defend herself. "It's not that easy."

"Did anyone say it was supposed to be?"

"You think you know it all."

"I know she can string words together. She did it today."

"What?"

"I was teaching her to catch a ball and she missed it every time, but when she finally caught it she jumped up and down and said 'I caught it' and didn't pause once. She said it twice." He held up two fingers.

Becky was tired, so tired, and this bickering was not helping, but she couldn't ignore that her baby had put words together for Bo and not her. "We're going to practice speaking tonight," she mumbled almost to herself.

"What if Luci cries?"

Becky sighed, wondering who Bo had been talking to. She couldn't deal with much more today. "Bo, please go home."

"Okay." He took a step toward her and she had to resist taking a step backward. A musky scent mixed with Irish Spring soap drifted to her, weakening her resolve. "I'll go, but first, I want to know who Luci's father is."

"Bo…"

"I'm her father, aren't I? You've kept it from me all these years."

"You are *not* Luci's father," she snapped, getting edgy from his dogged persistence.

"You said that just a little too quickly."

"Because it's true."

"I don't believe you. Luci responds to me and we have a connection. There has to be a reason for that."

"She's a little girl wanting attention. That's the only reason."

"I still don't believe you. How could you do that? I know I hurt you and I've apologized many times, but keeping my child from me is the worst."

"You're not Luci's father," she repeated, losing what little patience she had left.

"Prove it."

She stormed out of the room, went to the kitchen and found a plastic bag, and hurried back to the bedroom. Bo was still standing there as if he didn't know what to do and she was sure that was a first for him. He was a take-charge kind of guy. She went straight to Luci's little dressing table where she kept her brush and comb and her ribbons, hundreds of pink ribbons. Putting the bag under her arm she picked up Luci's brush, removed several hairs and stuffed them into the bag. She handed the bag to Bo.

"You're a cop and I'm sure you can have a DNA test run quickly. If she's your child, this will tell you the truth."

He took the bag from her. "You think I won't do it."

"I dare you to do it."

He shook his head. "What's going on, Bec?"

"Just stay out of my life. I don't need you anymore." She walked out of the room with as much dignity as possible and headed to the kitchen. She heard the front door close and her body sagged with relief.

Luci was watching cartoons on a mini iPad and Becky hurried to her bedroom. She needed a moment. Sitting on the bed, she tried to calm her nerves, trying to figure out what Bo would do. She had to be prepared for the next round because Bo wasn't through disrupting her life.

LATER THAT NIGHT, Bo sat in his bedroom staring at the strands of hair in the bag. She thought he wouldn't have it tested. Becky had said Luci wasn't his in a voice strong enough to cut through steel. But...there was always that *but*. The problem was that he *felt* like Luci was his. All the signs were there and he couldn't ignore that. He'd played a lot of poker when he was in the army and now sometimes played with the SWAT guys. And he was willing to make a big bet on this. He picked up the bag.

"Becky Tullous, I'm calling your bluff," he said to no one in particular.

His mother had gotten a call and had to go back to the store. It closed at ten and there was a problem, so he was all alone with his thoughts. With nothing to do but watch mindless TV, he called Cole and told him about the hair.

"She gave it to you?"

"She did, and she thinks I won't have it tested."

"Bo, you really need to go back to work. You're fixated on this little girl."

"I know. I feel there's something there and I can't let it go."

"Do the DNA test then, but you have to accept whatever it says."

"Yeah." As he put his phone down Bo

wondered if he could. All his feelings for Becky were tied up with his feelings for Luci. He recognized that and he had to deal with it in his own way. He'd never thought love would hurt this damn much. With that thought on his mind he went to bed.

The next morning his mom left early for work, as usual. It was after eleven when she'd come in the previous night and she had to be tired, but she was financially independent now and he wasn't going to question her about her life.

He placed the hair in his briefcase and headed for Austin. Since it was Sunday, there was only minimal help in the lab. He texted one of the technicians and told her what he was bringing in. She thought it had to do with a case and he had to tell her differently. When she took his DNA, she had a smirk on her face, but didn't say a word. He told her to bill him privately and since he'd been with the force so long she didn't question it.

After that he drove to Temple to visit with his grandmother, as promised, and he braced himself for another round of *why aren't you married?* Enchanted Oaks was a new retirement villa and he had to agree with his mother that it was a very nice place. The

Austin-stone structure was nestled among large oaks and pines, and had a fresh, appealing look. The building was a large square with rows of apartments facing inside the square, downstairs and upstairs. Blooming flowers and well-maintained shrubs dressed up the manicured lawn.

He went through the large foyer decorated in a Southwestern motif of oranges, yellows and browns. Strolling down a long hallway he headed for the back door and the center of the complex, which was also well maintained with a waterfall and flowers. The babbling water and the birds chirping gave the place a tranquil feel.

His grandmother's apartment was downstairs, and as he walked along he spoke to people as he made his way there. He knocked on the door and no one answered. He knocked louder. Still nothing. He tried the knob and the door was open.

"Grandma!" he hollered.

She came out of the bedroom in her customary polyester pants, print blouse and comfortable shoes. That wasn't what caught his attention, though. It was her hair, which was now a yellowish gray and resembled an

Afro. She had naturally curly red hair, but he'd never seen it like this.

"Beauregard!" she shouted. "Come give your grandma a hug." She was the only person who called him Beauregard because she'd named him.

He walked forward and she grabbed him in a bear hug and then slapped him on the shoulder. "Where have you been? You should come see your grandma more often."

"I work a lot."

She sat in her chair with a groan. "That's what Ava told me."

He moved her big purse out of the way and sat on the sofa. "Grandma, your door was unlocked."

"I know. I hardly ever lock it. Lost my keys three times and I got tired of looking for them. Besides, it's a safe place and I don't have anything in here that's worth stealing."

As a cop that bothered him. "You really need to lock your door, especially at night."

"Oh, I do that, if I remember. Like I told you, there's nothing in here that anybody wants, including me."

"Grandma..."

"Haven't you learned by now not to argue

with me?" She frowned, looking closely at his face. "How old are you now?"

She knew how old he was because he was the oldest of her grandchildren.

"When are you getting married?"

He gritted his teeth. "Not anytime soon."

She clicked her tongue. "I have six grand-children, five girls and one boy, and that boy is determined to stay single. I don't know if it's you or the girls you date."

To turn the tables on her, he asked, "What happened to your hair?"

She slapped her leg with her hand. "Now that's a story. Flora told me this ol' wives' tale…"

"Who's Flora?"

"Beauregard, you know Flora. Lamar's mother."

Lamar Jones lived in Horseshoe and owned an auto repair shop. The Joneses had been in Horseshoe as long as anyone, and his family was a big part of the community. If Bo had anything wrong with his truck, he always took it to Lamar. His mother was usu-ally sitting in a rocking chair on the porch.

"I had no idea Lamar put his mother here."

His grandmother shook her head. "No one *put* her here. She came of her own free will because she was tired of her daughter-in-law telling her what to do, just like I was tired of Lois telling me what to do. Here, we can do whatever we please and we don't have to cook and we don't have to clean or put up with anybody's crap." She reached down and pulled up her support hose.

"I'm glad you're happy here. What was the old wives' tale?" He thought he'd better change the subject before she gave him one of her come-to-Jesus talks.

"You know, I'm always complaining about my curly hair and Flora said her mother heard that if a Black woman gave herself a permanent it would straighten her hair. We figured that might work on mine. I told the beautician I wanted a perm. And, of course, she asked what for, since I had naturally curly hair. We went round and round and finally I threatened her and she gave me the permanent." She pointed to her head. "This is the result."

Bo tried not to laugh and it was hard. "Guess the old wives' tale was false."

"Yep, but we had a good laugh about it. If ol' Sam could see me now."

"Grandpa would laugh, too."

"Nah, Sam wasn't into laughing that much."

"Sure he was. He used to tell me and Cole all kinds of stories and laugh."

"That was when he was drunk. When he drank he talked and carried on."

"I don't like it when you say things like that about Grandpa."

"It's the truth, Beauregard. Ask your mom. Ask Lois."

He shifted uncomfortably on the sofa. Grandpa had been Bo's hero all his life and he couldn't make himself believe otherwise. His grandfather would say, "Forget about your father. You got me." That made Bo feel safe and reassured that he would never be left alone. For a kid, that had been important.

"I know you put your grandfather on a pedestal and he could do no wrong, but I've held my tongue long enough."

Bo's patience snapped. "He was more of a father to me than Mason ever was."

"And do you know why?" His grandmother's voice rose in a tone that, when he was a kid, usually had him running for the back door. But he stood his ground on this one.

"Because I was his grandson. That meant something to him."

Grandma nodded. "You got it. You were a boy and he'd been waiting for one just like you. All boy, tough and rowdy with grit in your gut. You see, Mason wasn't the son he wanted. My boy had gentle ways and your grandfather tried to break him, but it didn't work because I made sure he had music lessons to further the talent that he had.

"My Mason didn't care about ranching and farming, and he couldn't throw bales of hay onto a trailer or fix fence in the hot sun. It just wasn't something he liked to do and your grandfather couldn't understand it. So he belittled Mason every opportunity he had. He called him sissy and called him other words I'd rather not use. He tried to break his spirit, but I was there to make sure he didn't."

Bo rubbed his hands together, wondering if Grandma was off some of her medications, making her talk crazy. But with his grandmother he could never tell.

"I don't want to talk about my father."

"Well, then, you can just listen. When you were born, Sam thought he'd hit the jackpot. His son had had a son and he went on and on about how Mason had finally done something right. As you grew it was plain to see you were not like your father and your grandfather delighted in that. You followed Sam around like a little puppy and learned everything from him. Mason never had a chance to be a father."

Bo stood, anger swelling in his chest. "Because he was always running off with some woman, leaving his kids and his wife. That's the kind of man he is and I'm not going to have you talk like that about my grandpa. Without him I'd probably have ended up on the wrong side of the law. He taught me right from wrong and he taught me everything I know about good and bad."

His grandmother looked straight at him, her green eyes a little dull, but as strong as cast iron. "When Lois was born, Sam left the hospital and didn't return for hours. He was mad because she wasn't a boy. Yes, that's the man who walks on water to you. He ignored Lois most of her life. Just ask her.

"And ask Kelsey how much interest her grandfather showed in her. He bought you things and took you places, but he never took Kelsey anywhere or bought her anything. Now Sam has five granddaughters and I imagine he's turning over in his grave. Keep your dream of Sam, but I want you to know that your father is still living and it's time for you to forgive him and have a man-to-man talk."

That's what this was about. His grandma was always on Mason's side and she'd do anything he asked of her. "Are you giving this same speech to my mother? He was at her house the other day. I assume he needs a place to stay and you know how weak my mother is where he's concerned. But he will never move back into the house because I own it."

"Oh, Beauregard, you're too young to have this much anger. And I don't have to tell your mother anything. She lived through it." She reached down and pulled up her support hose one more time. "And Mason doesn't need a place to stay. He's doing very well now."

"If not for him, you'd still be living on the farm."

Her head jerked up. "Living on the farm? Are you insane? The house had no insulation or air conditioning. It was cold in the wintertime and hot as a firecracker in the summertime. Do you think I wanted to work that farm at my age? Here—" she glanced around "—I'm free to enjoy my life and not worry about too much, just a grandson who can't seem to get his act together. Hand me my purse."

He picked up the big purse and passed it to her, giving him time to cool off. His mind was whirling like a fan, going back through all the memories, trying to prove his grandmother wrong. His grandfather hadn't treated women differently. Bo had never seen that.

His grandmother was fishing coins out of her purse and placing them on the end table beside her.

"What are you doing?"

"Getting my poker money ready for this afternoon."

"Poker? Grandma, you're Baptist. You don't play poker."

"Nah, they kicked me out long time ago."

"No, they didn't."

She looked up, her green eyes narrowed. "Sure they did. I bumped my toe on the pew and said a cuss word, and the pastor suggested I not come back until I could speak in a more pleasant manner. I started to tell him what he could do with his suggestion, but Lois pulled me out of the church. I haven't been back since. But that's okay, they have services here every Sunday morning and I go with Flora and Imogene. We just walk to the chapel." She slapped her hand against her leg again. "Oh, did I tell you Mason came by on Friday? He brought his guitar and we sang so loud everybody started gathering outside and listening. The director suggested we take it to the family room and did we have a good time. You know Mason gets his talent from me."

The only fond memory he had of his father was his singing. Bo had woken up many mornings to his father singing in the bathroom, and then his dad would get his guitar and he and Kelsey would sing with him. And laugh because Kelsey's singing was similar to that of a cat with its tail caught in a screen door. That was a good memory, but his father had ruined it all by leaving, as if they meant nothing to him.

Grandma pulled up her hose again and diverted his thoughts. "Grandma, you need new support hose."

"Lois bought me some, but I'm getting the goodie out of these first. What time is it?"

Bo looked at the large clock on the wall that had big numbers. He was sure she could see it all the way from Austin, so why was she asking him? Maybe she needed new glasses. "A little after one," he answered as politely as possible.

She sat up straight in her chair. "I gotta go. The game starts at two and I like to visit a little bit before we start playing." She rummaged in the purse again and glanced around the room. "I can't find my glasses."

"They're on your face."

She reached up to touch them. "Oh, that's good. Sometimes I lose them."

A question burned in his mind and he had to ask it. "Did you love Grandpa?"

She stopped digging in her purse to look at him. "Oh, my gosh, yes. The first time I set eyes on Sam Goodnight I fell in love for the first and only time in my life. There were some things about him I didn't like and one of them was his disrespect for women. And I didn't like his drinking either, but that didn't change my love for him. It just made me want to kill him a time or two, but we survived."

She stood and patted his chest. "Hold on to your views of your grandpa, but don't let them destroy what could be."

He hugged her. "I better go, but I'll try to get back soon."

"You do that." She patted his chest again.

"Oh, wait, I have something I want you to do."

She hurried down a small hallway and came back with a pair of brown slacks in her hands. "You take these to Target and get my money back."

"Do you have a receipt?"

"No. Who keeps receipts?"

"What's wrong with them?"

"They're uncomfortable and I want my money back."

She'd never asked him to do anything before and he wondered what she was up to. He fingered the slacks and saw food stains.

"Grandma, have you worn these?"

"Yeah, that's how I know they're uncomfortable."

"You can't take back something you've worn."

"Wear your badge and your gun and tell him your grandma wants her money back. It'll work."

"Grandma, I don't use my gun and badge in that way."

"You can do it for your grandma who lives on a fixed income."

He knew this was a losing battle. His

grandmother had her own way of thinking and she was never going to see Bo's side.

"How much did they cost?"

"Nine ninety-nine plus tax."

He took out his wallet. "Tell you what. I'll give you ten dollars and it'll save me a trip from having to bring you the money."

"Deal."

He handed her a ten dollar bill.

"Plus tax."

He groaned inwardly and gave her another dollar. "Is that good enough?"

"Perfect. Now I have to run. I just have to find my glasses."

Bo gritted his teeth. "They're on your head."

"Sometimes I forget that."

At that moment Bo wondered just how much she remembered about the past. At eighty-one her memory was a little faulty. As he drove home, the past ran through his mind like pages from a photo album and his grandfather was in all the pictures—fishing, hunting, baling hay, riding a four-wheeler, riding horses, playing cards, cutting down a Christmas tree—but his dad wasn't.

Could his grandmother be right? Could Mason have been left out for a reason? He pushed the thought aside. Mason had had many chances and Bo wasn't giving him another one. Everyone had different memories, but he was almost certain he would never forgive his father and see him as the man his grandmother did.

CHAPTER SEVEN

ON SUNDAY MORNING, Becky, her father and Luci got up late and Becky fixed breakfast for the three of them. Luci sat in her booster seat, stuffing pancakes dripping with maple syrup into her mouth. Becky didn't allow her daughter to eat too many sweets, but Sunday was always a special day when she made pancakes or waffles.

Sipping her coffee, she watched as Luci carefully speared a cut-up piece of pancake and shoved it into her mouth. Becky had waited so long for Luci to learn to use a fork and now she was good at it. Everything was improving, except her speech.

Last night Becky had intended to have Luci do some of the speech exercises, but her daughter must've read her mind because she said no before Becky could even start. *No* was her favorite word. Then she cried and held her hands over her ears. Becky gave up and admitted she needed help with Luci.

She reached over and wiped syrup from Luci's chin. She loved this little girl with all her heart and it hurt that she might not start school when she turned four. That was Becky's goal—for Luci to speak so she could go to school with other children her age. If things didn't change, Becky might have to send her to a special school. That hurt even worse. And it was her fault. The truth of that cut into her conscience with a big *Mother Fail*.

When Luci finished, Becky picked her up and carried her to the sink to wash her hands and face. "We're going to the park today so go to your room and pick out something to wear."

"Grand-pa. Go-ing?"

Becky looked at her father for the answer.

"No, grandpa's going to work in the yard today."

Luci ran to her room and Becky sank into a chair. "I'm not sure how to deal with Bo."

Her dad pushed his plate back. "The truth might work."

"It's hard to talk to him."

"Why?"

"Because I'm afraid I'll fall for every line he feeds me."

"You're not sixteen anymore—trust yourself." Her father carried his plate to the sink. "But I'll tell you one thing. He's very good with Luci. She kind of looks up to him and will do anything he asks of her, which I find very unusual. I watched it yesterday. She strung three words together without pausing and I think she's on the precipice of speaking correctly."

"I know I need help."

"Yes, you do."

"But I don't want it to be from him."

"Rebecca, you once loved the man with all your heart, and I think if you spend some time together you might find some of those feelings are still there."

"That's what I'm afraid of." She got up and started putting the dishes in the dishwasher. She feared it, dreaded it and agonized over it. The only way to prevent it was to stay away from him. In her heart she knew she would always love him, but she couldn't give in to that emotion. It had almost destroyed her once and that panic of being abandoned when she had needed him the most was always uppermost in her mind and kept her grounded.

When he found out the truth about Luci, he

would forever be a thorn in her side. Could she continue to fight him? Maybe that talk was long overdue.

They spent most of the day in the park and Becky didn't think about Bo once. Luci ran and played, going up slides and down slides, and jumping on and off the swings and carousels. Becky was right behind her.

Luci played with a little boy who was almost three and the son of Bubba and Margie Wiznowski. They now owned the bakery in town that had been there as long as the town had existed. Bubba was a deputy with the Sheriff's Department and Margie was entertaining their son until Bubba got off. It was nice to talk to another mother and share concerns and worries over their children. The little boy was too young to notice Luci's speech, so the park adventure was going very well.

Later that afternoon she noticed Bo's truck was at his mother's house. It hadn't been there earlier that morning and she was hoping he'd returned to Austin. But he was back and now she waited for his next move.

Bo STOOD AT the living room window and watched as Becky drove up, got Luci out and walked into the house with Luci on her hip. In denim cutoffs and a sleeveless blouse, she looked as beautiful as ever and the sun highlighted her flawless skin. The look of motherhood suited her. She thrived in it.

As his grandmother had said, you could love a person and still not like some things about them. And he really didn't like her unwillingness to forgive. Then again, he had to admit he was the same way. They had that in common. But he had never hurt her like his father had hurt him and Kelsey and his mother. There had to be a way to make this right between them, and the only way to do that was to talk. That was another thing he didn't like about her: her refusal to talk.

He ran a hand through his hair. He really needed to go back to work. All this introspection was driving him crazy. It had been simmering for years on the back burner of his thoughts and he'd just as soon have left it there. But there was Luci… Until he knew something for sure, he was hanging in.

Other things were on his mind, too. He pulled out his phone and called his sister.

"Hey, Kel."

"Bo? Is something wrong? Is it Mom?"

"Can't I call my sister without something being wrong?"

He could almost see her green eyes flashing as her mind struggled with a retort. She had their mother's eyes and their grandmother's personality.

"Sure. What's up?"

"I went to see Grandma today."

"And…?"

"She told me some things that I think she has mixed up and I wanted to check them with you."

"Grandma may not act like it sometimes, but she's very sharp. What did she say?"

"Grandpa bought you things, didn't he?"

"Are you kidding? Grandpa bought *you* things and he never bought me one blessed thing, nor did he buy our cousins, Mitzi and Sarah, anything. But Grandma made up for it by taking us all to Walmart and letting us pick out what we wanted. Those were fun times."

"Wait a minute. He bought the ATV for us, remember?"

"He bought the ATV for *you*, and you and Cole drove the wheels off it. Not in any way was that ATV any part mine."

"He bought us the horses." Bo was desperately trying to think of something that Grandpa had bought Kelsey, but now there was just a dark truth he couldn't escape. Grandma had been right.

"I didn't see one for me. Are you having temporary amnesia?"

"I guess I am. I thought the world of him and thought he treated us all equally, but I'm beginning to see that wasn't so."

"Don't let it bother you too much. Mom and Grandma made up for his lack of interest and I got used to it. Doesn't bother me at all. What bothers me the most was that our dad showed no interest in us. That will probably always hurt."

"He was here on Friday when I got home."

"Dad was there?"

"Mom wasn't expecting me, and when I drove up a strange truck was in the driveway. He was talking to Mom in the kitchen and they were looking very guilty when I walked in."

"She's talking to him again? Oh no, here we go."

"Yeah, kind of blew my top, and she said she's not in love with him anymore and I wasn't to worry, like I haven't heard that a hundred times."

"Well, we're out of the house and on our own and it's Mom's decision to make. If she's happier with him, so be it. Maybe we can get to know him now and not feel so dejected when he leaves."

"Oh, please, don't give me some kind of woman mumbo jumbo."

"Shut up."

"Let's don't argue. Did Grandma ever tell you why Mason is the way he is?"

"No. Could there be a reason?"

Bo told her what his grandmother had told him.

"You know, Bo, you need to talk to Mom. She would know more about that than anyone and it does sound believable. There had to be a reason."

Bo looked out the window again and saw Luci sitting on her front step with the dog and cat and the ball in her lap. Those pink glasses were pointed right at his house. She was waiting for him.

"I don't want to talk about him anymore. It just brings back all the hurt from when I was a kid."

"We're grown now and you should be able to handle it."

"Guess what? I'm not. Because of our

childhood I don't think you and I will ever recognize love when we find it."

"I'm not giving up. I intend to get married and have kids and have that damn happy-ever-after if it kills me."

"Keep dreaming, Kel."

"What are you doing home anyway? Don't you usually work around the clock?"

"I'm on a forced vacation."

"Good gracious! They have to force you to take a vacation?"

"Something like that."

"You're nuts, do you know that?"

"Becky's home, too," he said, for some reason unclear to himself.

"Well, now, isn't that something."

"I met her little girl. Her name is Luci."

"Bo, please don't open that wound."

"Do you know who Luci's father is?"

His sister groaned. "Becky and I work in the same hospital, but we rarely see each other and how would I know that? And why do you want to know?"

"I'm just trying to make peace with the past. That's it."

"Yeah, right. Gotta love a man who can bluff as good as you can."

"Gotta go. I'll talk to you later." He had

said enough and there was a little girl waiting on him.

"If Dad comes back, let me know."

Bo slipped his phone into his pocket and went out the front door. Try as he might, he couldn't stay away.

When he reached Luci, she stood and held up the ball. "Play. Ball."

He sat on the stoop, as did she. "We'll have to ask your mom."

Luci went into the house and he followed. Becky was at the kitchen table on a laptop. She pushed tortoiseshell glasses to the top of her head.

"Bo, what are you doing here?" she asked in a very calm voice.

"Play. Mom-my. Ball. Bo."

"I don't know, baby. Aren't you tired from the park? You ran around a lot and your cheeks were flushed."

Luci shook her head. "I. Not."

Craig came in through the French doors with dirt on his jeans. "Hey, Bo."

Luci pulled on Bo's hand. "Ball."

Bo glanced at Becky. "Go ahead, but make sure she doesn't get overtired."

That was just too easy, he thought as he followed Luci out into the backyard.

"You're okay with Bo playing with Luci?" her father asked as the French doors closed.

"Yes. You're right. I'm not sixteen and naive anymore, and if he can help my daughter then I'm going to let it happen, but I will maintain my distance."

"That's better than being antagonistic." Her dad looked down at his hands. "I have to get cleaned up."

Becky got to her feet and went to the French doors to watch Bo and Luci. They were throwing the big blue ball. Luci missed it almost every time, but Bo was very patient, coaxing and cajoling her, and she giggled and laughed until Becky couldn't stand it. She opened the door and went outside and sat on the patio. Pink and Purr followed her out.

"Now let's kick it," Bo said.

He set the ball on the ground and kicked it. It hit the board fence and bounced into her dad's flower bed, the one he'd been painstakingly working on.

Luci put her hands over her mouth. "O-ops. Grand-pa. Mad."

"Didn't hurt a thing." Bo placed the ball in front of Luci. "Your turn."

Luci tried to kick it, but she missed it every time. It broke Becky's heart and she started to go back into the house, but then Bo started talking to Luci.

He squatted in front of her. "Remember? Keep your eyes on the ball and make your foot connect with it. Eyes. Foot. Ball."

Luci nodded and drew back her leg and kicked. The ball went flying into her grandfather's famed flower bed. Luci jumped up and down screeching, "I did it. I did it!"

Becky got to her feet and couldn't believe her ears. So many times she'd tried to help Luci and all her efforts had been for naught, but Luci responded to Bo in a way that Becky couldn't explain. She sat back down and watched.

"More. Bo."

They threw and kicked the ball, and Luci ran screeching across the backyard like any almost-four-year-old. It was a delight to watch. When Luci's cheeks grew red, Becky called a halt and Luci ran to her and crawled into her lap, her heated face resting in the crook of Becky's neck.

"I. Good. Mom-my."

"Yes, you are." Becky kissed the warmth of her daughter's face and stared into the dark eyes of a man she'd thought she would hate for the rest of her life.

"Go inside and rest for a minute and I'll be in soon."

"'Kay."

Bo sat in the patio chair opposite her. "What's up, Bec?"

"Stop talking in that sarcastic voice. It doesn't become you."

"Why are you letting Luci play with me?"

"Because she wants to," Becky answered as honestly as possible. "And for some reason she responds to you. I've lost my patience with getting her to do anything. She mostly cries and just wants me to hold her."

"Then let me help her."

She stared at him, and a wealth of emotions flooded her. She tried to push them away, but all she could see was his broad shoulders stretching a black T-shirt to the max. He hadn't had those muscles back in the day, and his workout routine must be a killer. But she understood he had to be fit for his job.

"She's not your child, Bo." She felt she needed to get that point across before her strength completely collapsed.

"We'll see."

"So you did the test?"

"Yes, but I don't see why you just can't

be honest with me. I know I hurt you, but I don't deserve this."

"You're not Luci's father. How many times do I have to say that? That's the reason I wanted you to do the test, because you're not going to believe me until you see it in writing."

"Then who is?"

She got to her feet, tired of the conversation. "I'll be leaving early in the morning for work."

"You're taking Luci back to Austin?" His anxious voice imparted to her just how strong his connection to Luci was.

"No, she's staying here with my dad. If you want to see her, you can, if my dad approves. Just be very aware she's not your child."

He stood slowly and her muscles tightened at the impending doom she glimpsed in his eyes. "When the test comes back, you be very aware that I want to talk. This time you're going to talk and we're going to get all the good and bad out into the open."

"Okay. You just be prepared to handle the truth."

"I don't understand all this secrecy, but I have a whole week to wait, and during that time you and I are coming to grips with the past. And then maybe both of us can walk away or maybe we can salvage something out of our relationship." He strolled toward the gate and out of view. She exhaled deeply.

The truth? How in the world would he ever understand the truth?

CHAPTER EIGHT

THE NEXT MORNING Bo stood at the living room window, sipping coffee and watching as Becky left for the day. He didn't know if she was coming back or staying in Austin for the week. But he had a sneaking suspicion she would be back for the night. She wasn't going to leave Luci that long.

All night he'd thought about her change of heart that would let him see Luci without a big argument. She was up to something but he really didn't care what it was. Talking about the past was uppermost in his mind. If they could do that, they might be able to bridge the gulf between them. And if Luci was his, the talk would be even more important. One he had been waiting on for eighteen years.

He locked the house and headed for a training morning in Austin. A cop had to put in so many hours of training each week, but as a SWAT member his training was more vigorous and more frequent. The lieutenant hadn't mentioned keeping up his training while he was on vacation. As a sergeant, he knew the drill and his butt would be in the fire if he didn't.

He did his full routine at the police gym, from lifting weights to working with the machines, and then he put on his full tactical gear and ran the obstacle course: up stairs and down stairs, up walls and over to the other side, crawling through brush and falling to his belly to shoot at a moving target. By the time he dragged himself into the locker room he thought he might not want to do this for the rest of his life. It took a lot of stamina, and at his age he had to wonder how long his stamina would last. At thirty he used to fly over that wall. Today it took a little more energy.

There were other cops in the gym and on the practice field, but he hadn't seen anyone he worked with on SWAT. He was sure the lieutenant would get a full report of his workout, though.

Driving back to Horseshoe, he hoped Luci wasn't sitting on the step waiting for him.

As he pulled into the driveway, he saw her sitting there, once again, with the ball on her lap and Pink and Purr beside her. When she saw him she got up and ran toward him, but she fell and the ball bounced out into the street. He lifted her into his arms and brushed the grass from her pink outfit.

"Hey, little angel, are you okay?"

"Yeah. Wait. You." Her eyes were as bright as the sky.

He was going to ask about her grandpa, but then he saw Craig standing in the doorway. Bo walked toward him.

"I was watching her," Craig said. "I couldn't get her back into the house."

"Play." Luci pointed to the backyard.

Bo picked a piece of grass from her pink top. "Have you had lunch?"

Luci nodded.

Craig handed him some papers. With a frown, Bo took them. "Becky left some notes for you."

Luci wiggled down and ran to the back door. Looking through Becky's notes, the frown on Bo's forehead deepened. Was she kidding? It was a list of things to do to help Luci speak. *Singing helps. Reading helps. Try to get her to repeat sentences after you. Anything to engage her in speech.* Well now, this was a nice turn of events.

"Does Becky think I have some magical powers?"

"You'll have to ask her that. This is her decision and I hope you two can be amicable for Luci."

"Yeah." This was looking more and more like Luci was his and Becky was giving him time to adjust. He didn't think beyond that. Right now, a little girl was waiting for him. He ran outside and got the ball from the street. He was looking forward to spending the rest of the afternoon with Luci.

They kicked the ball. They threw the ball. Luci laughed and giggled, running around the backyard. She was full of energy.

"Catch. Me," she screeched. He ran behind her, caught her and threw her up into the air. Her screams of delight echoed around the neighborhood. But her face was red and she was hot. The summer heat still lingered in the air. He saw the hose that Craig had left out while he was watering the yard and flower beds. He turned it on and sprayed Luci. She giggled uncontrollably and tried to run away. He followed with the hose and she doubled over with childish laughter and fell to the ground.

He lifted her into his arms and held her

close to his chest. She was soaking wet and so was he. But he was having the time of his life with this little girl.

He sat her on the grass beneath a large oak tree and held her on his lap, trying to remember some of the things Becky had written in the note.

"I like Luci."

She smiled broadly, the water drops glistening off her eyelashes. But she wasn't getting the message.

"I like Luci. I like Luci. I like Luci. Your turn."

She shook her head.

"I like Luci. I like Luci. I like Luci. Your turn." He didn't want to come out and say *repeat the words* because she'd become more resistant, as she was with Becky. He had to try something else.

He stood. "I guess I better go back to my house since no one wants to talk to me."

"No! I. Talk."

He squatted in front of her. "I like Luci. I like Luci. I like Luci. Your turn."

"I." She paused and Bo shook his head.

"I like Luci." He said the words slowly but he didn't pause. "I like Luci."

"I like Luci." She said the words fast and

all together without pausing. He grabbed her and held her close.

"Thank you." He had meant for her to say *I like Bo* in return, but he'd take what he could get. He got to his feet and noticed Becky standing on the patio in her scrubs. She'd come home early.

Luci noticed her too, and went running. "Mom-my!" She tripped and fell into a water puddle they'd made while playing.

Bo picked her up by the waist and carried her to Becky. "I believe this belongs to you."

Luci giggled.

"She's soaking wet."

Craig brought out some towels. Becky wrapped them around Luci and they went into the house. Becky didn't say a word to him. "Thank you, too," he said to himself and turned off the water hose.

Becky put dry clothes on her daughter and ran back outside to catch Bo. She reached him as he headed down the sidewalk toward his house. "Bo."

His clothes were wet and that black T-shirt was clinging to muscles she'd never touched. And it scared her that she still wanted to. "Could we talk?"

He sauntered toward her with a glint in

his dark eyes and she wanted to smack him. "What did you say? Talk? How many times have I asked you that?"

"Well, it took me this long to make up my mind," she replied with more sass than she was feeling.

He sat on the step and she eased down beside him, careful not to sit too close.

"If you're going to tell me not to splash her with water or not to take her out in the sun, I'm already aware of those problems. I kept her in the shade and made sure she was hydrated. She was never in any danger. I do have some medical training."

"It's not about that. I just want to know how she did today. Did she say anything in a full sentence?"

He turned to look at her and his dark eyes rivaled the heat level of the sun. "So when it benefits you, it's okay to talk to me." She could hear the hurt in his voice and she remained steadfast.

"You started this by playing with her when I told you not to, and now you have somehow become her hero."

"Oh, Bec." His eyes glittered with humor. "I used to be *your* hero."

"Can we have a conversation without going back to our relationship?"

"Honestly, no. Until we resolve the issues from our past we can't go forward. I read that in a book somewhere. Aren't you proud of me?"

She gritted her teeth. "I'd be prouder if you could stick to the conversation. How did Luci do this afternoon?"

"I had to push her, but she said a sentence and then reverted back to her old way of speaking."

The knot in her chest eased. "That's a step. She won't do anything for me. She knows I'm her protector and won't hurt her."

"And I will?"

"You took that the wrong way."

He got to his feet, six foot two of muscle and strength. "Yeah, I take a lot of things the wrong way. Like a woman who won't admit who's the father of her child and makes a mystery out of it. That I don't understand at all, but obviously I'm taking it the wrong way."

She stood, her hands clenched at her sides. "You are so aggravating and…"

"It would help if I knew a little more about the situation." He interrupted her as if she hadn't spoken. "Exactly what is Craig's schedule? Evidently he's not working at the bank."

"Dad is retiring permanently in January and he goes in part-time now to train the new president of the bank. He takes Luci with him and she colors and does puzzles and things. She's very good and she thinks she's working. He brings her home for lunch and puts her down for a nap."

"I don't know if I can be here every afternoon. I do have things to do, you know."

That threw her. "Oh, of course. I don't want to intrude on your time off from work."

He pointed to her face. "Your eye's doing that little thing it does when you're upset."

"It is not." Instinctively she put a hand over her left eye. Ever since she was small, when she was upset or stressed her left eye would twitch for a moment. She hated that she couldn't control it, but as she'd gotten older it didn't happen as often. Why did it have to happen now?

He touched her arm and a surge of energy similar to electricity shot through her. An explosive energy she'd forgotten. Almost. Her hands were clammy and the sweat coating her body had nothing to do with the temperature.

"I... I better get back to Luci." She turned to go into the house. She couldn't stand being this close to him and not be affected. "Thank you for helping Luci. I appreciate it and if..."

"I'll be here tomorrow." He strolled across the street and she watched, unable to look away from his long strides. Heaven help her.

ON TUESDAY MORNING Bo did the laundry, mostly to wash his gym clothes. His mother had been late getting in again the previous night, and against his better judgment he intended to talk to her about it. She couldn't continue with those long hours. She needed some rest. And in that moment he realized he did the same thing, working so he didn't have to deal with everyday life or memories—just work. He definitely would talk to her.

He spent the afternoon with Luci. They played with the ball and the water hose, and then sat under the oak tree while Bo read to her from one of her books. He read through the whole book and then started over. Luci listened avidly, her blue eyes wide.

"Let's read it together."

Luci shook her head.

"Once upon a time. Your turn."

Luci shook her head again.

"Once upon a time," he repeated, and a stubborn look marred her pretty face.

He scooted over to where Purr was stretched out in the sun. "If you won't read with me, Purr will."

"No. Me. Read."

He scooted back to sit in front of her. "Once upon a time."

"Once." She paused.

He shook his head and said, "Once upon a time."

"Once upon a time." The words flew from her mouth.

He read the next sentence and she repeated it after him. He went through the whole book and she never paused or shook her head.

"The end."

"The end."

"Perfect." He leaned over and kissed her forehead. "You are perfect."

She giggled and he carried her into the house for dry clothes. She ran to her bedroom and Craig started to follow her, but stopped when Bo held out the small recorder he'd had in his pocket.

"Would you mind giving this to Becky?"

Bo had put the recorder in his pocket hoping he could get Luci to talk. Now, Becky would be able to hear her daughter speaking in complete sentences. Tomorrow he would do the same thing because he wanted Luci to speak as much as Becky did. Deep down he knew Luci was his daughter and he would do anything for her.

Craig looked puzzled, but he took the recorder.

Back at his house, Bo called his mother to find out if she was working late again that night.

"Yes, son, do you need anything?"

"Not a thing. I'm just worried about you working so many hours."

His mother laughed. "Really? How many times have I said those same words to you?"

"You got me. I think I'll get in touch with Cole and see what he's doing. We haven't visited much since I've been home."

"That's a good idea."

He slipped out of his wet clothes, took a shower and put on a clean pair of shorts and T-shirt. As he dressed he thought about the DNA test. He should've heard something by now.

He reached for his phone, called the lab

and within seconds Marla was on the line. "I sent it to you yesterday."

"I didn't get it."

She read the email address to him and asked if it was correct.

Damn! "I wanted it to come to my cell. I gave you the information." He was trying very hard not to get ticked off.

"Sorry, Sergeant. It went to your email."

"Never mind. I'll check my email." He cursed himself for not checking them like always, but he'd had other things on his mind. He sat at his desk, opened his laptop and brought up the document. He read through it with a sense of disappointment and a sharp pain pierced his chest. Luci wasn't his, not even close.

Dammit! Dammit! Dammit!

He jerked to his feet. It didn't make sense. He had a connection to Luci; he'd just known she was his. How could she not be? He shoved his hands through his hair and paced in his bedroom. He couldn't run over and confront Becky because she wasn't home. But the confrontation was coming.

He yanked off his clothes, put on his running shorts and sneakers and hit the front door. He ran through Horseshoe, up and down streets, and found himself on the county road where his grandparents used to live.

As his chest was about to explode he stopped, drew in a ragged breath and stared at the old house. It was now a pale yellow and Grandma's flowers were all gone, replaced with cacti and something else he didn't recognize. The chain-link fence was rusted in spots and in one area it was held up by boards. A man on an old tractor was plowing under the cornstalks where his grandfather's cornfield used to be. The place looked so small compared to the picture in his memory. Two air conditioners were stuck in windows and some kids played in the yard. They waved at him and he waved back.

Through all the pain and agony of the past all he had to do was bring up the memories of this home and they gave him peace. They kept him sane. But his memories were slightly flawed.

As he watched the tractor, a recollection wedged its way into his brain. His grandfather would say, "Never let a woman get the best of you. You're the man. Be the man."

He'd believed that one straight into the biggest heartbreak of his life. Yeah, his memories were flawed.

"Treat it kindly," he said under his breath and continued running.

While he was running he tried to keep Becky out of his mind. She'd known Luci wasn't his and yet she kept tempting him and asking him to help Luci. She worked him. She played him. And now he would get the answers he wanted.

He ran by the sheriff's office and saw Cole's truck. He darted in, going straight to where Cole was sitting and collapsed into a chair. Sweat soaked his clothes and his breath came in shallow gasps. He'd overdone it.

Cole got up, went into another room and came back with a towel and bottled water. Bo wiped his face and patted his chest, then twisted off the bottle top and took a big swig.

"What's going on?" Cole asked in his calm, steady voice.

Bo took another gulp of water. "Luci's not mine."

"Then it's time to back away."

Bo leaned forward. "Not until I've had my say. She led me on, letting me believe Luci was mine and even letting me visit with her, even asking me to help her with Luci's speech. How could she do that?"

"How many times does anyone have to tell you that you and Becky need to talk?"

"Obviously no one has told that to Becky, but it's going to happen tonight."

"Don't do anything stupid."

"She's been with someone else and has a kid by him." Bo couldn't get past that fact.

"She's been married before, so obviously she's been with someone else."

"Did you have to remind me of that?" Bo ran a hand through his damp hair. "It's time to face reality and I'm having a hard time doing that. I got really attached to that little girl and I'm going to miss her." He wiped his face with a towel. "I should've stayed in Austin, especially when I found out Becky was here. Now..." He got to his feet. "I'll see you later."

"Bo," Cole called before he could make it to the door. "Come out to the house and we'll have a beer in the barn like we used to, except we don't have to hide it from Grandpa anymore."

"Thanks, but I'm going home to handle this the best way I can."

When he reached the door, Bubba Wiznowski, a deputy, was coming in. "Hey, Bubba."

"Hey, Bo. I didn't mean to scare your parents the other night."

Bo couldn't stop a frown from spreading across his face. "What are you talking about?"

"I got a call the other night about loud voices in the park so I went to check it out. You know people call about every little thing these days. It was your mom and dad and I apologize for disturbing them."

"What were they doing?"

Bubba shrugged. "They were just sitting there on the bench talking."

Cole came out of his office and stood behind him. Now he knew the reason his mom was staying out so late. She was spending time with Mason and didn't want Bo to find out. In that moment he realized Kelsey was right. His mother had to make her own decisions, and he and his sister were grown and had their own lives. He was through getting angry over something he couldn't change.

"Thanks, Bubba."

Bubba sat at one of the desks in the outer office and Cole looked at Bo. "Where's the fireworks? The anger?"

"I'm tired of fighting this and I don't want to fight it for the rest of my life. If my mom is happy, that's all that matters. I'm just beginning to wonder what kind of dark cloud is hanging over my head. I don't need anything else to mess with my mind."

"Let's go get a beer."

"No, I don't need that either. I need to be an adult and handle the situation on my own. I'll talk to you tomorrow."

As Bo walked home darkness crept in, easing the heat of the day, and he breathed a little easier. He'd left his phone at the house so he couldn't call anyone. He didn't really want to talk, but he braced himself for what was to come and he didn't know which situation to address first. He didn't have anything to say about his parents. He was through fighting that battle. But with Becky and Luci he had a lot to say. And tonight was the night to unravel the mystery that he was caught in.

CHAPTER NINE

TUESDAY WAS SURGERY day for Dr. Eames and Becky always assisted. They had two patients who needed to have lumps removed. It was a full morning and then they saw patients in the office in the afternoon.

The day ran longer than Becky had planned. She wanted to be home to talk to Bo before he left her dad's house. His playtime with Luci was proving very beneficial, but once the DNA results came back she didn't know how long Bo's time with Luci would last. She just hoped he believed her when they talked.

As she turned the corner onto Liberty Street she saw Bo's truck and she hurriedly parked and ran in. Her dad was sitting in his chair watching television.

She threw her purse on the sofa and looked around. "Are Bo and Luci outside?"

"No. Luci's in her room playing with her dolls and Bo left a long time ago." Her heart sank almost into her shoes and that reaction made her angry. Just as she had thought— if she let her emotions get involved it would be the same old thing, ending with her getting hurt. She'd managed to protect herself all these years and now she was caught between her love of Luci and her desire to never see Bo again.

Becky walked down the hall to see her daughter and stood in the doorway, watching her for a moment. Dolls were all over the place and Luci knelt on the floor, feeding one and combing the hair of another one, her face soft and loving. Her daughter was a very affectionate child and Becky wanted to do all the right things for her.

Luci noticed her. "Mom-my." She got up and ran to Becky.

Becky lifted Luci into her arms. "How's my baby?"

"Good. Got. Wet."

"Did you? Was Bo here?"

Luci nodded. "Play."

Becky thought she would leave the Bo situation alone.

Luci nodded and they set off to the kitchen. Her dad met her in the hallway.

"I forgot to give you this. Bo left it."

Luci ran to get her iPad and Becky turned to her father. "This looks like a small digital recorder. Did you listen to it?"

"No. He said it was for you."

"Please watch Luci. I'm going to play this in my room."

Becky sat on the bed and turned the recorder on. By the time it ended, tears were running down her cheeks. Her baby was speaking in sentences, over and over with Bo's prompting. She played it again. Luci could speak. She just had to be pushed and Bo did it in such a gentle way Luci didn't know she was being pushed. She had to talk to him and let him know what a special gift this was. In doing so she would break every rule she'd ever made about Bo Goodnight.

Her dad was sitting on the sofa with Luci, watching cartoons on the iPad. "I'm going across the street just for a minute."

She knocked on the Goodnights' door and Ava answered. "Becky, what a surprise."

"I'd like to talk to Bo. Is he here?"

"Come in. Those are words I haven't heard in almost eighteen years."

"I know, but he did a really nice thing and I wanted to thank him."

"He's not here and I'm not sure where

he is. My guess is he's out running because his phone is in his room. I tried to call him and let him know I'm going back to the store and it rang in his bedroom. He should be back soon."

Becky couldn't believe how disappointed she was. Some habits were just too hard to break. "I'll catch him later."

"Does this mean you and Bo are talking?"

"Yes, about Luci. That's it."

"I don't understand my son's interest in Luci."

"He's just being Bo, sticking his nose in everything with his unwavering persistence because he wants to help. I've been waiting a long time for Luci to speak in complete sentences and she does that with Bo."

Becky slowly walked back across the street feeling drained and vulnerable. Ava probably could see right through her. Her eager face gave her away. She and Bo were getting just a little too close for Becky's comfort and she didn't know how to stop it.

She made supper and afterward gave Luci a bath. Luci chatted on and on about Bo. "Bo. Play. Fun. Water. Hose. Bo." She paused after every word. The doctors and the therapist said Luci should be talking in complete sentences by now and her resistance to do so was stubbornness and laziness. And Becky had let her get away with it. The doctor had said that Luci was comfortable speaking that way. It was her pattern and she didn't want to change and that it would take discipline on Becky's part to get her to speak correctly. So far Becky hadn't accomplished that. Bo had. That should make her very angry, but she just wanted her baby to speak in full sentences. And she was on the edge of doing that, thanks to Bo.

Tucked in bed in her pink princess nightgown, Luci smiled at her and Becky's heart swelled to double its size. She sat on the bed beside Luci. "What book do you want Mommy to read?" She gathered several off Luci's nightstand. "*Cat in the Hat, If You Give a Mouse a Cookie, Green Eggs and Ham, To Catch a Mermaid* or..."

"Mer-maid!" Luci shouted.

Becky read the book all the way through and Luci listened closely. Becky thought she would use some of Bo techniques. "Let's read it together."

"No! No!" Luci covered her ears.

Frustration overtook Becky. There was no way Luci was going to talk for her. They'd done this a hundred times and Luci reacted the same way every time. Becky now had to face the fact that she needed Bo's help. It was either that or hire a professional to work with her every day. But she was afraid that would be too stressful for her daughter. She sucked at being a mother.

Feeling deflated, she took a shower and dressed in short pajama bottoms and a T-shirt. Looking out her window she saw the Goodnight house was in darkness. Bo hadn't come home. He'd been gone too long for him to be just running. He must be out with Cole.

In high school, she'd been jealous of Cole. Bo had seemed to want to spend more time with his friend than he did with her. That had been so childish of her and it had caused a lot of arguments. It was as if she always needed Bo to prove that he loved her. Oh, heavens, could she have been any more immature?

She tucked her hair behind her ear and returned to the living room, sitting cross-legged on the sofa with her laptop in her lap. She stared into space as their relationship unfolded before her eyes.

When she was a young girl, dreams and fairy tales had filled her head about a wild, dangerously handsome boy. The boy wanted freedom and the girl wanted a home and a family. At no time had Bo ever said he wanted the same things she did. He'd just wanted her to be happy, and her happiness was him. Memories were personal views of the past. Sometimes you could see them clearly and other times you couldn't see them at all. She could now see her childish behavior and foolish expectations had been very unrealistic.

She jumped as the front door opened.

In running shorts, T-shirt and sneakers, Bo stood in the living room, his dark eyes aflame with fury. "You lied to me."

She swallowed hard and got to her feet, carefully placing the laptop on the sofa. "Did you ring the doorbell? I didn't hear it."

"No. I didn't want to wake Luci and the door was unlocked." His words came out as abruptly as a whiplash.

"What did I lie to you about?"

"You led me to believe that Luci was mine."

"I did not. I told you repeatedly Luci wasn't yours and you refused to believe me. That's why I gave you her hair to do the DNA test and obviously the result has come back."

"Who's Luci's father?" The three words

were fired at her like bullets and she felt their sting. "And don't give me that crap about it being none of my business. You made Luci my business and now I want to know who her father is. No lies. No deception. Just the truth."

She weighed her options every which way from Sunday, but she could only find one that worked for her and Luci. She had to be honest and tell Bo the whole truth, and in doing so she would never be the same again. Bo would be forever embedded in her life. She knew that much about him. He wasn't going to walk away without another word.

Standing straight with her dignity intact, she replied, "Bradley Taylor."

Bo frowned. "The name sounds familiar. Do I know him?"

"You don't know him, but you've met."

"Does he work for the police department?"

"No."

"How did you meet him and why isn't he a part of Luci's life?"

"I've only met him a couple of times."

"That doesn't make any sense. Who is Bradley Taylor?"

"Think, Bo. You're a better police officer than that."

"Now it's a guessing game?"

"Think, Bo." She wanted him to get it on his own and not shove it down his throat.

He ran both hands through his hair. "Bradley Taylor... Bradley Taylor..." He snapped his fingers. "Bradley Taylor and Melissa Tate. I got it. They're the couple who were holed up in a house having a baby and no clue of what they were getting into. What does this have to do with Bradley Taylor? He's a teenager."

"You're not getting it."

His eyes narrowed. "You mean...?"

"Yes, Luci is that baby. I adopted her."

Disbelief sapped his strength and he struggled to understand the truth. That was the connection he and Luci had. It wasn't biological. It was something much deeper. He'd been there to save her life. God had put him there at that moment for a reason.

He went down the hall to Luci's room. He could see by the night-light that she lay on her back with the big stuffed bear in one arm. He bent down and placed his hand on her small chest and felt the thump against his palm. *Thump. Thump. Thump.* He knew this little girl by the beat of her heart. Oh, man.

Becky stood in the doorway watching him

and his anger floated away on a cloud of gratitude. Gratitude Luci was alive. He left Luci's bedroom and Becky followed him back into the living room.

"How come you couldn't say you adopted her?"

"It was complicated and I didn't want you involved in my life."

"You asked me to help her. Tell me where any of that makes sense."

Becky sat on the sofa and he noticed for the first time she was in her nightclothes. His mind went in a completely different direction, but he curbed it quickly. "Why all the secrecy, Bec?"

She looked down at her hands clasped in her lap. "After you brought her in that day, I couldn't stop thinking about her so I went to the pediatric ICU to see her. She was so tiny and had the most gorgeous blue eyes. I fell in love instantly.

"I was there when the police brought the father because he wanted to see his daughter. He wanted to keep her, but his mother wouldn't let him. He had a scholarship to Harvard and she made sure he was going. He cried and I felt sorry for him, but his mother wouldn't budge.

"Then his father came and he agreed with the mother that Bradley was too young to raise a child. He eventually signed away his paternal rights. He came again to see her when I was there, and I told him that I would make sure a nice family adopted her. I knew that I would try to keep her myself and I did. I was approved all the way down the line. She's my little girl and I love her just as much as if I'd given birth to her. Her happiness, health and well-being are my main concerns."

"Does my mother know Luci is adopted?"

"No. Very few people do. Luci became a ward of the state and when she was well enough to leave, she went into foster care. I visited with her every day, waiting for the paperwork to be finalized. When the approval finally went through, I took her home."

"Does Kelsey know?"

"No, just a few of my friends and the people in the office."

He sat beside her. "I went every day after work to see her and had to put on scrubs, a mask and a cap. They'd let me sit with her for a while. She had so many tubes in her and I had my doubts about her surviving, but each day she grew stronger and stronger.

"I would sit with my hand on her stomach and talk to her, and she would turn her head in my direction and her blue eyes just lit up the whole world. The nurses said someone was trying to adopt, but I never dreamed it was you. I was disappointed the day I went there and she was gone. I often wondered where she was and I sincerely hoped she was happy and had a good life. All the time her adoptive mother was just across the street. Is that ironic or not?"

"I wasn't across the street. I was in Austin." For some reason she seemed to want to make that clear.

"You will always be across the street to me."

She jumped up and paced in front of the coffee table. "Okay, you're not going to like this, but I'm going to tell you the truth. I didn't want you to know I had the baby."

"Why?"

"The nurses told me about your visits to see Luci and I knew she meant something to you. I didn't want to have to deal with you wanting to see her and spend time with her. I couldn't handle that."

"Why? I told you many times I'm sorry

for what happened when I joined the army. I wasn't thinking. I just wanted to get away."

"And you forgot about me." The words were thrown at him like a dead fish, the stink hitting him in the face.

"I never forgot about you. You were the first person I went to see when I came home on leave. You were the first person I went to see every time I came home, even after you married that doofus. And I tried through all the intervening years to talk to you and I hit a brick wall every time. You carry a grudge like the devil carries a pitchfork, and with each rejection you stabbed me through the heart. I'd like to know why."

"So now you're the hurt one?" Her voice rose in defiance.

"No, I'm the one who did wrong, but I need to know why you can't forgive me. Why is that so hard for you?"

She sat beside him again and the scent of her hair drifted to him. Mimosa Rain. She'd used that shampoo years ago and it still triggered his senses. "Okay. Back then my whole world was you. My dad was busy at the bank, late meetings, card games with his friends and I was alone a lot. But I really wasn't alone, I had you. All my hopes and dreams were centered on you and our lives. I would never, ever love anyone like I did you. I wanted a home and lots of children, and to see your face every morning when I woke up. I thought you wanted the same things, but evidently you didn't. I didn't realize it until I woke up that morning and watched you drive away without even saying goodbye one last time."

"We said goodbye the night before."

She turned to face him, brushing tears from her eyes, and his heart shattered like a target hit by an M24 rifle. "I stood at my window and watched you leave and not once did you look back. Did you not even think about coming over here for a hug or a kiss? You were going to be gone for a long time. And don't say you're sorry. I don't want to hear it. I heard it about a hundred times or more and it still doesn't have any effect on what you broke in me. I can't get those feelings back. They died that day."

His throat closed up. He had no words to explain his actions. That morning he hadn't even thought of her. Adrenaline had been pumping through his veins as he anticipated the new phase of his life, and he couldn't wait to pick up Cole and get his new life started.

He hadn't even thought about her. As the memory ran through his mind, words from his grandfather came to him and he had to tell her about his misguided thinking.

"I went to see my grandmother the other day."

"Oh?" She sounded confused and was probably wondering what that had to do with what they were talking about.

"My grandpa was my hero. He was there for me when my dad wasn't and I put him up on a pedestal."

"You talked a lot about him."

Bo rubbed his hands together, trying to gather words that would make sense. "My grandmother was saying bad things about my grandfather and I told her I didn't want to hear them. Then she unloaded on me, some home truths I also didn't want to hear. I thought she didn't remember the past like I did, so I called my sister and she confirmed what my grandmother had said."

He took a deep breath. "My grandfather had issues with women. He treated them like second-class citizens. I never saw that. I guess I was blinded by my love for him. When I got the results of Luci's DNA test, I was upset and took off running. I found myself on the old county road where my grand-parents used to live.

"Some of those home truths hit me hard as I remembered some of the things my grand-father had said to me. The gospel according to my grandpa was *never let a woman get the upper hand.* You're the man. Be a man. Never let a woman tell you what to do.

"You're the man. Be a man. Never give in to a woman. You're the man. Be a man. It was all garbage ingrained in me by the narrow-minded prejudices of my grandfather. I ar-rogantly believed you would be waiting for me. I was the man. What crap!"

"You weren't like that. You never made me feel that way."

He looked at her then and had to tell her the truth. "I never thought of you the morn-ing I left. I was eager to leave and that was all that was on my mind. I never thought of your feelings and that makes me just like my grandfather."

She blinked. "You never thought of me that morning?" Her voice held a tinge of hope that she'd heard him wrong.

He exhaled deeply. "No." He wanted to say he was sorry, but that word was just an excuse for his behavior and it couldn't heal wounds or mend her broken heart. The only thing he could do was to prove he wasn't that arrogant, misguided teenager anymore and to be there for her now.

She got to her feet, her shoulders squared. "I was right across the street, crying my eyes out, and you never thought of me, the person you professed to love." She gulped a breath. "It's over and done and we can't go back and change a thing. Right now, my focus is on Luci."

"Mine, too."

"Yeah." She pleated the hem of her T-shirt in a nervous gesture. He had a feeling she wanted to say a lot more and was holding her breath.

"What do we do about Luci?"

Her eyes narrowed. "She's my daughter."

"I'm well aware of that, but I can't just walk away, if that's what you're expecting me to do."

"That's exactly what I'm expecting you to do."

"What about her speech?"

Becky bit her lip and he knew that gesture well. She was upset. "You can still see Luci when I'm not here. She likes you and I won't keep her from seeing you. That doesn't mean I have to see you. I'd just as soon we kept our distance."

"If that's what you want."

"I do, and now I want you to leave."

He dragged his sweat-coated body from the sofa with a heavy heart and walked to the door without a backward glance. He'd walk over hot coals for her if she wanted him to. He owed her that.

CHAPTER TEN

BECKY CLOSED THE door and wanted to sink to her knees and cry like she had when she was six years old and a friend had broken her favorite doll. The head had been ripped right off and tonight Bo had ripped her heart out. But she wasn't going to shed one tear. She walked into the kitchen and turned the light out, then did the same thing in the living room. She went to bed, stopping only to check on Luci.

Curling beneath the sheets, Becky tried to block his words from her mind, but she couldn't. *He never thought of me.* How could she be in love with someone who hadn't cared enough about her to say one last goodbye? He'd be away for months and she hadn't been his top priority. She never had been. It was so clear now.

When she'd first met him, he and Cole were always together. They'd become a trio. Eventually, they'd made time for themselves apart from Cole. Bo had pushed her for sex, but she hadn't been ready. He'd hung in there until she decided she wanted it, too. And she'd paid for that with a shattered heart that could never be put back together again.

With his close connection to Luci, Becky had hesitated about adoption. But the baby had stolen her heart and Becky couldn't walk away. Still, Bo and Luci had that connection and the nurses told Becky about it every day. They told her how Bo would sit by her incubator with his hand on her chest, talking to her. They were in awe. So was she. There were times she'd wanted to talk when he'd asked her. She was glad now she never had. She was strong enough now to hear it without breaking down. *He never thought of me.*

That's when the tears she'd sworn not to shed came, rolling down her cheeks, soaking her T-shirt. Some things she just couldn't stop.

She must have fallen asleep because the next thing she heard was a tiny voice calling, "Mom-my. Mom-my." And it was close. She reached down and pulled Luci into the bed on top of her.

"What's the matter, baby?"

"Sleep. Mom-my."

Usually Becky would take her back to her bed, but tonight she settled Luci beside her and snuggled close. "Go to sleep, baby." She brushed the hair from her child's face and kissed her forehead.

There were times she questioned her interest in Luci as an infant. Was it because of Bo and what the nurses had said about him? It had shown her a different side of him and she'd liked it. But her interest in Luci had been all about the baby from the first moment Becky had seen her. It was love, a pure mother's love.

She kissed Luci one more time. "I love you." And because of that love she would allow Bo to see Luci and help with her speech. Beyond that, she would put Bo Goodnight in her rearview mirror.

Bo TOOK A shower and lay across his bed in his underwear, feeling depleted. He'd always thought that talking to Becky would solve all their problems. Wrong! Talking to Becky had highlighted his problem, his personality, his way of thinking. And it had all been wrong.

His stomach cramped as he closed his eyes and saw the hurt in hers. He had hurt her one more time, but he'd wanted to be honest. He'd wanted her to know and now…he had nothing. Not even hope.

He got up and turned off the light, flipped on the ceiling fan and crashed, shutting out everything. He stirred when he heard his mom in the kitchen. He glanced at the clock and saw it wasn't even five yet. Slipping on a pair of shorts and a T-shirt, he prepared to go through another agonizing conversation.

"Bo." His mom jumped back from the coffee maker and held a hand to her chest. "You startled me. I thought you were sleeping."

Bo poured a cup of coffee and leaned against the kitchen counter. "I had a talk with Bubba yesterday." Since they both had been through this before, he didn't beat around the bush. He just wanted her to know it didn't matter to him anymore.

She poured coffee into an insulated container and screwed the top on. "What does that mean?"

"It means you're seeing Mason again and trying to hide it. I talked to Kelsey about him and we both decided that you both need to do what you want and leave us out of it. We're grown and you can make your own decisions. I'm done. Kelsey's done."

"It's not what you're thinking."

"I think it is. This house is in my name so you'll have a place to live when he leaves you for another woman again. But that's your choice. I'll probably go back to Austin today." He walked toward his bedroom.

"He's dying."

Bo stopped in his tracks and swung around to face his mother. "He pulled that on you and you fell for it? Mom... I have no words."

"He has stage IV lung cancer and they gave him six months to live. That was three months ago. He just wanted to talk about his kids and I couldn't do that here because of you. Yes, he's done a lot of bad things, but I wanted him to know about his children and how good they turned out in spite of us."

"In spite of him."

"Let it go, son. He doesn't have much longer and if you have anything to say to him, I'd advise you to say it now."

"You just took his word for it?"

She shook her head. "I went with Mason to tell your grandmother. She's pretty torn up. You might want to visit her if you can keep your temper in check."

My father is dying. Bo couldn't wrap his head around that. For years he'd just wanted Mason to disappear and not come back, but now…now Bo realized he didn't want that. He wanted Mason to stay and be a man. *Be a man.* The words resounded in his head and he realized again they were his grandfather's words. Be a man! He wondered how many times Mason had heard those words. Dammit. How wrong could he be about so many things?

His mother put her arms around him and held him tight. The coffee cup shook in his hand and he held on to her like he had when he was twelve years old. After a moment, he stepped back.

"I'm okay, Mom."

"No, you're not. You need time to digest this. Your father wants to talk to you and it's up to you if you want to do that. Just think about it. I'm not pressuring you and neither is your father."

"I need to think about this."

"Sure." She touched his hair. "You need a haircut. I have to go to work, but I'll try to be back by noon."

"I don't know where I'll be at noon. I have to do a lot of thinking."

Bo sat on his bed staring out the window toward Becky's house. His mind was blank as he tried to absorb everything he'd learned in the past twenty-four hours. He watched as Becky came out dressed in her blue scrubs, got into her car and left. A little later Craig appeared, carrying Luci. He put her into the car seat and they drove away. For the first time in a long time, loneliness pierced Bo's heart and he wasn't sure what to do next. Thinking was too hard and he couldn't re-live all the years of anger toward his father. He had to go forward, just as he had to with Becky.

He pulled out his phone and called his sister.

"Hey, I was just going to call you," Kelsey responded.

"I guess you heard, then."

"Yeah. I was just thinking about what I was going to do, but before I made that decision I wanted to talk to you."

Bo squeezed his eyes shut and tried to leave the anger behind. "I don't know, sis. I'm taking this slow."

"I'm going to see him," Kelsey announced. "I couldn't live with myself if I didn't. He's my father and I want to say goodbye, and I hope you do the same thing for your own piece of mind."

"Okay."

"Bo…"

"I'll think about it, Kel."

"I'll give you a couple of days and maybe we can do it together."

"Okay."

He leaned back on the bed and watched the ceiling fan go round and round until it lulled him into sleep. He woke up with a start and wondered what time it was. His phone was on his chest and he quickly glanced at it. It was after one. He hadn't gotten much sleep the previous night and his body and brain had been tired. As he walked by his bedroom window he saw Luci sitting on the step across the street with the ball in her lap and the cat and dog beside her. In her pink glasses and pigtails she was about the cutest thing he'd ever seen.

Through all the heartache, this little girl was a blessing and he wasn't going to run out on her. He wasn't going to hide and try to leave his past behind. He had to face it head-on, all of it, the pain, the sadness and the tears. The only way to go forward was to admit he'd been wrong.

As soon as he opened his front door and started toward her, Luci got up and ran to the curb. Of course, she tripped and he grabbed her and threw her up into the air. She giggled. He lifted her onto his shoulders and they went to her backyard to play. They did the same things they had done the previous day and later sat under the oak tree reading a book. The temperature was in the nineties and stifling at times, but with their wet clothes and the breeze they were cool.

Luci sat in his lap as he read to her. She repeated everything without pausing, as he'd asked her. They'd made so much progress in a few days and he knew he had to keep helping her. He couldn't run back to Austin to soothe his injured male pride.

He left before Becky got home, not leaving her a tape this time. He felt it was best that way. At his house he called his lieutenant. If he was going to help Luci, he needed more time. And he needed time to face whatever he had to do about his father.

"Hey, Lieutenant."

"Goodnight? Don't ask to come back to work."

"I'm not. I'd like an extra week off."

"What?"

"I have vacation time coming and I'd like to take it now."

"This is a little startling, coming from you, but take the time."

"Thank you."

It was the last thing Bo had thought he would ever want, but things changed and now he had to be the man he wanted to be—not the one his grandfather had created.

He quickly changed into jeans and shirt and went to see his grandma.

BECKY WAS BUSY and she didn't have much time to think about Bo. They had a patient, Kathy Purcell, who was twenty-eight years old and four months pregnant. The doctors had just discovered she had stage I breast cancer and Mrs. Purcell had an appointment to discuss her options.

It was an emotional meeting, as Kathy's top priority was her baby. The cancer had to come out before it spread. It wasn't in the lymph nodes and that was good. Dr. Eames felt once they removed the cancerous tumor that Kathy could have a healthy baby. Kathy wanted time to think about it.

All Becky wanted to do at the end of the day was to go home and hold her own baby. Life was so precious, and too many times she had taken it for granted, but today she was well aware of how valuable every moment was.

She went into the house through the garage and the first thing she heard was screeching. Then a flash of color dashed down the hall and away again. Had that been Luci?

Walking into the kitchen, she saw her dad fixing supper. She placed her briefcase and purse on the counter. "Is that Luci running around screaming?"

"Yes. She has a lot more energy these days, running around and babbling. All because of Bo. He has a way with her. She wanted me to tie a towel around her neck and she said something about super."

"She has a book about that and I guess Bo read to her today. He was here, right?"

Her dad wiped his hands on a dishtowel. "Yep. He was here and played all afternoon out there in the yard."

"Did he say anything about how she did?"

"No. He didn't say a thing, but from Luci's actions I think it went very well."

Luci ran into the kitchen, out of breath. "Mom-my. 'atch. Me."

Luci ran off, fell down, got back up without a whimper and took off down the hall into her room and back again. "Me. Super."

Becky swung her up into her arms and kissed her. "Yes, you are."

Luci wiggled down and was off again.

Becky gazed after her. "She has an appointment tomorrow with the doctor and the therapist. I hate to tell her because she always cries and doesn't want to go."

Her dad pointed across the street. "Get Bo to take her. She'll do anything he asks and he's not doing anything."

"Dad, I can't dump my problems on Bo."

Her dad hugged her around the shoulders. "It'll give you a reason to talk away from the house. It could be a good thing."

"I've already talked to Bo and it was a disaster." She told him about the conversation and what Bo had said.

Her dad shrugged. "So he didn't think about you at that precise moment. You spent half the night with him and were late getting home, and I allowed it because he was leaving.

"He didn't run over here the next morning and you were upset about it. That's a little self-centered and I didn't raise you that way. The boy had a tortured life and he was eager to get away and make something of himself, and I admire that. So should you. I would advise you to stop wearing those eggshell feelings. They don't become you."

The rebuke startled her. Her dad was always on her side. She stood there with words tripping over themselves to be heard, and none of them soothed her bruised ego because deep down she knew her father was right. She had been selfish. She squeezed her eyes shut and knew what she needed to do. Her life was about Luci and she had to do what was best for her. As her dad had said, she needed to stop with the eggshell feelings.

"That was a little strong," she mumbled.

"Think about it and you'll see your old dad is right."

"I'd rather you pamper me." She shot him a sly grin.

"Hmmph." He turned back to the stove.

"Dad, can you bring Luci into Austin tomorrow around three?" She wasn't quite ready to give in and see Bo again.

"You know I hate driving in traffic now. I'd rather not, especially since you have someone who can easily do it."

"You're aggravating, do you know that?"

"Bo has gotten more out of Luci than we have, and in just a few days. Sink your pride and do the right thing. He needs to know what's going on with Luci, health-wise."

"What are you cooking?" she asked, to change the subject.

"Spaghetti, of course. My granddaughter's favorite."

Becky thought about it and wondered if her life was always going to be tangled up in Bo's. She thought about Kathy and her unborn baby, and Becky knew she would do anything to help Luci, even if that meant spending time with Bo.

Bo KNOCKED ON his grandmother's door but there was no response. He turned the doorknob and, of course, it was unlocked. He heard music. It was his dad's voice singing "Rock of Ages." He stepped into the apartment and saw his grandmother sitting in her recliner, listening to a CD of his father's. She dabbed at her eyes with a tissue and he took a deep breath and walked closer.

"Grandma…"

She turned around, her eyes red. Someone must've cut her hair because it was short. She turned off the CD player. "Beauregard. Have you heard?"

He swallowed to speak. "Yes, I heard." He

squatted by her chair and she put her arm around him and hugged him. He hugged her back. "I'm sorry, Grandma."

She wiped at her eyes and he took a seat on the sofa facing her.

"He was such a tortured little boy and he never recovered from it. That's my fault. I should've hit Sam upside the head with an iron skillet. I should've done something. I keep thinking of what I should've done."

"Grandma, you can't change a thing."

She nodded. "It's just not fair. He's getting his life together and this happens."

"I'm sorry, Grandma," Bo said again.

She pointed a finger at him. "That's what I wanted to hear. I want you to forgive your dad because all you've got left now is forgiveness. Do you hear me?"

"Yes, ma'am."

"Good. I'll sleep a little easier knowing that." She looked around. "Have you seen my glasses?

"They're on the top of your head."

"Oh. I forget sometimes." She turned the CD player back on. "Listen to this with me."

He sat and listened to his father's voice, and something inside him snapped, something he had been holding on to for a long time with a deathly grip—his anger. It disappeared into his father's melodious voice and Bo didn't try to grab it back. He didn't need it anymore.

After a while his grandmother turned the CD player off and she talked about her son. Bo listened with an open heart. He didn't want to gag and run away from the words. It was almost the same thing she'd told him before, but he let her talk.

When she stopped, he said, "Grandma, I'm gonna go now, but I'll be back."

"You always were such a good boy."

He didn't know about that. He was just trying to find his way right now. After kissing her forehead, he started for the door.

"Wait, Beauregard. Did you take my pants back?"

"Huh… I gave you the money for them, remember? So I wouldn't have to come back."

"No, you didn't. You're supposed to use your gun and badge to get my money back."

"It doesn't work like that. Grandma…" A smart man always knew when he'd been conned and he knew he'd been had by his grandmother. He pulled out his wallet and handed her ten dollars.

"Plus tax."

He gritted his teeth and handed her another dollar.

"Did you tell them they were uncomfortable?"

The trash can hadn't responded when he threw them away, so he replied, "You got your money back so be grateful for that."

"You bet I am."

He leaned over and whispered in her ear. "Never try to con a cop."

She chuckled as he went out the door and he was glad she was in a better mood. But the worst was yet to come.

CHAPTER ELEVEN

BECKY LOOKED OUT the window to see if Bo was home, and his truck still wasn't there. It was getting late and she wondered where he could be. She gave Luci a bath and tucked her in. Her baby was tired and fell asleep almost instantly.

The next time she peeped out the window she saw Bo's truck. "Dad, I'm going over to talk to Bo. Listen for Luci."

"Use your charm. He won't know what hit him."

"Dad!"

She didn't know she had that kind of charm anymore, and she certainly wasn't using it on Bo. After last night, he'd probably laugh at her about-face. But her dad was right. She had gotten all bent out of shape over something trivial, though little things could mean a lot to a seventeen-year-old girl.

She knocked at the front door and waited. She knocked again.

"It's open." She heard Bo's deep voice.

Becky tentatively opened the door and walked in. Bo was sprawled on the couch. His head rested on one of the cushions and his legs stretched out in front of him. He'd taken his boots off and he had a look on his face she'd seen many times. He was in pain. The pain that could only be caused by one person—his father.

"What's wrong?" she asked, as if they were the best of friends.

He sat up and rubbed his hands between his knees. "A whole lot of heartache, Bec. That's what's wrong."

He wasn't making any sense. She sat beside him and she couldn't believe how her emotions were focused totally on him now. "What happened?"

"My dad has three months to live."

She touched his arm. "I'm sorry."

"Yeah, everybody is. My mom wants me to talk to him. My sister wants me to go with her to see him and my grandma wants me to forgive him. They're in my face, but they don't understand how hard that is for me, even though I know the past didn't happen exactly as I remember it."

She bit her lip, trying not to give him advice, but she couldn't help herself. "I think you'll regret it if you don't see him one last time."

"He'll only say he's sorry, which is something I've heard many times."

"Then listen to him say it one more time. He needs to say it and you need to hear it."

He looked at her and the pain in his dark eyes made her tremble. "I thought you weren't talking to me."

"I… I didn't say I wouldn't talk to you." She was trying to find an explanation for her actions and she couldn't. "Okay, I was out of line last night and overreacted, but when you said you never thought of me, I turned into that seventeen-year-old girl who was across the street crying her eyes out. I really have matured beyond that."

"Really?"

She lifted her chin. "Yes."

He didn't come back with a sarcastic retort. He rubbed his hands together once again and stared at them. "I don't think I can do what my mother, sister and grandmother want me to do."

She touched his leg. "Yes, you can. You're stronger than that, Bo."

He reached out and pulled her close, and

she leaned against him as if she was starving for his touch. Her head rested just below his chin and the musky masculine scent reached senses that had been dead for too many years. She'd missed him and she hadn't realized until that moment just how much. She'd heard it said that love hurt—she could honestly say that it did.

He leaned back with her in his arms and they sat there for a long time as she listened to the beat of his heart. They used to sit like this in his truck, on her sofa, and talk. They could talk about anything and it was one of the things she'd loved most about him.

He kissed her forehead. "This is nice. I'd rather do this than argue with you."

She would, too, but she didn't say the words.

"We can't go back, Bo. We have different lives now."

"Yeah. I'm like my grandma. I sometimes forget."

That ache in his voice was almost her undoing. She patted his chest and resisted the urge to let her hands linger. "You'll do fine talking to your father. Just listen and don't react out of anger. This will be your last chance and you need to take it. Tell him how you feel and how you felt all those years when he would leave. That's all you have to do."

He lifted her chin and kissed her for a brief moment, and she was lost in all the emotions that he created in her. It was nice. It was perfect. And she just wanted to go with the moment and not think about anything else. But then there was Luci...

She slid out of his arms and got to her feet. "I better go."

"Did you come over here for a reason?"

A few minutes in his arms and she'd forgotten all about it. She was a total mess.

"Yeah." She slipped her hands into the pockets of her shorts. "I wanted to ask you a favor."

"A favor?"

"Luci has a three o'clock appointment tomorrow in Austin."

"Okay. I won't come over tomorrow."

"No, that's not it. Since the accident, my dad doesn't like to drive in heavy traffic and I was hoping you'd bring Luci to Austin for me."

He got to his feet. "You trust me with her?"

"Of course. Why wouldn't I? You saved

her life and I know you wouldn't do anything to jeopardize it."

"I guess I can work it into my busy schedule." That confident gleam was back in his eyes.

"If you want, you can stay and visit with the doctor and therapist with me, so you'll know what's going on with Luci."

"I'd like that. Thank you for asking me."

His soft demeanor was weakening every bit of resolve in her, but she felt this could only be a good thing. She pulled out her phone. "Can I have your cell number, please?"

They exchange numbers and Becky opened the door to go. "Oh, I should probably tell you not to mention doctor or therapist to Luci. If she knows she's going to see them, she will cry and plead and beg until your ears ring from all the drama."

"I've been thrown to the wolves, huh?"

She smiled and it felt good. Bo used to make her smile all the time and she'd missed that, too. "I'll send the doctor's address and meet you there."

"Thanks, Bec." He brushed a hand through his dark hair and she had the urge to stay a little longer just to make sure he was okay. Bo was strong enough to handle his own battles and she knew he would make the right decisions concerning his father. She just hoped she'd done the right thing by inviting Bo back into her life.

Bo WAS UP early the next morning. He wanted to talk to his mother. They sat at the kitchen table eating breakfast.

"Tell me about Mason." The words were easy to say and his mother was eager to talk. They were basically the same things his grandmother had told him. Bo's grandpa had called Mason all kinds of names when he was younger. Grandpa never let up on trying to make Mason into the kind of "man" Grandpa thought he should be.

"He made our lives miserable," his mom said. "Remember that time you caught your father in bed with that woman?"

"It's burned into my memory, Mom."

"Your grandfather showed up a little later. Do you remember that?"

"Yeah. He was cussing and calling Mason names because of what he'd done." It was exactly what Bo had wanted to hear. He'd wanted his father to hurt like he was hurting.

"I asked him to leave."

Bo frowned. "You did? I don't remember that."

"Yes, after what my son had been put through it angered me that Sam thought he had a right to come in here and take over. He pointed a finger at me and said no woman told him what to do. I then told him that if he didn't leave I would call the sheriff.

"He left in a huff. I didn't care. I didn't want you to listen to that kind of talk. Sam had always been a thorn in our marriage. I know Mason caused a lot of our problems, but if he hadn't heard he was a loser, half a man and good for nothing all his life, he might have turned out differently."

Bo took a sip of his coffee. "I don't know if I can see him and talk to him. I'm struggling with that. I just want to be honest with you."

His mother patted his hand on the table. "You do what you feel you have to. I'll understand."

"Grandma says forgiveness is all I have left."

"She might be right." His mom got up and gave him a quick hug. "I have to go to work."

Bo stood and stretched, feeling like his brain was going to explode. He needed a distraction. He sat on the sofa, pulled out his phone and called Hutch. "Hey, how's it going?"

"Like always. We had a convenience store robbery and the guy was still in there holding the clerk as hostage. We had to go in and take him. It went smoothly. He's sitting in a jail cell now."

"No one got hurt?"

"No. We can actually run a call without you, Sarge. The lieutenant kept him talking while Cruz and I snuck in the back and took him down within seconds. Then the rest of the team rushed in and took charge of the scene."

"Good job. I just wanted you and the guys to know I won't be back for another week. I have some family matters I need to take care of."

"Sorry to hear that, Sarge. Just get back as soon as you can. It's not the same without you."

Bo ended the call with a smile. They could do very well without him; they were all highly trained professionals. But the words were good to hear.

He slipped on his shorts and T-shirt, and drove into Temple to get a haircut, first one in over two months. The stylist left a little length and combed it all back. He then stopped and bought a car seat, and installed it in his truck. When he got home, he shaved off his beard. He stared a moment at the man in the mirror, hardly recognizing him. He had been a little shaggy lately and now he was squeaky clean, just like Cole.

He made a sandwich and drank a glass of milk with his eye on the clock. Luci woke up about one thirty and they had to leave before two. Actually, he wanted to leave earlier so he could deal with Luci.

His phone pinged. Pulling it out of his pocket, he saw it was a text from Becky. It provided the address of the doctor's office and he knew exactly where it was.

There was a note beneath: When she sees the office, she'll know where she is and she'll probably throw a hissy fit. Don't let her cry too much.

He texted back: I can handle it.

She texted: You're in for such a surprise.

He tapped a smiley emoji and put the phone in his pocket. Marching across the street, a smile spread across his face. Becky and her notes. She was very organized and he remembered it had driven him crazy in high school. Craig opened the door with Luci in his arms. She rubbed her eyes, still sleepy.

Craig handed him a note. It was a list from Becky of things he needed to do. Like what clothes for Luci to wear.

"Are you kidding me? What's wrong with the clothes she has on?"

Craig shrugged. "I put the pink bows around her pigtails that came undone while she was sleeping and combed her hair. I do that every morning anyway."

Luci's feet were bare. "Where's your shoes, little angel?"

Luci pointed to her room.

It took a minute to put on her white sandals. He glanced at the white shorts and a pink top that had a white heart and colorful flowers. It looked fine to him. He lifted the girl into his arms.

"Ready to go with Bo?"

She nodded.

Before he could open the door, Craig was there with a large bag.

"What's that?" Bo asked.

"Luci's bag. Her water and juice are in there and an extra set of clothes if she has an accident. Some wipes and…"

"I got it," Bo interrupted.

"I already took her to the potty so you're set to go."

An accident? Potty? When he and Luci played outside and she had to potty, she would go inside and Craig was there to help her. Now Bo had to do that? He was totally clueless and out of his comfort zone.

"You can take the car seat out of my car," Craig said.

"I bought one," Bo replied, going out the door.

With Luci secure in her car seat they were off.

"Where. Bo?"

"We're going for a drive." He evaded the question.

"Play."

"Not today, little angel. We have something more important to do."

Luci watched the traffic and didn't say anything else. Soon she was sound asleep. It didn't take him long to find the glass-and-brick building that housed doctors' offices near the hospital. When he parked and turned off the engine, Luci woke up and looked around.

"No! Home!"

Bo got out and went around and opened

the door so he could talk to her. "What's wrong?"

Luci shook her head. "No!"

When he tried to take her out of the seat, she pulled away. "No!"

This was a problem. He wasn't used to disciplining children, but if he could discipline men he should be able to handle this.

"Luci, look at me."

She turned her head, a big frown on her face.

"Everybody has to see the doctor. Even I have to see the doctor. I'm a cop so I have to go to the doctor for checkups to make sure I'm healthy. And that's what we're going to do today to make sure you're healthy. You told me once that you were different. The only way to change that is to see the doctor so we can make sure that you're not different anymore."

"Mean!"

"Me or the doctor?"

"You!"

He was the bad guy now, but he knew how to deal with this little angel. He squatted and placed a hand over his heart. "That breaks my heart and makes me so sad. I guess you're not my friend anymore and we can't play together."

"No! No! You. My. Friend."

"Then we're going to go see the doctor and afterward we'll get an ice cream, any kind you want."

She stretched out her arms. "Big."

"As big as you want." He reached in, unhooked her from the car seat and made his way to the entrance. Luci buried her face in his neck, whimpering. It shook his strong resolve.

He patted her back. "You're not going to cry on me, are you?"

Luci didn't say anything and they went up in the elevator to the designated floor. Inside the office, two mothers, each with a child on her lap, sat in chairs, but Becky wasn't there. He started to call her, but decided to wait.

"Potty," Luci whispered in his ear.

Oh, man. He'd have to wing this.

He asked the receptionist where the bathroom was and she pointed to the hallway. Once inside Luci wiggled down from his arms.

"Me. Do." She went to the children's toilet and pushed her shorts and panties down. "No. Look."

He turned around to face the door, smiling. "Do you need any help?"

"No."

A tinkling sound filled the room and he peeked to see if she needed help. But she hopped down and pulled her panties and shorts up, although they were crooked.

"Can I turn around?"

"Yes. Wash. Hands."

He held her up to the sink while she washed her hands and he had a chance to straighten her shorts.

She pointed to the toilet.

"What?"

She walked over and pointed to the handle.

"You can't push it?"

She shook her head.

"You have to push it down hard. Try it."

She used both hands and pushed, and the toilet flushed. Her eyes grew big and her mouth formed a big O.

"You did it." He swung her into his arms and kissed her cheek. "You're a big girl."

"Yeah."

She had to wash her hands again and he would have expected no less of the daughter of a physician's assistant who made lists.

Going out the door, Luci buried her face

in Bo's neck and he was amazed at the feelings this little girl generated in him. Fatherly feelings. It was almost as if Luci was his and Becky's. Almost.

BECKY WAS RUNNING LATE. The last patient appointment had gone long and she was rushing to make it to Luci's appointment on time.

She pushed the button for the elevator. She had to wait for people to get off and then she hurried inside. Zooming up to the third floor she hoped Bo had made it on time. She opened the door to the office and froze.

A man stood with Luci and she blinked to see who it was. For a moment she didn't recognize him with the shorter hair and clean-shaven face. She took in his full appearance in jeans, boots and a white shirt, and it took her back to being a young girl who had fallen in love at first sight. That boy was standing in front of her, all grown up and a danger to her blood pressure. He still was the most handsome guy she'd ever met.

"Mom-my." Luci ran to her and her flash-back ended.

"Potty."

"You have to go potty?"

Luci shook her head. "No." She pointed to Bo and Becky knew what she meant.

"Bo helped you go potty?"

Luci nodded. The nurse called them back and Bo followed them down the hall into a room. The nurse took Luci's vitals and she didn't cry or resist. She even went with the nurse to get weighed and measured without a word. Becky wanted to talk to Bo, but Dr. Beasley came in.

"We have a guest today," Dr. Beasley said when he noticed Bo.

Bo shook his hand. "Sergeant Bo Goodnight with Austin SWAT."

The doctor sat on a roll-around stool and opened Luci's file. "What's your interest in Luci, Sergeant?"

"He's the cop who saved Luci when she was born," Becky explained. "I thought it would be nice if he heard how good she's doing." It was easy to say the words, to give Bo credit for what he'd done. It didn't hurt one little bit.

The doctor reached out and shook Bo's hand again. "Marvelous work in saving that baby. I had my doubts when I first saw Luci, but she's a fighter. And she's got a good mother."

"To me she seems like a normal little girl, except for her speech," Bo said.

"At first I didn't think so," the doctor replied. "Usually babies that have the umbilical cord around their neck are born dead. Luci is a miracle. At first we thought she would have global developmental delay. And I thought it would be severe. I was wrong. Her cognitive skills and social skills developed quickly. We're still working on her fine motor skills and speech, and I expect by the time she turns four she'll catch up with children her own age."

"She seems small to me."

Becky felt invisible as the two men talked. She'd once fiercely protected Luci, but now she wanted Luci to know the man who had saved her life. Time changed everything and it had certainly changed her heart.

"She's in the lower fiftieth percentile in height and weight, but I expect a growth spurt pretty soon."

"Is there a reason she's unable to string words together?"

"No. There is no problem with her tongue or palate or frenulum, and there is no medical reason she cannot put words together in a sentence. She's done it for Dr. Cox, the therapist, when she's pushed. The problem is Luci learned to speak by saying one word and waited for her brain to tell her the next word. Now she knows the word, but she still pauses. It's a technique she uses and it's become a pattern, a habit of hers. It's hard to break, but we must break it for her to speak in sentences."

The talk went on until Luci came back and the nurse handed the doctor a piece of paper. The doctor looked at Luci.

"You've grown a fourth of an inch and gained two pounds. I'm so proud of all you've accomplished."

Luci beamed and she was different from the crying child who usually visited with Dr. Beasley. What kind of magic did Bo have?

Later they walked down the hall and Becky marveled at the difference in all three of them. A week ago she'd rather have died than talk to Bo, and Luci had been adamant about not talking. The difference made Becky's heart happy and she didn't analyze it any further than that.

"Luci has a thirty-minute appointment with the therapist. You can go if you want. I can handle it from here."

That gleam sparked in his dark eyes. "Trying to get rid of me, huh?"

"No. This must be so boring for you and…"

"It's not. I want Luci to be the best she can be."

"Me, too." Their eyes met and a sizzle of electricity scorched her skin. And for the first time in a long time she didn't want him to leave. She wanted him to stay.

CHAPTER TWELVE

Bo sat on the sofa, staring at a piece of paper. Another list. But not from Becky. This time it was from the therapist, Dr. Cox. Luci's session with Dr. Cox had been private, but he'd talked with the therapist for a little while afterward. It seemed Luci was enthusiastic about their playtime and the doctor had written a list of things that he could do to help her.

What was it with women and lists? She said that singing helped a lot and provided a list of songs that he should learn and sing to Luci and get her to sing with him. There were lots of other things, too. Evidently, she thought he had superpowers.

The next day he found himself singing "Itsy-Bitsy Spider," "Baa Baa Black Sheep," "The Wheels on the Bus," and "Baby Shark." "The Wheels on the Bus" was her favorite and they sang it over and over. She never paused once, but when they talked afterward, she paused after every word. On Sunday Becky joined them and they sang and played in the backyard, sitting on the swing under the oak tree. Luci sang and jumped around.

"Why can't she do this all the time?" Becky asked.

"She will, but I think we're going to have to be more disciplined."

She turned in the swing to face him, the beautiful lines of her face edged with worry. The days had turned into October, but the heat of the summer still hung in the air and sweat dotted her smooth skin. He found he couldn't look away from the blue of her eyes.

"I think we're going to have to stop her and remind her not to pause," he said. "There'll probably be tears as she will resist. Like Dr. Beasley said, she's more comfortable pausing. It's a habit and habits are hard to break."

"Like I resisted talking to you for years and it's really not so bad. It was my stubborn pride and I wish now I had been more grown-up and able to handle the situation."

He was dumbfounded by her words, and also humbled. They really had come a long way. He tucked blond hair behind her ear and stared at her pink lips. The urge to kiss her was stronger than his need to breathe. He needed her in a way he had never needed anyone.

The splash of water broke them apart. Luci had turned on the water hose and sprayed them, giggling.

Becky jumped up. "Luci Diane Tullous!"

Bo grabbed the hose and turned it off. Becky was drenched and it was hard for Bo not to laugh.

"Play. Mom-my."

"No. We're going into the house now."

Luci ran to the door and tried to open it.

"Look at it this way. She's learning how to do things." He tried to bring a smile back to her face.

She wiped water from her arms. "Yeah."

At her forlorn look he turned the water back on and sprayed her. She ran screeching and he followed. They both were laughing so hard it was hard for him to catch his breath.

"Stop it! Stop it!" But she was laughing so much he barely heard the words.

He threw the hose down and took her into his arms and kissed her there in the bright sunshine in the backyard. The sun was warm, but not as warm as the kiss that welded their soaked bodies together. It had been a long time, but it felt as good as the first time.

She finally pushed him away. "How could you, Bo? How could you?" She stormed into the house.

A deep sigh erupted from his throat and he slowly turned off the water. He made his way back to his own house and thought maybe he should stay there for a while. He'd crossed a line after just gaining her trust again. Now he'd blown it.

He was still sitting in the living room, pondering his actions, when his mother came home. She made iced tea and they sat together, talking.

"How's Mason?" he asked, because he knew she expected him to, and if he was anything, he was a good son to his mother.

She pulled off her sneakers and rubbed her feet. It reminded him of all the hours she stood on them to work.

"He's the same. The tumor on his lungs is growing, but he's refused chemo and radiation. He's seen what people have to go through when they do that and he's chosen not to. He'll take his chances and deal with the pain the best way he can."

"But chemo might shrink the tumor."

"It's his choice." She got to her feet. "Now I'm going to take a shower and meet your father for supper." She watched him for a moment. "No comeback?"

He rubbed his hands together. "I'm still trying to find that elusive thing called forgiveness. If I say the words, it won't change a thing. It won't change the feelings I have inside. All those bad feelings are a part of me."

She touched his shoulder. "Give it time." She headed for the hall and turned back. "Oh, I forgot to tell you. I got the raise for myself and my employees, and a lot of other things I asked for."

"Good for you, Mom. You deserve it."

He got up and stared out the window to the Tullous house. As he'd been talking to his mom something had occurred to him. Becky couldn't forgive him because it would just be words without any meaning. She'd still feel the same way inside. She'd said she was broken. That's why forgiveness was so elusive. It had to be felt in the heart. He wasn't there yet and neither was Becky. He understood it now, but it didn't make it any easier.

BECKY HADN'T SEEN much of Bo since the sizzling kiss in the backyard. She wasn't avoiding him. She was just very busy, and all the time she was working she was trying to get her head straight and decide what she wanted. She wanted her daughter to speak in full sentences and she wanted Bo not to have such an effect on her heart. But she figured that ship had already left the harbor.

The two weeks was almost over and Bo would be leaving on Sunday for Austin. The singing was working better than they could've ever imagined. At night she could hear Luci singing "The Wheels on the Bus." She'd sing until she fell asleep. But the next morning she'd pause after every word. They still hadn't accomplished their goal. Tough love had to happen, but Becky would rather leave that up to Bo. She was hopeless in that area.

On Saturday Becky had to work and check on patients since Dr. Eames was out of town. Kathy was one of those patients. She'd had the lumpectomy and everything had gone well. She was still in the hospital because Dr. Eames and the obstetrician wanted to monitor the baby a little longer, but the baby was doing well, too.

Becky was surprised that the husband hadn't been there for the surgery. When she walked into Kathy's room, she was putting her things into a carryall.

"Are you ready to leave?"

Kathy brushed blond hair out of her face. "Yes. I can't wait to get home."

"Is your husband picking you up?"

Kathy zipped the carryall. "No, my mother is. I guess you want to check my breast before you discharge me."

"Yes." Kathy sat on the bed while Becky removed the small bandage they'd put on the incision. "Everything looks good. Call the office and make an appointment in about a week. Any questions?"

"My arm hurts."

"That's normal. We talked about that, remember? It will go away and then you can concentrate on having a healthy baby."

"Thank you, Becky. I appreciate all the encouragement."

Becky wanted to ask about the husband, but decided it was none of her business. She just wanted Kathy to be well and be happy in her pregnancy.

She had lunch in the cafeteria and it was after one before Becky left the hospital. She was ready to spend some time with her own baby and hopefully get her to sing some of the catchy children songs with her. When she opened the front door, loud music filled her ears. Creedence Clearwater Revival was singing "Proud Mary." Becky didn't know where the sound was coming from, but Luci and Bo were dancing around the room using their arms as paddles and singing, "Rollin', rollin', rollin' on the river." Becky's dad sat in his chair smiling.

"We rollin', Mommy," Luci shouted above the music.

Becky dropped her purse and briefcase. Luci hadn't paused. "Oh, my goodness!"

Bo started singing the words and Luci sang along with him. She never realized he had such a great voice. He'd probably gotten that from his dad, which was something he likely didn't want to hear.

"Play rollin', Mommy," Luci called and Becky eagerly joined them.

"Like this," Luci told her, moving her arms like she was swimming. "Gotta get rollin', Mommy."

Becky laughed and laughed and didn't bother being proper or professional. She was just Becky enjoying the moment. She laughed so much she could barely breathe. She fell down on the sofa and Bo fell down beside her. It wasn't long before Luci joined them. Bo reached over and turned off the music and the room became quiet.

Luci climbed onto Bo's lap. "I. Like. To. Dance."

"No! No! No!" Bo pointed a finger in Luci's face. "Say it correctly."

Luci glanced at Becky and she could see a temper tantrum looming.

"Say it," Bo prompted.

"I like to dance." Luci said it fast and got it all out in one sentence.

Becky kissed her child's nose. "I'm so proud of you, baby."

"Baby Lu."

"What?"

"George Strait's 'Baby Blue,'" Bo explained. "It was playing and I called her Baby Lu. She likes it."

"Where did you get the boom box?"

"We got tired of 'Itsy-Bitsy Spider' and all those other songs, and I remembered this boom box I had when I was a teenager. I'd left a tape inside with a lot of country songs on it and we just let it play. Didn't we, Baby Lu?"

Luci nodded. "Can I take it to my room?"

"Yes, but you have to turn it off when your mom tells you to."

Luci nodded.

Craig got to his feet. "I'll help her." He picked up the boom box. "You'll have to keep the volume down low so we don't bother the neighbors. Okay?"

Luci nodded again and the two walked down the hall.

"How did you accomplish that?" Becky asked. "In two weeks?"

"She just needed someone to push her and I'm good at that. If she gives you any lip, just tell her you'll call Bo. And if she pauses, just correct her and make her say it the right way. Eventually she'll get into the habit of speaking correctly."

Becky clapped her hands together. "A miracle worker, I do declare. But it makes me so happy. Thank you."

"You're welcome, and thank you for letting me spend some time with Luci. I told her today that I would be going back to work tomorrow and she seemed okay with it, but I don't think she really understood what I was saying."

There it was. He was leaving again and

Luci wouldn't be the only one who would miss him.

"My sitter called and said she'd be able to keep Luci on Monday, so we'll be leaving for Austin late tomorrow, too. This was kind of like a moment out of time, wasn't it?"

"Yeah. We talked and that was the main thing. I guess it's best if we go our different ways now, but I would like to see Luci from time to time if you wouldn't mind."

What about me? She couldn't believe she was vulnerable once again. But she was so much stronger this time.

"No, I don't mind."

"She can keep the boom box."

"Oh, no. I'll bring it back to you."

"Whatever."

She followed him to the door.

He looked back at her and she really couldn't read anything in those dark eyes. "Take care of Luci."

She nodded and he strolled across the street. They were acting like strangers. And maybe that's all they ever really were, two strangers who'd deeply loved, but had never understood each other.

Bo hated goodbyes. Yesterday he'd wanted to say so much to Becky, but words were useless when real feelings got in the way, like heartache and pain. He took his carryall and laptop to his truck and waited for his mother. She was supposed to be home by noon.

She came through the back door like a whirlwind. "Sorry, I'm late."

"You didn't have to come home. I'll try to get back on my day off. I don't know which day until I look at the schedule."

"It's just been so nice having you home for two weeks."

"You were hardly ever here," he reminded her.

She touched his face. "It was nice to know you were nearby and I could see you anytime I wanted. And I have to say, I love the new look. You look just like my favorite son."

He kissed her cheek. "I'll call when I can."

"Just be careful. You know, I have this fear of getting a call that you've been injured and I don't really want that to ever happen. I don't want to ever get that call. You understand? Take care of yourself."

"I'm very good at what I do so don't worry. I'm always looking out for me and the guys."

"Mothers worry. We just can't help it."

She hugged him tightly and he hugged her back. Without a backward glance, he walked out the back door. Getting into his truck, he paused and glanced at the Tullous house. No, he decided he was going to do it differently this time. He marched across the street and knocked on the door.

Becky opened it, her eyes wide. "Bo."

"Could we talk for a minute?"

"Sure." She came out wearing skinny jeans and a long-sleeved knit blouse. A cold front had blown through and the air was fresh and snappy. She sat on the step and he sat beside her. "Luci is in her room dancing to the music. She has so much energy."

"Did she give you any trouble with pausing?"

"A couple of times, but then I told her to say it correctly and she did, which surprised the devil out of me because I've been trying to get her to do that for over a year."

"Keep at it. I think she's made the turn and is confident she knows the words."

"I'm just happy she'll be able to start school next year." She glanced at him. "Did you want to talk about something?"

Bo rubbed his hands together. "The last time I didn't say goodbye like I should have, and this time I want to say goodbye the right way."

"Bo, you're not going to be gone forever and I'm trying really hard to forget my immature behavior."

"No, you were right. I've learned a lot of things about myself since I've been home and the major thing I've learned about is forgiveness. Anyone can say they're sorry, but it doesn't mean anything if it doesn't change the way that person feels in their heart."

He placed a hand on his chest. "It's hard for me to forgive my father because when I say I'm sorry it's not going to change the way I feel inside about him. I know I said I was sorry a hundred times to you and it's never going to change the way you feel inside about what I did. I hurt you and that scar is always going to be there. I understand that now."

"Oh, Bo."

"And I apologize for kissing you the other day, but some things are just too hard to resist and that's my attraction for you. I just want us to remain on friendly terms for Luci's sake."

"I don't see a problem there."

"I'll miss her."

"She…she'll miss you, too. Bo…"

The door opened and Luci ran out, interrupting them. Her hair was out of its usual pigtails and disheveled. And she wasn't wearing her glasses. "Bo, we gonna play?"

He gathered her into his arms. "Not today, little angel. Remember I told you I'm going back to work and I'm leaving today."

"Oh. Where. You."

Becky pointed a finger in her face. "No."

Luci giggled. "Where you going?"

"Austin." He kissed her cheek. "You be good for your mother and I'll come visit you one day."

"'Kay."

"Where are your glasses?" Becky asked Luci.

Luci shrugged. "I don't know."

"Say goodbye to Bo and go find them."

Luci raised her hand in goodbye and went back into the house.

"She's acting just like any three-year-old," Becky remarked.

Bo got to his feet and wanted to take Becky into his arms, but they'd grown past that. Today they would part as friends. "I'm glad we had the opportunity to air out our feelings."

She stood beside him. "Yeah. It's an eye-opener when you find out that what you've been upset about for eighteen years was something trivial."

"Goodbye, Bec. Maybe I'll see you in Austin."

"Bye, Bo." There was a forlorn note in her voice and he turned back to see if she expected something more from him. But she was already headed toward the front door.

Goodbye, Becky. He really hoped that it wasn't forever.

Bo DROVE TO the end of Liberty Street and saw the courthouse and the sheriff's office. He'd talked to Cole a few times on the phone, but hadn't seen him much in the last two weeks. He swerved into a parking spot next to Cole's truck.

Bubba was sitting at the front desk. "Hey, Bubba," Bo said as he walked into Cole's office. He sat in a chair facing Cole.

"What's going on?" Cole asked, leaning back.

"I'm headed back to work."

"I think that's a good idea, considering everything that's going on." Cole knew about Bo's dad and he knew about Luci. They knew everything about each other's lives but they'd been growing apart since Cole now had a family.

"I have so many conflicting emotions in my head it's about to explode."

"Catching criminals will force you to concentrate on something else."

Bo ran his hands through his hair. "I feel as if I'm letting everyone down, but I can't change the way I feel."

"Go to work and things will look different in a week. Dealing with the seedier side of life will give you an appreciation of what you have."

"What I have is a headache."

Cole twirled a pencil in his hand. "How did you leave it with Becky?"

"As friends."

"That's gotta hurt."

"Yeah." Bo got to his feet. "But I understand now what she went through and I wish I could take it back, but back then I was all puffed up and there was no way she wouldn't be waiting for me. I can't believe how arrogant I was. Grandpa filled my head with a lot of nonsense and I'm working my way through that situation, too."

"You're grown, man. It takes a lot of courage to admit that."

"I get A-plus for being a jerk."

"Come on, man. It's over, and you and Becky are talking and that's what's important. And for the record, you're not a jerk."

Bo knew Cole would always take his side, no matter what. That's the way they'd grown up, being there for each other because their parents weren't.

"Daddy! Daddy! Daddy!"

Zoe came running through the front door and straight to Cole. He swung her up into his arms and kissed her cheek. "How's my girl?"

"Good. We come to take you…"

Cole's wife, Grace, and his grandfather, Mr. Walt, followed more slowly.

"Hey, Bo." Mr. Walt slapped him on the shoulder. "How come you haven't been to see me?"

"Grandpa." He'd always called Mr. Walt grandpa, and it had always seemed natural. "I've been busy with family problems."

"Heard about your dad. I'm sorry."

"Thanks, Grandpa. I'm still coming to grips with that."

Grace hugged him. "I'm sorry, too."

"Thank you." He didn't know what else to say so he didn't say anything.

"So, where are you guys taking me?" Cole asked to break the tension.

"To dinner," Zoe shouted.

Grace moved to Cole's side and he put an arm around her waist. She was a dark-haired, dark-eyed beauty, and Cole was lucky to have found his soul mate. Bo was happy for his friend.

"Come with us," Grace suggested. At five months pregnant she was really showing and she absolutely glowed.

"Thanks, but I have to get back to Austin." He wasn't in the mood for a family get-together. He told everyone goodbye and kissed Zoe.

"No ouchie." She rubbed Bo's clean-shaven cheek.

"I like the new look," Grace said.

"He's hard to recognize," Cole joked.

"See you guys later," Bo called, going out the door. He got in his truck and drove toward Temple to see his grandma. He'd get a lecture, but he was used to that. He was getting used to a lot of things.

In his line of work he knew what to do and how to do it without any emotional entanglements. He was good at gauging actions and reactions when it came to criminals. But he was hopeless when it came to women, especially Becky. There was no way she was ever going to love him the way he wanted her to love him. Sometimes hindsight was pure torture.

CHAPTER THIRTEEN

BECKY SETTLED BACK into her condo with ease when she and Luci returned to Austin, but her heart was heavy. She wanted to say so many things to Bo, but she'd held on to her fear and she wasn't sure what she'd been afraid of. He'd been so sincere. He'd meant every word he'd said and she just wanted to throw her arms around him and forgive every pain he'd ever caused her.

But it didn't work like that. He was right. She had to find a way to ease the pain inside, and the only way to do that was to continue to talk and continue to share Luci with him. She'd already seen so many breakthroughs she thought would never happen. But there was hope in her heart and she clung to that.

Luci asked where Bo was a couple of times, but she was glad to see Ruby and Thomas Edwards after their two weeks away. They were a couple in their sixties, and their daughter, Leesha, was a nurse who worked in Dr. Eames's office. Leesha's daughter, Zia, had been born a month before Luci. When Becky had frantically been searching for someone she could trust to keep Luci so she could go back to work, Leesha had said she would ask her mother, who was keeping Zia, and it had been a godsend.

It was nice being back in the condo, but she worried about her dad being alone again. She would make sure they visited this weekend so Luci could see her grandfather and maybe, just maybe, Bo might be home, too. So many years she hadn't wanted to talk to him, but now that was all she wanted to do. Well, not all.

Bo FELL BACK into his regular routine and tried not to think about Becky or his dad. He put them on the back burner, as he'd always been able to do. That was why he liked to work. He was good at shutting out the memories, but eventually he had to face them and he couldn't put it off much longer.

"Goodnight." The lieutenant's voice came over the intercom. "My office."

As he opened the door he could see the lieutenant leaning over something that looked like a map.

"We have a situation." She pointed to a spot on the map. "A rural area outside of Bastrop. A deputy tried to serve a warrant on a guy in a house trailer and was shot before he made it to the door. He called for backup and the next officer was shot as he got out of his patrol car. The Bastrop PD and sheriff's deputies are at the scene, but the shooter has them pinned behind their vehicles. They tried to go through the back way and an officer was shot there, too. There are three officers down and no one can get to them for the shooter's constant firing. We got a call asking for help. Take the team and get this done so those officers can get medical attention."

"Yes, ma'am."

She handed him some papers. "That's a map of the fastest route and a sketch of the layout of the trailer. The sheriff knows you're coming."

He nodded and joined his men. "Let's go. We have an emergency." They loaded into the Hummer. Bo took the passenger side. "Listen up." He told them what the lieutenant had told him. He handed the map to Patel. "The lieutenant said that's the fastest way. Make sure it is. We need to get there as soon as possible. Officers are down."

"Sarge, we can shave about eight minutes off by going a different route."

"Give Speed the directions."

"Got it," Speed said, putting the route into the GPS.

"This is an extremely volatile situation. Make sure you're in full tactical gear for safety. We don't need any more casualties today."

As they rode, Bo studied the layout of the trailer. Two doors. One in front and one in the back. Two windows in the front and three in the back. One was a double. There were no windows on either end of the trailer.

As they neared the site, gunshots echoed through the cool afternoon breeze. They topped a small hill and could see the scene in the distance. An old trailer sat under scattered oak trees. An abandoned truck rested in tall weeds and another truck was next to it.

Police and sheriff's cars were about a hundred yards away and were set up as a barricade in front of the trailer with officers behind them. Ambulances and other first responders waited patiently behind the officers. The man in the trailer was firing shots at anything that moved. As they got closer, Bo could see two officers lying in the front yard, one on his back and the other with his face to the ground. His heart rate sped up at the sight.

He told Speed to park behind the sheriff's car, which was clearly visible. They had to be careful. Bullets were flying everywhere and ricocheting off vehicles. A man with a badge bent over and ran to the Hummer. The bullets stopped for a moment. Bo got out, crouched and met the man. His crew waited for orders.

"Sheriff Laskey," the man said, shaking Bo's hand.

"Sergeant Bo Goodnight." They squatted on the ground to avoid being hit by a bullet.

"We have officers down and we could use your help. We can't get near them. The guy inside is Duane Hopkins, and he just keeps firing. He's on drugs, for sure."

"Have you tried a high-powered rifle?"

"Yes, but it's hard to get a shot at him. He's at the window for a second to get off some shots, then he quickly disappears, either against the wall or farther into the room. We tried to get to the front and back door, but he seems to know when we're coming and I'm not risking another officer's life."

Bo peeked over the car to the shattered

trailer and saw something at the top under the roof. "Is that a security camera?"

The sheriff took a look. "Well, I'll be damned. It looks like it, but I'm not sure. I didn't think Duane was that smart, but at this point, I'm almost positive it is."

"That's how he knows when you're coming. He's seeing everything you do."

"Do you think you can get that armored car in there to get my men out? They need medical attention."

"Yeah, I was thinking about it, but that would put a lot of people at risk, especially the officers who are down. We don't know what kind of injuries they have, and if we pull them to safety we might injure them more. If we get the ambulance in, then the EMTs are at risk. I think the best plan is just to take the shooter out."

"We've tried that."

"Have you tried gas?"

"Yes. The damn man has a gas mask."

"I guess that rules out smoke bombs."

"Yep."

"Tell your men to wait for orders and we'll take it from here."

The sheriff nodded. "Sure thing."

Bo motioned to his crew and they came

out and squatted around him. "What's the plan?" Cruz asked.

"I'm going to see if I can get a bead on him."

"That's dangerous," the sheriff said. "I have a wounded guy because of that."

"Thanks, Sheriff." Bo turned to his guys. "Here's the plan. Speed, I want you to take Cruz, Preacher and Patel in the Hummer and get as close to the end of the trailer as you can. He'll fire at you, but he'll just put marks on the Hummer.

"Once you're there, wait for orders. Hutch will take out the security camera first. Then Cruz and Patel will go to the front door and Preacher and Speed will go to the back door. Preacher and Speed, look for a security camera on the back of the trailer. He'll have it well hidden. Let me know if you see one. Then slither up against the trailer as if you're glued to it and don't give him a shot.

"Hutch will back me up. Once you're in position I'm going to take a shot and see if I can bring him down. When I give you the word to go, that means breach the front and back doors and make sure he's completely down."

"Got it," they said in unison.

The Hummer made its way to the end of the trailer. Hopkins fired several rounds at it until it was out of sight.

Bo turned to Hutch. "Take out the security camera."

Hutch stood quickly and aimed his M16. He pulled the trigger and the camera shattered into a million pieces.

"Go," he said to the others.

The guys climbed out of the Hummer and got into position.

"The back door is locked," Preacher said through the mic. "Security camera is located on the end of the trailer."

"Take it out."

They heard a boom and he knew the camera was gone. They'd leveled the playing field now.

Curse words blasted from the trailer.

"The front door is open." Cruz came on the mic.

"Preacher, wait for my orders to kick in the back door. Cruz, you know the drill. Patel and Speed, back them up."

"Yes, Sarge."

Bo lifted his M24 with its scope into his hands. He looked at the sheriff. "Have your guys fire a couple of rounds. I want him to come to the window." As the bullets slapped against the trailer, Bo placed his rifle on a squad car, putting his head and shoulders in plain sight and putting himself at risk. He glanced through his scope. He could see the guy clearly. Long dirty hair and a beard, but Bo didn't take time to critique his appearance. A bullet zinged past his helmet. As soon as he had Hopkins centered in the scope, he pulled the trigger and shouted into his mic, "Go, go, go!"

Bo lowered the rifle and took a deep breath. He watched as Cruz and Patel went through the front door and in a second he heard Cruz on his mic. "We got him. We got him. He's shot in the shoulder, but he's still breathing. All is safe."

"Good shot," Hutch whispered. "But I didn't expect anything else.

"Get the ambulances in here," Bo shouted, ignoring Hutch.

The sheriff ran to his men, helping to get them on stretchers and to the hospital. Bo walked into the trailer with Hutch. He paused in the doorway to the bedroom. Hopkins lay on the floor in a pool of blood. Cruz pressed a towel to the man's shoulder, trying to stop the bleeding.

Bo took a moment to glance around the room. It was full of rifles and handguns. They were stacked to the ceiling with tons of ammunition, enough to be holed up in here for a week or more. A stained mattress lay on the floor, more guns were stacked on it. A broken doll, a toy truck and some Lego were scattered about. Children had been in this room. His gut tightened.

The sheriff entered. "Oh, man."

"Did Hopkins have kids?"

"Yeah. Two. His wife left him a week ago and that's what started this rampage. He robbed a liquor store and shot the clerk. There's been a warrant out for his arrest for days. We finally located him here." The sheriff stared at the body. "Is he dead?"

"No. We need another ambulance." Within minutes they had Hopkins on a stretcher on the way to a hospital.

"Stay with him," Laskey ordered two of his deputies. Then the sheriff held out his hand. "Thank you for finding a way to end this nightmare. Now I have to go to the hospital and check on the officers who were shot. Keep your fingers crossed."

The rumble of engines sounded and soon Bo and his team were the only ones left, besides those dealing with the weapons and gathering evidence.

Bo looked around the room and touched the security monitor, which was now black. Hopkins had had a clear view of anyone coming into his back or front yards. That's how he'd been able to keep shooting for so long.

"Ingenious. Criminals are getting smarter."

Speed stepped over several rifles. "I think his wish was not to come out of here alive."

Hutch slapped Bo on the back. "You ruined that, Sarge."

"Let's head back to Austin."

They didn't understand why he didn't shoot to kill. Sometimes he didn't understand it himself, but his goal was never to kill. It was always to save lives, even when dealing with a scumbag like Hopkins. But tonight, when he was lying in bed alone, he would relive the moment he'd been in the open, bullets aimed at him, whizzing past his head.

Yeah, the night after a shooting was always hard.

BECKY GOT HOME a little after five and Luci was soon telling her about her day. She was talking in full sentences and learning more all the time. Her baby was gaining confidence and Becky couldn't have been happier. Luci had reached all her sought-after milestones and the future looked bright.

"Mommy?"

"What?" Becky asked as she put milk into the refrigerator.

"What does *married* mean?"

Becky swung around, puzzled. "Where did you hear that word?"

"Z's cousin is getting married and she has a pretty white dress with a long tail. A long tail, Mommy." Luci called Zia Z because, at first, she hadn't been able to say her name.

Luci sat at the table, coloring, and Becky pulled up a chair, searching for words to explain the best way she could. It seemed surreal to be having a conversation about this with her daughter.

"When two people meet and fall in love and want to spend the rest of their lives together, they get married. He gives her a ring and she gives him a ring and they're bound together forever."

Becky drifted off to la-la land as she thought of all the years she'd planned to marry Bo and spend the rest of her life with him. And now, here they were—friends. Could they really be friends?

"I want to get married so I can have a dress with a tail."

Becky kissed her cheek. "You're too young to get married. You have to be older and you have to have a boyfriend."

"Bo is my friend. I can marry him."

Her dream wish. Becky smiled inwardly at all the thoughts of that young seventeen-year-old and how real they'd been to her. The rest of her life had been Bo and that was the reason for so much pain. Becky could see that clearly now. She'd been too young to love that deeply.

"Why he not come see me?"

Luci's question brought her out of her agonizing thoughts. "Bo's a cop and he's busy. Why don't you go play with your iPad while I fix supper."

Luci ran into the living room, picked up the remote control to the TV and flipped it on. Becky started to tell her to turn it off, but she noticed the news was on and heard the announcer say something about the SWAT team. Luci wasn't interested in the news and curled up on the sofa with the iPad. Purr crawled all over her while Pink took her position on the floor.

Becky walked farther into the living room and listened closely.

The Austin SWAT team was called to assist a rural community outside of Bastrop where a deranged gunman had officers pinned down behind their cars for over two hours. The SWAT team arrived and had the situation under control within ten minutes. The officer you see in this video is Sergeant Bo Goodnight, who took out the alleged gunman. Video is courtesy of a local rancher.

No. No!

Becky watched in horror as Bo stood up with a rifle in his hand as gunfire blasted around him. He fired his gun with an ear-splitting sound. Then there was silence. Was Bo hurt? What happened?

We're happy to announce that two of the officers who were injured are in stable condition and expected to recover. The other is in critical condition.

What about Bo? What about Bo?

But the announcer went on to another story. Becky stood there, completely numb. If he was hurt… She couldn't think beyond that. All those feelings she kept inside that were hers and she could control were suddenly zapped by a power much stronger than herself—the fear that she might never see him again.

She grabbed her purse from the counter and fished out her phone. She couldn't call her friends because no one knew about Bo. There was only one person who might know something and that was her father. He never missed the news.

"Hi, Rebecca. How's Luci?"

"She's fine. Did you watch the Austin news tonight?"

"Yes."

"Did you see Bo?"

"Yes. Ava saw it, too. She knew her son worked SWAT, but it was the first time she'd seen him in action and it really upset her."

Becky had the same feeling. She just hadn't realized Bo put his life at risk every day. Maybe she just hadn't wanted to know that part. But it had been right there in living color today.

"Do you know if he's okay?"

"I'm sure he is, and Ava hasn't heard anything."

"Is Ava there?" Something in her dad's

voice alerted her. He was speaking as if Ava was with him.

"Yes, she's here."

How much time did they spend together? It was the first time Becky had thought of it. After the accident she supposed they'd hung out a lot. She worried about her dad being alone all the time, but maybe she didn't need to worry anymore. But her dad hadn't said anything to indicate otherwise. It would be nice if her dad could find someone, and if that someone was Ava, it would be okay with Becky.

"Could you call me if you hear anything?"

"Sure, sweetheart. I'll call you, but I'm sure he's okay. I'm just wondering why you're so worried."

Oh, why did parents do that? He'd done that all her life, making her look inside for the answer, wanting her to discover it herself. But she already knew. She just needed... Time was what she needed.

She hung up quickly, made supper, got Luci to bed and took a shower, and all the while she was wondering if there were any easy answers to her situation with Bo.

She crawled under a sheet and comforter,

but sleep eluded her. The scene of the shooting played vividly in her mind. What would she have done if Bo had been killed? She never would have had the chance to say she'd forgiven him. That's what it all came down to—her stubborn unwillingness to forgive.

Frustrated, she reached for her phone on the nightstand and called Bo. That was the only way she was going to get any sleep. He answered immediately.

"Hey, Bec."

"Are you okay?"

"Why wouldn't I be?"

"I saw you on the news tonight. A guy was shooting at you and they didn't say if you are okay or not."

"Are you worried about me?"

"Of course I am. I never realized what a high-risk job you have."

"I'm in SWAT, Bec."

"I guess I try not to think about it."

"You haven't done too badly all these years. You haven't thought about me at all."

"You haven't thought about me, either."

"Oh, Bec, you'll never know all the times I've thought about you."

Her heart did a funny dance in her chest

and she was falling hard once again. "Luci is asking about you, and since Halloween is coming up I thought you might like to help take her trick-or-treating, just a few houses in our neighborhood. She's a ballerina with a tiara."

"In pink?"

"You guessed it."

"After a shooting, we usually get a couple of days off, so sign me up."

"Okay. I'll see you then."

"Thanks, Bec, for worrying about me."

"Call your mother. She worries, too."

"My mom is used to my job."

"Call your mother. Take my word for it, a mother is never used to that."

She laid her cell on the nightstand and with a smile, sank into the covers. Now she could sleep. He was okay.

Bo GOT UP from the sofa in his underwear and made his way to the bedroom. He'd been putting off going to bed, but after hearing Becky's voice he decided to give it a try. Her soothing, soft voice always had an effect on him. With his phone in his hand he decided to call his mother. He never did after a shooting, but tonight after listening to Becky, he did.

"Oh, Bo, I'm so glad you called. I've been so worried."

"I'm fine, Mom. I told you not to worry."

"But it's different when I have to see what you're doing. It made the hair stand up on my arms. I just knew that man was going to shoot you."

"It's a risk everyone takes every day. We never know what's going to come out of the blue and I've been trained to deal with that."

"I don't care how much training you've had," she snapped. "A bullet kills."

"I'm fine," he said again. "I have a couple days off and I might come home for a night."

"You don't have to do that. Just hearing your voice is all I need."

He cleared his throat. "How's Mason?"

"He's in a lot of pain, but hospice is taking care of that."

"Good. I'll call you soon." He couldn't say one more word. After the day, all he needed was peace.

He crawled beneath the covers and stared into the darkness for a moment and then turned onto his side. Usually sleep would elude him, but tonight he continued to hear her voice. Not his mother's. Becky's. He let it wash over him and the scene of the day disappeared as he got lost in the tangled web of his feelings for her.

CHAPTER FOURTEEN

ON HALLOWEEN BO drove up to the curb in front of Becky's condo. She didn't live too far from the hospital. It was a clear, cold night and kids were already out trick-or-treating. He slipped on his jacket and walked to Becky's front door. Before his hand could touch the doorbell, the door opened and Luci stood there in a ballerina outfit. All pink with long sleeves, leggings, a frilly skirt and ballerina shoes. A sparkly tiara rested on her head. Her eyes beamed behind the pink glasses.

She darted out and wrapped her arms around his knees. "Bo, you came to see me."

He lifted her into his arms. "Hey, little angel. I think you've grown."

Wiggling down, she waved toward the kitchen and ran inside. Becky stood in the living room in black tights and a blue turtle-neck sweater. The blue of the sweater made her eyes pop and he couldn't look away from her beauty.

"Bo," Luci shouted, demanding his attention.

Walking to her, he saw she was pointing to a ruler attached to the wall. It had red marks at certain heights. "See how I grow."

"Yes, I see."

"She's grown another half inch," Becky said and Bo's eyes clung to hers. He hadn't seen her in weeks and he was starved for the sight of her.

"Look, Bo, I'm a…" Luci glanced at Becky.

"A ballerina," Becky said for her.

"Yes, that."

Bo squatted in front of her. "Say it. Say the word. Ballerina. Ballerina."

"Bal…la…rina. Ballerina." Luci lifted her arms above her head and tried to spin around, but she fell.

"We're still working on coordination." Becky smiled and Bo thought he could grow old looking at her smile.

"I get my pumpkin." Luci scrambled to her feet. "Mommy made me a pumpkin." She ran into the living room.

"She's changed a lot," Bo said.

"Yes. She's talking up a storm. There are some words she has problems with, but we're working on that. You can actually have a conversation with her now."

"I could always have a conversation with her," he pointed out in a smug voice.

"Oh, yes. I remember."

"It's cold out. She's going to need a jacket."

"Okay, magic maker." Becky reached for a coat over the sofa. "Get her to put it on." Now there was smugness in her voice.

"I got my pumpkin. We have to go." Luci came running and Bo held up the coat.

"You have to put this on. It's cold outside," Bo said.

"No. It covers up my pretty clothes."

"Then we don't go." Bo laid the coat back on the sofa.

"Mommy," Luci wailed.

Becky folded her arms across her chest. "Coat or we don't go. I don't want you to catch a cold."

Luci hung her head. "'Kay."

Bo helped her into the coat. "When you go up to the door, we'll unzip it so everyone can see your pretty outfit."

"'Kay." She was all bouncy and excited again.

Becky slipped into her jacket and they went out the door for the adventure of trick-or-treating. Becky grilled Luci on what to say. When they went to the first house, Bo unzipped Luci's jacket, rang the doorbell and stepped back.

A young woman of about thirty answered the door. There was a long pause as Luci didn't say anything. Becky started for the front door, but Bo held her back.

"Let her do it," he whispered.

Finally Luci said, "My name is Luci. What's your name?"

Becky groaned.

The woman bent over and said, "Aren't you the sweetest little thing. My name is Marcia."

"Trick or tweet," Luci replied.

The woman proceeded to dump a lot of candy into Luci's pumpkin.

"Thank you." Luci ran back to them, all smiles.

Becky's zipped up Luci's coat and they walked to the next house.

"Don't say anything," he whispered to Becky.

"How did you know I was going to say something?"

"You're itching to correct her. Don't."

"You don't know Luci better than I do."

"Let her do it her way," he insisted.

"You're infuriating. I want her to learn the right way."

"There's nothing wrong with her way. I'm guessing *trick-or-treat* is a little hard for her to say. So let it be."

They did the same at the next house. A man answered this time. Luci stood there as if she were searching for words and said, "My name is Luci. What's your name?"

"My name is Bob. Debra," he shouted to someone in the house. "Come see this."

A woman in her fifties came to the door. "Oh, my goodness. You're so cute. Are you a ballerina?"

Luci nodded and then said, "Trick or tweet."

"Go get those cookies I made," Debra said to Bob. "I want to give her something special."

As they walked away, Bo nudged Becky with his elbow. "Told you. There's nothing wrong with her way."

By the time they made it back to the condo, Luci was worn out and asleep on Bo's shoulder. Her pumpkin was overflowing and Bo even had some stuff in his pockets. The people had been more than generous. He helped Becky get Luci's clothes off and put her to bed.

He glanced around the room. "I've never asked, but what is it with pink?"

"I asked the doctor about it and he said it would pass. I'm still waiting." She poked him in the chest. "With your magic powers, it's your job to get her off of pink."

"No, no." He followed her downstairs to the living room. "That is completely your job."

She pushed hair from her face. "She does so much better with you."

Bo sat beside her. "I'm looking at it this way. She'll outgrow it."

A faraway look entered Becky's eyes. "She's come so far in the past weeks. The doctor said when she started talking everything else would fall into place and he was right. When I pick her up from Ruby's, she talks and talks and talks. She's understanding and putting things together and it is so wonderful to watch." Becky got to her feet. "How about if I order pizza? I have beer in the refrigerator."

"Deal." He could think of nothing better than to spend the evening with her.

They ate the pizza at the coffee table. She kicked off her boots and sat on the floor while he took the sofa.

"I thought about something the other day and I really couldn't answer the question. What do you think we would be doing if we had gotten married so young?"

"I'd probably be stocking shelves at my mother's grocery store," he replied flippantly.

"No you wouldn't. You wanted to do bigger things, and you and Cole always talked about being cops."

He thought about that for a moment. "Yes, I guess we did." He looked into her blue eyes. "What are you getting at?"

"Through all my soul-searching I realized something important. I was too young to get married. I had no idea about what life could be like. All I wanted was to be with you. That's how every seventeen-year-old girl thinks when they have a boyfriend."

He wanted to be honest, so he said what was in his heart. "After seeing my parents' disastrous marriage, the last thing I wanted was to get married, but I loved you and would have done anything you wanted."

"Except stay. And I'm not saying that to be mean. I take full responsibility for my part in being a selfish teenager wanting only what I wanted. And it was so unrealistic I can't even believe I wanted that back then."

Bo laid his half-eaten pizza slice in the cardboard container. "When my dad came back, all my conflicting thoughts about you, the army and Cole became clear. I'd had to go for my own peace of mind and there was no doubt in my mind that you would be waiting for me."

"Remember that line we learned in English class? 'Hell hath no fury like a woman scorned.'"

He tipped his beer to her. "I should have paid more attention."

"We've talked the past to death," she said. "When I saw you in the video being shot at, I thought if you had gotten killed you would've never known I had forgiven you. Sometime in the last few weeks I realized I didn't have that pain in my chest anymore."

His heart stilled. He'd waited so long for her to say that, and for a moment he wondered if he was dreaming.

She placed the beer bottle on the coffee table and looked at him. "I would like very much for us to start over without bitterness or resentment over what happened in the past. Start over with a clean slate as two mature adults wanting to spend time with each other."

"Do you think that's possible?"

She got up and sat beside him, so close he got a whiff of her delicate perfume. "Why not? We're both in our late thirties and know how hard life is and how good it can be at times. I'm willing to take a risk."

When he'd come here tonight he'd had no idea she would offer this—an opportunity to get back together. He'd wanted that for years and now it seemed too good to be true.

His eyes met hers. "I am, too."

Her tongue moistened her lips and he was captivated. Before his lips took hers, her phone went off. He hated that phone! But she reached for it because it could be the hospital or something important.

She looked at the caller ID. "It's the hospital. I have to take it."

Bo got up and watched her talk. Her anxious voice matched her face. She paced around the room talking. "Okay. I'll be right there."

She went into the kitchen and grabbed her purse, dropping her phone into it, and then she came back into the living room and reached for her boots. Sitting on the sofa she shoved her feet into her boots. "We have a patient named Kathy Purcell and we did a lumpectomy on her a few weeks ago. She's four months pregnant and she's in the emergency room with spotting. Dr. Eames is out of town and Kathy is asking for me so I have to go."

"Then go." He felt a little let down, but he was mature enough to accept what she did in her job.

"I have to call the teenager down the street who sits with Luci when I have to go to the hospital."

"I'll stay until you get back."

One eyebrow lifted. "You sure?"

"I'm not doing anything else and I have tomorrow off."

"Thank you. I'll be back as soon as I can." She picked up her purse and headed for the kitchen, and he supposed there was a door to a garage back there. She turned and smiled at him. "I'm sorry we got interrupted."

He waved at her to go. "How much beer do you have?"

She laughed as she disappeared out of sight. He cleaned up the mess and thought about what she'd said and wondered if they could start over after everything that had happened between them. He didn't want to look that gift horse in the mouth. For now, he would take one day at a time and hopefully somewhere in those days they would find the love they'd shared years ago. And maybe this time it would be better.

BECKY PARKED IN the hospital parking lot and rushed into the ER. A nurse she knew stopped her. "Are you here about Kathy Purcell?"

"Yes. Where is she?"

She motioned for Becky to walk down the hall out of earshot. "She miscarried and is now in surgery. They're doing a D & C."

"Oh, no! She so wanted that baby." All of Becky's fears liquefied and flowed through her veins like a red-hot fever. She tried to push them away, but they were right there.

"There were bruises on her arm and her face when she came in. I had to notify police."

"Are you saying…?"

"Yeah, someone hit her and held her arm so tight you can see the imprints of fingers. The police are waiting to question her."

"Did she say anything?"

"She said she fell, but she was crying so hard it was very difficult to get anything out of her. She was worried about the baby."

"Anything else?"

"No. When she asked for you, I called. A few minutes later she started cramping and that was it."

"Thank you. I'll wait until she gets to her room to talk to her." Becky took a chair in the small waiting area staring down at the inlaid floor. Squares and triangles fit perfectly together to create a pleasing effect. As a teenager she hadn't known if she was a square or a triangle. She'd just known she didn't fit anywhere. Until Bo. He'd made her fit in and become part of a group, and her plans for the future had become happy ones.

A tear rolled down her cheek and she quickly brushed it away. Not now! She couldn't remember, not here in this hospital. All these years she'd been able to push it to the farthest corner of her mind, but…

The nurse walked up and handed Becky a piece of paper. "They're taking her to her room. That's the room number. The cops are waiting for her."

"Thank you."

Bracing herself for the scene she was about to witness, she took the elevator up to Kathy's room. She knew the drill. She knew exactly what was going to happen. She introduced herself to officers Spellman and Lopez, trying desperately to keep everything inside.

"Do you know Mrs. Purcell?" Officer Lopez asked.

"Yes. I'm a physician's assistant to Dr. Eames and Kathy is one of our patients. Dr. Eames found a cancerous lump in her breast and it was removed. Kathy chose to wait on the radiation until after the baby was born."

"Do you know her husband?"

Becky shook her head. "I've never met him."

"Not even when she had the surgery?" Officer Spellman wanted to know.

"No. He wasn't there."

Officer Lopez held out some photos taken by the hospital. "These don't look good. Someone hit this woman."

Becky stared at the bruise on Kathy's face and the marks on her arm. Anger roiled in her stomach. How could she live with someone who would do this?

She looked up to see nurses pushing a gurney into a room. In a minute they were out. "She's a little groggy, but she's awake," one of the nurses said to Becky.

"Let me talk to her first," Becky said to the officers.

"We'll be right behind you," Officer Spellman said.

The blinds were drawn in the small room and it was almost in total darkness, except for a small light above the bed. Kathy still had an IV and a nurse was checking a heart monitor.

"Everything seems fine," the nurse said. "She'll probably sleep the rest of the night."

"Thank you."

Becky moved closer to the bed, feeling a knot in her stomach so big she could barely breathe. "Kathy." She spoke gently.

At the sound of her voice, Kathy turned her head toward Becky. Her dark hair was pulled back, emphasizing the purple bruise on her face. "You came." Her voice was low, but Becky caught it.

"Yes. I'm so sorry."

Kathy closed her eyes and tears squeezed through. "I lost my baby."

"I know, and I'm so sorry." Becky looked over her shoulder. "These officers would like to ask you some questions. Do you think you can handle it?"

Kathy nodded.

Becky stepped back and listened while Kathy told them what happened. "He found the medical bills for the lumpectomy and saw it was from the Women's Center and he said I had an abortion. I told him the center didn't do abortions, but he wouldn't believe me. I tried to tell him I was still pregnant but he was enraged and wouldn't listen. That's when he slapped me and I stumbled backward and fell. He yanked me up, but I managed to get away and lock myself in the bathroom. He beat on the door for a long time and then finally left. I... I..."

"It's okay," Officer Lopez said. "Take your time."

"He's very controlling and my friends don't come around anymore because of that."

"Why did your husband think you had an abortion?" Officer Spellman asked. "Didn't he know about the cancer?"

"No. I didn't tell him. I was scared. I didn't know what he would do. After a year of marriage, I wanted out, but then I discovered I was pregnant. I wanted to wait to have children because I'm still in school, but my husband wanted a baby now. We argued about it and that's why he jumped to the conclusion that I had an abortion."

The officers got a description of her husband, their address and the make of his vehicle. "I'd advise that when you are released, you go somewhere else until we catch him."

"My mother is coming and I'm going to stay with her for a while."

The officers left and Becky walked to the bed. "Why don't you try to get some sleep? I'll stay until your mother gets here." Becky didn't think the woman should be alone. Being alone was a terrible thing at a time like this. It ate away at your heart until there was nothing left to feel but a chilling emptiness.

"I don't think I'll ever sleep again."

"I'm not going to lie to you. The days ahead are going to be hard and you'll really need your mother. Everyone will say how sorry they are until you want to scream. But each 'I'm sorry' will start the healing process. This day you'll never forget, though." *How did she ever think she could forget?* "It will always be a part of you. That baby will always be a part of you." *That part stayed forever in her heart. Why didn't she realize that?* "No one understands that but other women who have lived through this pain. You will survive because you're strong."

As Becky talked, Kathy fell asleep, and

soon her mother came in and Becky was able to leave. She got into her car and couldn't stop the tears trailing down her cheeks. For years she'd had this under lock and key, and now it was all coming back. She rested her head on the steering wheel and fought for an elusive control. There was no way to go forward until she took a step back into the past. That's what she should've done from the first.

She wiped away her tears and headed for home, knowing what she had to do. It was way past time. She'd been dancing around the truth for weeks now, ignoring it, thinking no one need ever know. But she was lying to herself. She couldn't live with lies.

She went into the house and placed her purse and keys on the kitchen table. Bo sat on the sofa, his legs stretched out in front of him and his head resting on the cushions. The moment she walked in he woke up.

"You're back." His sleepy eyes made her want to forget all the churning feelings in her.

"Yes. It was a rough night."

"You look tired."

She walked farther into the living room,

bracing herself for the onslaught of emotions. "The patient had a miscarriage."

"I'm sorry." His eyes darkened.

She hated those words. They meant nothing. They were only a response, just like she'd given to Kathy. But it was the only thing a person had in these kinds of times.

"It's almost three in the morning." He flexed his shoulders. "I better go so you can get some rest."

She drew a deep breath and prayed for courage. "Bo, I know you wondered why I couldn't forgive you for all these years."

He slipped his feet into his boots, which had been sitting by the couch. "You said it was because I didn't say a final goodbye. Isn't that true?"

"No. I lied." She held her head high.

He got to his feet and his intimidating height made her want to take a step backward, but she would never do that. "I thought we were being honest."

"Yes, but I didn't tell you the whole truth. I didn't tell you why I was so angry and it was more than the fact that you didn't come over to my house and say goodbye, even though I was upset about that, too."

He shook his head. "Bec, what are you trying to say?"

"After you left, I discovered I was pregnant."

CHAPTER FIFTEEN

"W-WHAT?"

Becky's words hit him like a sucker punch and he was unable to process what she was saying.

"That first week you were gone, I cried and cried and my dad said I had to pull myself together, but I didn't know how to do that. The next week I got sick and I thought it was because I was an emotional wreck. I kept throwing up every morning and that's when the light bulb went off in my head. I made an appointment to see a doctor in Temple and he confirmed my suspicion. I was pregnant. You were thousands of miles away and I didn't know what to do."

"My mother knew how to get in touch with me," he snapped, unable to believe what he was hearing.

"That's nice, Bo. Your mother knew, but I didn't and I was the one who needed you the most."

"What happened?"

Becky walked around him to sit on the sofa. "I didn't know how to tell my dad so I didn't, the usual reaction of every teenage girl. I just ignored it for the first few weeks, and then I realized I was having a baby and I got excited. It was just what I needed while you were away. I asked your mom so many times if she'd heard from you, and every time she said no. I went out and bought this little white baby outfit. When you came home I was going to give it to you. That's how I was going to tell you. In case you're wondering, I had every intention of waiting for you."

"Bec..." His throat closed up and he couldn't push words through.

"I was registered to start nursing school in September and my dad went with me to Austin to look for apartments. We found one and I rented it. Dad was glad I had found a way to cope. I still hadn't told him about the baby. In the tenth week I started feeling bad and I noticed I was spotting so I drove to Temple to get checked out. I never left. I started cramping on the way and as soon as I reached the ER I lost it on the table. Tons of blood everywhere. I was so scared. The baby was gone and I was left alone to deal with the aftermath."

Bo swallowed hard and wanted to shut out her words. Years of asking for forgiveness came down to this moment—a moment of reality.

"I still hadn't told my dad about the baby, so I called him and told him I was spending a night with a friend. The next day I drove myself home and still didn't tell my dad. I don't know why that was so hard for me because my dad has always been very supportive. I guess I didn't want to disappoint him.

"I lay around the next few days as my world crumbled. My fever spiked on the fourth day and my dad found me in bed, shivering and unresponsive. He immediately called an ambulance. That's how he found out I had a miscarriage and he didn't understand why I couldn't tell him. I stayed in the hospital for a few days and then my dad brought me home and took care of me. I don't know what I would've done without him."

"Bec…"

"Don't say another word. I don't need your sympathy now and I have to get all of this out because I'll never be able to say it again." She took a long breath and pushed hair from her face. "The next week Ava said you'd called and that you were doing good and to tell me hi. Tell me 'hi'?"

Her voice rose and a surge of guilt ripped through him. "That was your message to me. You called your mother, but not me. That stung and it still stings and it was one of the main reasons I thought I would never forgive you." She jumped to her feet, her eyes blazing. "How do you think I felt when I got that message? After losing your child, should I have been happy that you said *hi*?"

"After basic training, Cole and I came home and I couldn't find you anywhere," he said almost to himself.

"I couldn't stay in Horseshoe and listen to your mother giving me reports of how you were, so I moved into the apartment in Austin and my dad went with me. He wouldn't leave me alone. We grew close during that time. I always thought I needed my mother, but I also needed my dad. He got me through the worst part. I then had to find a way to live with it. The next time you came home I refused to see you. That's how I dealt with it—by not seeing you or talking to you."

"Why did you marry someone else?" It came from the depths of his chest.

"To get you out of my head!" she shouted. "I wanted to remove you from my heart, but I found it almost impossible to do. I couldn't sleep with him so it was over quickly. By then, anger at your behavior had consumed me and I really never wanted to see you again."

He bowed his head as the weight of her words almost brought him to his knees. He'd lost track of the times he'd tried to talk to her, even after she was married, and he never understood her anger. But now he did. It was clear at the many missteps he'd made in the name of love. At this point, he wasn't sure what love was. All he knew was that she filled his every waking thought and many of his dreams. Then how could he have treated her that way?

"I want you to leave," she said in a calm tone.

He reached for his jacket. Words gathered in his throat like little soldiers waiting for enemy fire. "I don't know what to say."

"There's nothing left to say. I should've told you from the start, but my pride wouldn't let me."

"You should've found a way to tell me

when it happened," he replied with a touch of anger.

She shook her head. "Oh, no. You don't get to pull that on me. You made the choices that separated our lives. I don't believe there's any way to go forward anymore."

Bo walked out the door, unable to defend himself.

Totally spent, Becky walked up the stairs to check on Luci and then fell across her bed and wondered if this night could get any worse. She'd really thought she could forget the past. Bo had been incredible with Luci and Becky had seen a whole different side of him, loving, caring and compassionate, and dreams of a life with him had tempted her. How could she be so stupid? Bo was grown now and different than the wild living-life-on-the-edge teenager she'd known, but she would never forget that little life who had lived in her for a moment in time.

She got up, went to her closet and reached for a small box she kept there. Sitting on the bed, she removed the lid and the tissue and pulled out the white onesie she'd bought eighteen years ago. She'd gone with white because she hadn't known if it was a boy or a girl. On the front of the onesie it said

I Love My Daddy. There were white booties to match. She held them to her heart as tears rolled down her cheeks. They'd been a gift for Bo. She lay on the bed, holding them to her chest.

As she lay there, precious memories washed over her, the good and the bad. Back then she'd understood Bo's need to get away since his father was in town. Or, at least, she'd tried to understand. He became a completely different person around his father, someone she didn't like. She'd tried to talk to Bo about it, but he always grew defensive and she'd let it go.

Looking back through realistic glasses, she knew there was nothing she could have done to change him. The way he felt about his father had been shaped long before she'd met him. Knowing he had issues with his father, she'd still fallen in love with him and tried to be supportive.

She got up and removed her clothes, grabbed her pajamas and crawled back into bed, clutching the onesie and booties to herself. She'd hurt Bo tonight, but she hadn't seen any other way.

He had to know the whole story. He had to know about the child they'd created and lost. Her keeping it locked inside wasn't doing either of them any good. They had to mourn and grieve for that child together, but she didn't know if he ever wanted to see her again. That was the big question now: Would Bo ever forgive her?

BO DIDN'T KNOW where he was going and he didn't care. He just had to keep moving. He found himself at the cattle guard at the entrance to Cole's grandfather's place. He pulled his phone out of his pocket and called Cole.

"Meet me at the barn."

"Huh… Okay." The two of them had always been there for each other and tonight was no different. Cole didn't ask any questions because he knew Bo wouldn't make this request if it wasn't important. Bo turned off his headlights and drove down the lane to the barn.

He pushed the door open and a donkey brayed. Mr. Walt's animals were in the barn because it was cold. There was a donkey, a potbellied pig and a goat. Chickens roosted in the hay and he knew if he looked up there would be a cat perched in the rafters.

Bo sat on a bale of hay and the pungent

scent of alfalfa reached him, reminding him of all the times he and Cole had met in this barn to deal with life and its many problems. They'd first tried smoking here and almost burned down the barn. They'd tried making beer and almost blown up the barn. A lot of their life had been in this barn, making plans. But nothing had prepared him for the shock he had received tonight.

Cole came in dressed in jeans and a jacket and pulled the door closed. He flipped a switch, flooding the barn with iridescent light. "What's going on?" he asked as he sat by Bo.

He got up and paced in front of his friend. "I'm going crazy, man."

"Why?"

"We took Luci trick-or-treating tonight, and Becky and I were getting along really well, but she got called to the hospital. One of her patients had a miscarriage. It affected her deeply. I could see she'd been crying when she got back and then she unloaded a whole lot of hurt on me. Turns out, after you and I left for the army, she found out she was pregnant."

"What?"

"My reaction exactly." Bo went on to tell

Cole everything that had happened while they'd been gone.

"Why would she keep it a secret?"

"She was dealing with a lot on her own. I was keeping in touch with my mom instead of her. Why did I do that? I told my mom to tell her hi. Why, Cole? Why did I do that? I should've called her. I should've done a lot of things, but I didn't and the truth is now slapping me in the face. I'm just like my father. I judged him and look what I did."

"Come on."

"It's true. At least he was there when we were born. I wasn't there for Becky or the baby. I was off living my dream while she was in pain."

"She could've gotten a message to you."

"Yeah." Bo sank back onto the bale of hay. "I don't know whether to be mad at her or me."

"Take a deep breath and think about it. She wouldn't talk to you for years, but now you're talking and all the bad stuff is coming out. You need to keep talking."

"I've said I'm sorry so many times that the words are redundant now. There's not enough sorries in the world to cover this. I behaved badly toward the woman I loved." He jumped up and started pacing again. His guilty feelings were eating away at him. "You know that saying about paying the piper?"

"Yeah."

"Well, I'm paying through the heart and I don't think this pain is ever going to go away. I let her down. How do I get over that?"

Cole didn't say anything as Bo sat back down on the bale of hay. His senses calmed into a steady numbness. "My father is dying and a man with any guts would go see him, but I keep putting it off. All my life he's been a thorn in my side, but you know what? That was his life and I couldn't change it.

"As a child I took on his role, to try and make our family a family. It didn't happen and the thorn got deeper. Out of responsibility I took on a lot of my mom's pain. And that made my hatred of him grow, an uncontrollable hatred that I see now as childish. It wasn't my problem to carry. I should've been dealing with my own issues. I should have been thinking about Becky and our lives. I certainly missed the boat on that one."

"You're sounding very mature and grown-up."

"It's like looking in a mirror and seeing myself for the first time—the real me, the one who lights up like a firecracker whenever he's around, the guy who made his mom's life miserable because he would never give up on the issue, and the guy who abandoned the woman he loved and their child. It's staggering when you look at the whole picture. Like Grandpa always said, I'm the man. Be a man. I guess I proved him right."

"I'm not going to listen to this, Bo. You're taking the blame for everything. I think your mother would agree that you're the one who kept pulling your family together. And you didn't abandon Becky. You had planned on coming back and making a life with her. Yes, you should've called her, but if you remember, we were rather busy since we chose Intelligence and had to take extra training. Our minds were focused on a war. And if you say you're like your grandfather or dad one more time, I'm going to hit you."

Bo laughed and the sound echoed through the barn, frightening the chickens, which squawked and then settled down. "Remember all the fights we had in this barn?"

"Yeah. Grandpa Chisum had to break us apart one time with the blast of a shotgun."

"What were we fighting about?"

"I liked that dark-haired girl in tenth

grade and you had flirted with her. We had an agreement not to trespass on the girls we dated. When we got back to the barn, I lit into you."

"What was her name?"

"I can't remember."

"Me neither." Bo threw his arm around Cole's shoulder. "We had a code of honor and I broke it. We promised each other we would never get married, but once you met Grace…"

"I was happy to break it." There was silence for a moment and then Cole added, "I think you have to ask yourself a big question now. Do you still love Becky?"

Bo didn't hesitate with his response. "I'm always going to love her. I just don't know if she can ever love me again."

"My advice is, and remember you asked for it, go visit your father and be the man you want to be and not the one your grandfather groomed. Get that garbage out of your system that you've been carrying around since the day you found your dad with another woman. And the next step would be to tell Becky how you really feel."

"Sounds easy."

"Yeah."

"But why is it so incredibly hard?"

"Nothing worth fighting for has ever been easy."

Becky meant everything to him and now he had to prove it. Bo got to his feet. "Sorry for waking you up so early. I think I'll go see my mom for a few minutes before I head back to Austin. Thanks for listening."

"Anytime."

They walked out of the barn and a lot of the guilt around Bo's heart eased. As he got into his truck he vowed that from this day forward Becky would always be number one in his heart. He just had to make her believe it.

It was five o'clock when he drove into his mom's driveway. The lights were on and he knew she was either going to the grocery store or to church. He had a key, but he didn't want to frighten her so he knocked at the front door. She answered in a bathrobe.

"Bo, what are you doing knocking?"

"I didn't want to alarm you."

She patted his cheek. "You're such a sweet boy."

"Mom, I'm not a boy anymore," he told her as they walked into the house.

"I'm well aware of that. Get a cup of coffee and I'll make breakfast before I go to church."

Pouring a cup of coffee, he asked, "Isn't it a little early for church?"

"Yes, but I go by the grocery store to make sure everything is running smoothly."

For the first time, he realized how strong his mother was. She didn't need her son running her life or worrying about her. She had that down. She owned it. Mason was her kryptonite and she had that under control, too.

He shifted uncomfortably in a chair. "Mom, I'd like to ask some questions."

She pulled out a chair with a coffee cup in her hand. "Sure. Craig said you and Becky took Luci trick-or-treating. Did she have fun?"

"Yeah, she was so cute. You wouldn't believe what she did." He told his mother how Luci would forget to say trick-or-treat and just introduce herself. As he talked, he realized how much he loved that little girl and he wasn't going to bail on her. He wasn't going to bail on Becky, either. He shook his head. "That's not what I want to talk about."

"By the expression on your face, I'm guessing it's something important."

"Were you aware that Becky was pregnant when I left for the army?"

"What?"

"I found out last night that Becky was pregnant and she had a miscarriage at ten weeks. It devastated her."

"Oh my goodness." His mom held a hand to her chest. "That's why she called all the time, asking where you were."

"Why didn't you get in touch with me?"

"I thought she was just missing you. She never said otherwise. Oh, heavens, what did I do?"

"She wanted to let me know about the baby."

"Oh, son, I'm so sorry. I didn't pick up on the clues."

"She went through it alone, not even telling her father. But she caught an infection and Craig had to call an ambulance. That's when he found out his daughter had a miscarriage. He was there for her then."

"I heard about the ambulance in the neighborhood, and when I asked Craig, he said Becky wasn't feeling well. She came home, but before I could visit her, they left and were gone for a long time. I didn't know what was wrong and I didn't ask. I should've asked."

"It's not your fault. It's mine."

"Craig and I have been so happy that you two were getting along so well."

"Yeah, me too, but I don't know where we go from here."

"Why did she tell you now?"

He told his mom about the lady having a miscarriage. "It brought it back all back and she said she had to tell me."

"And?"

"She asked me to leave and I did."

"Oh, son, I'm so sorry." His mother stood. "I'll fix you a good breakfast and that will cheer you up."

"Yeah, right." Food fixes everything. While she cooked he went into his bedroom and looked out the window to the Tullous house. It was in darkness. Craig wasn't up yet. Craig's sharp attitude toward Bo become clear now. He didn't want Bo in his house and Bo didn't blame him. But because of Luci he'd held his tongue. Bo wondered if the man would ever accept him.

"Breakfast," his mom called.

She placed bacon, eggs and biscuits on the table and he dug in. He was hungry.

"I was going to call you about Thanksgiving," she said.

He shoved scrambled eggs into his mouth. "Why?"

"We're having the Goodnight Thanksgiving at Lois's, like always. Mason will be there for the first time in years and your grandmother is worried you won't come."

He took a sip of coffee. "I'll be there."

His mother's eyes opened wide. "Just like that, you'll be there."

"Yes."

She jumped up and hugged him. "Thank you, son. I don't believe you'll regret it."

He got up and filled his coffee cup. "Who am I to judge? I ran out on Becky and my baby, and that's about as low as you can get."

"Don't say that. Becky is to blame for a lot of this. She could have told me."

"Becky is not to blame," he snapped. "She went through hell because of me and I never want to hear you say that again."

His mother raised her hands. "Okay. I'm getting dressed and going to church. The family could use some prayers right now." She swung toward her bedroom and glanced over her shoulder. "Are you staying or going?"

"I'm going back to Austin. I have to work tomorrow and I need some sleep." He realized he'd been up all night and was beginning to feel the pull of that.

"I'll call you with details for Thanksgiving."

Details? He just showed up. What kind of details could there be?

His mom left for church and he sat on the sofa and fell asleep. It was one o'clock when he woke up. He hurriedly took a shower and changed clothes. He seemed to have clothes everywhere. One day he would live in one house with one family and not be such a vagabond. His future dream, but would it be Becky's?

As he backed his truck out he noticed Craig's garage door was up. He steered into Craig's driveway, walked to the front door and rang the bell.

"Bo." Craig was surprised to see him.

"Can I talk to you for a minute?" Bo followed Craig into the house.

"Have you talked to Becky?"

"Yes. She's fine and I'm glad the truth is out. She carried it long enough."

"Why didn't you get her to tell my mother? I'm not placing blame, but I would like to know."

"My daughter was lying in a hospital bed

with 105-degree fever and crying for her own mother. I would have done anything to ease her pain. She wanted to tell you herself and I gave in to her wishes. She'd lost her mother and then she lost her baby, and there was no way to soothe her injured soul. She didn't want anyone to know and I respected her wishes. I would do it all over again. You're the one who left, Bo, and now you have to deal with the consequences. I'm not placing blame, either. The time for blame is over."

"How is she this morning?"

"She sounded okay and she assured me she was. Maybe now that the secret is out you and Becky can talk and go forward or never see each other again."

Bo held out his hand. "I'm sorry for all I put Becky through, and you, too."

Craig shook his hand and Bo walked out the door to his truck with a butt-load of guilt weighing him down. *Talk and go forward or never see each other again.* If those were his options, he'd take the former.

CHAPTER SIXTEEN

WHEN BECKY WOKE UP, her body felt light, weightless and free. That deep pain in her heart that she'd carried like a badge was gone. Not completely, but it didn't have the power to reduce her to a pile of tears. Could it really have been that easy? Telling Bo had worked wonders, and now she could put the miscarriage behind her along with the memories of a baby who wasn't meant to be.

She tucked the onesie into the box, covered it with tissue and put it in its place in the closet. Throwing it away was out of the question. She hurriedly dressed and went to check on Luci.

Her baby was waking up, rubbing her eyes. "Mommy."

She lifted Luci into her arms and kissed her cheek. "Morning, baby. Let's go potty."

Luci liked to do things for herself so Becky let her. There was a small stool at the sink she could step on to wash her hands. She was fond of doing this, over and over.

"That's enough," Becky said.

At that moment, the memory of the night before came to Luci. "Candy, Mommy," she cried and took off running. Becky caught her at the bottom of the stairs. "Hold on, hold on."

Next followed a long conversation about how much candy one could eat or how little candy one should eat. Luci picked out the candy she was allowed to eat that day and put the rest into the cabinet, except for the cookies.

"After breakfast, you can have a cookie."

Luci clapped her hands.

While Luci was eating breakfast, Becky's phone binged. It was Dr. Berger from the hospital.

"Good morning, Becky, Kathy wants to go home with her mother and I see no reason to keep her here. She's nervous her husband will find her. I'm going to release her and I thought I'd let you know."

"Thank you. Just be sure she makes an appointment. Dr. Eames needs to see her."

"Will do. But I examined her this morning and she's fine."

Becky clicked off. Kathy wasn't fine. She wouldn't be fine for a very long time.

"Cookie, Mommy, cookie."

Becky handed her daughter a cookie and fervently hoped it wouldn't take a long time for Bo to adjust. She knew him, and right now he was experiencing a lot of guilty feelings. He had to experience them. That was the only way to deal with what had happened. After that, maybe he would talk to her again and they could meet on equal ground, sharing and loving a child they had created for that brief moment.

Bo THREW HIMSELF into work like he always did. If there was a lull in SWAT duties, they usually helped out the cops or trained, but they were always on call for emergencies. *Keep busy* was again his mantra. It kept him from thinking, but later at night, when he was lying in bed, Becky interrupted his dreams, and he wasn't sure if they could ever recover from the past.

Days turned into weeks and he had to face the big Thanksgiving coming up. He'd told his mother he would be there and he wasn't backing out. If he did anything now, it would be to stand up and be the man he was supposed to be. And forgiveness wasn't so hard anymore. He'd been through a lot of life's lessons and there were many more to come.

On Thanksgiving morning he left early to beat the traffic and was at his mother's by six. She was up already and busy cooking. There were pots and pans and dishes everywhere.

"Are you cooking the whole meal?"

"Lois and I have to make the whole meal. Lois's daughters are hopeless in the kitchen and what do you think Kelsey's going to bring? I don't know what I did, but that girl hates to cook."

"Because you always took care of it."

"Yeah." His mom brushed a strand of hair from her face.

"Do you need me to do anything?"

"Just stay out of my way. Oh." She changed her mind. "Could you get that big ice chest from the garage? I have lined it with tinfoil."

He brought the ice chest in and placed it on the floor in the kitchen. "Is Kel meeting us there?"

"Yes. Once I get all of this packed, you can put the chest into the car for me."

He helped her pack and carried everything to her SUV. She then took a shower and got dressed. Standing in the living room, she glanced at him as he was drinking coffee in the kitchen. "Bo, you are coming, right?"

"Yes, Mom, I'm coming, but I'd rather not go this early."

She stood there, staring at him, and he knew something was up. "What?"

"Uh…your father's girlfriend will be with him and I hope you won't cause a scene."

"He has a girlfriend?" For the life of him Bo didn't know why that surprised him, but it didn't matter. What mattered was his relationship with his father. Or the lack of one.

"No problem. Don't worry about it. Two months ago I probably would've pitched a fit, but who am I to throw stones? I promise you there won't be a scene."

"Well, you do seem rather calm."

"It's called growing up and facing facts."

"I'm speechless."

After his mom left, he strolled through the house and stopped at the window in his bedroom. His heart skipped a beat. Luci sat on the step of Craig's house with pink ribbons around her pigtails, wearing her pink glasses and a pink outfit he'd never seen before. Pink lay beside her and Purr trailed around the potted plant on the porch. Becky was home.

He stared at the blue ball on Luci's lap and before he knew it he was out the front door, walking across the street. Luci jumped up when she saw him and ran to him.

"Bo, you wanna play?" Such a change from the little girl he'd met weeks ago. A smile split her face as she spoke in a full sentence.

He lifted her into his arms. "Little angel, it's Thanksgiving and your mommy probably has plans for you."

"Grandpa's cooking."

He sat on the step with her in his lap, and took the ball from her and placed it on the porch. "You're all dressed up."

She looked down at her pink outfit. "Me pretty."

"Yes, you are."

The door opened and Becky stood there in black slacks and a white turtleneck sweater. Her hair was tousled around her face in a new style. She looked gorgeous. "Lu… Oh, Bo."

He got to his feet, letting Luci go, and was unsure of what to say. "I was just talking to Luci."

"I see," she replied in a nervous voice. "Luci, your grandfather needs you."

"'Kay." Luci ran into the house and left him and Becky to face the past between them. It was as big as all outdoors and stretched as far as they could see.

"I'm sorry for everything you had to go through." The words came out of Bo in a rush.

Becky sat on the step and he eased down by her. The scent of Mimosa Rain was all around him and memories, beautiful memories, floated through him.

"And I'm sorry for blurting it out like that," she said, "but I had to tell you. You needed to know."

"Yes, I needed to know." He didn't say he needed to know years ago or that she should've found a way to get in touch with him. He didn't lay the blame at her door. He accepted it squarely at his.

"Are you okay?" she asked in a soft voice.

"I'm getting there."

"I never realized what a burden I was carrying until I told you. I feel much better now and with less guilt. There's no way for us to go back and do things differently. We have to learn from our mistakes and try to do better. That's what I'm doing. I don't have that ache in my heart anymore or that resentment toward you. I finally set myself free and I suggest you do the same."

"I can't help thinking I'm just like my father."

"You're not. You never cheated on me."

"I can look him in the eye and talk to him as a son now."

"Oh, Bo. That's really a big leap for you and I hope it all goes well."

He could see through the warmth of her eyes that she did and that part of him that was wound so tight eased enough to let him breathe without angst.

"Bo, Bo, Bo." Luci came running out the door again, her blue eyes just as alive as Becky's. "We gonna get a—" She looked at Becky. "What we gonna get?"

Becky picked her up. "I have no idea what you're talking about, baby."

"You know, Grandpa said." Luci held her arms toward the sky. "It's big and..."

"Do you mean the Christmas tree?"

Luci nodded vigorously. "Yes. Grandpa says we gonna get a big Christmas tree... And I want... Bo to help. He's my friend."

"Anything you want, little angel, if it's okay with your mom," Bo responded without hesitation.

"Sure," Becky said. "We're going to get one in the morning. Are you off tomorrow?"

He remembered that Tullous tradition of getting the tree the day after Thanksgiving. He wasn't off, but he would be by tomorrow morning even if he had to quit. He was that serious about mending all the broken fences with Becky, and it started tomorrow.

As soon as he got into his truck he called the lieutenant. She was having Thanksgiving like everyone else, but he didn't hesitate. This was too important.

"Goodnight, what is it?"

"I would like some time off, Lieutenant. It's a family thing and I need to be here."

"Just schedule it like everyone else."

"I need tomorrow, Saturday and Sunday off."

There was a pause on the line. "You're very aware these need to be scheduled ahead of time."

"Yes, ma'am, and I wouldn't ask if wasn't something important."

"Okay, but you will be on call for an emergency in case we have a situation?"

"Yes, ma'am. Thank you."

He slipped the phone into his pocket. He was going to spend Thanksgiving like everyone else, but first he had to face the demon in him and the demon had a name—Mason.

BECKY WENT BACK into the house with Luci in her arms. She and Bo had had a good talk and she was happy about that. Maybe there was a way to talk through all the heartache and pain. Maybe there was a way to start the healing. Maybe there was a way to find love again.

"Grandpa," Luci said, slipping to the floor. "Bo's gonna help."

Her dad turned from the stove. He was wearing a big apron that had a turkey on the front of it. "What's she talking about?"

"Bo, Grandpa." Luci tried to make him understand, but failed.

"Bo's going to help us get the Christmas tree tomorrow."

"Good, then I'm going to sit in my chair and watch football."

Luci darted off to watch the Macy's Thanksgiving Day Parade.

"Bo's going to see his dad today."

"I know. Ava told me." Her dad stirred the potatoes on the stove and wiped his hands on a dishtowel. "I don't understand why Ava has to go. She's not married to Mason anymore, but I guess that's her family."

"Yes, I think they are. I hope she's going to be okay, since he's bringing a girlfriend."

"He's bringing a girlfriend! That's just…" Her dad couldn't find the words as he spit and sputtered.

"It's none of our business, Dad. You know Ava has a soft spot when it comes to Mason."

"I'm well aware of that. I just never understood her penchant for always forgiving that man." Anger coated her dad's voice and that was so unlike him. In all her growing-up years she hardly ever remembered him raising his voice.

"Did you say any of this to Ava?"

"Sure I did. I don't want to see her get hurt again. We're friends and we speak our minds."

"I see." But she really didn't. She had the same suspicion she'd had earlier about her dad and Ava's relationship. Were they more than friends? There were no signs if they were, but she and Bo were rarely home, so how would they know?

Bo's Aunt Lois lived in a nice Temple subdivision. The houses were on lots that were almost an acre and there was plenty of room for parking, but on this day cars were parked everywhere on the streets as families were home for the holiday. He parked at the curb behind cars in the driveway. He was leaving as quickly as he could, so it didn't matter if he was blocking some cars.

Someone got out of the car ahead of him and he looked closer. It was his sister, Kelsey. There was no mistaking that red hair. He used to call her the ugly duckling because of her hair, but he couldn't say that anymore. She'd turned into a beautiful young woman with deep coppery-colored hair and green eyes. He had to admit his sister was a knockout. Maybe a little clueless, stubborn, opinionated and sharp-tongued, too. His sister could get on his nerves better than anyone.

She tottered on high heels to him, carrying something in her hand. "I was waiting for you."

"I'm here now. What's the problem?"

"I'm not going in there alone."

"Why?"

"He's in there and I haven't seen him in years. I might need vodka for this."

Bo chuckled. "I've never known you to be afraid of anything."

"There's always a first time." She looked down at the glass thing she was holding. It was small at the bottom and wide at the top. It looked like a vase filled with something.

"What is that?" he asked.

"Mom told me to bring something sweet. What did she tell you to bring?"

"Uh…"

"I knew it. She didn't tell you to bring a thing, did she?"

"No," he admitted.

"It doesn't matter how old we get, you'll always be the favorite and I get diddly-squat nothing."

"Let's don't do the brother-sister thing today. Our concentration is elsewhere. What did you make?"

"Banana pudding."

He frowned. "It doesn't look like banana pudding. Is that a vase?"

She held it up. "Yeah. I didn't have anything else to put it in."

Bo tried very hard not to laugh, but this was classic Kelsey. "How did you make it?"

"I just mixed it all together and dumped it in the vase. It's glass and clean, so what's the difference?"

"It's supposed to be layered, I think."

Kelsey shrugged. "Who cares?"

Bo slung his arm around her shoulder. "Let's go meet the demon in our lives."

His mother answered the door. "Come in," she said, then whispered, "Be on your best behavior," as if they were five years old.

She looked at what Kelsey was holding in her hand. "What is that? Is that a vase?"

Kelsey handed it to her. "Yes, ma'am, and it's filled with banana pudding."

"Oh, good grief."

"Why did I have to bring something and not Bo? He's capable of cooking, you know."

"Not now, Kelsey."

"Beauregard, my grandson, is here." His grandmother threw her arms around his waist and hugged him, and then she hugged Kelsey. "Such beautiful grandchildren." She took their hands and led them toward Mason and the woman with him.

Bo had been trained to seek out the enemy and he zeroed in on Mason as soon as he stepped into the living room. His father stood at the back of the crowd with a drink in his hand and a beautiful woman wearing lots of makeup standing beside him. Bo's stomach tightened, just from habit.

On the way there he shook hands with

John and Nathan, the husbands of his cousins, Mitzi and Sarah. Uncle Jim's daughter, Andrea, and her husband, Mike, were also there. Mike was stationed at Fort Hood. Three little girls, four, three and two, milled around the room. Uncle Dale sat in his recliner watching a football game. Aunt Lois was in the kitchen.

Grandma had a death grip on Bo and Kelsey's hands and she practically dragged them to Mason and his girlfriend. They stopped in front of the couple and Grandma was the first to speak. "Look at your handsome children. I'm so proud of both of them."

"I am, too," Mason replied. "I'm glad you both came." He turned to the woman beside him. "This is Layla."

Before Bo or Kelsey could reply, Aunt Lois shouted from the kitchen, "Dinner. And turn that TV off, Dale."

Dale complied and they gathered around a long dining table. Aunt Lois and his mother had outdone themselves. The table was set for fourteen people with china and crystal, and flowers in the center. There were six places on each side and one at each end. There were place cards so everyone knew were to sit. Aunt Lois and Grandma sat on the ends. Two of the little girls sat at a table with their own special paper china. The two-year-old was in a high chair on Mitzi's right.

Dale stood and said the prayer and then Aunt Lois brought a big turkey on a platter to the table and set it in front of Dale, who promptly started to carve it.

Not a word was spoken during this process, and then everyone passed around the food and started to eat. All this was going through Bo's head and it was in slow motion, driving him crazy. He just wanted to get out of there.

Bo thought about Luci and how she would enjoy playing with the little girls. He tried not to look at his dad or the girlfriend. He concentrated on the food.

"There's too much salt in the dressing," Grandma said.

"Ava made it," Lois said and pointed a finger at her mother. "You thought I made it and wanted to criticize. Well, this time it backfired on you."

"The dressing is delicious," Mason said. "Ava's always is."

Bo kept eating and refused to look at his sister, who was sitting beside him.

Kelsey poked her fork into his thigh and he glared at her.

"Where did you meet Uncle Mason?" Mitzi asked Layla.

Layla wiped her mouth. "I met him at the Veterans Hospital in Temple. His band came to play and since I'm a singer I didn't want to miss it. They let me sing a couple of numbers and afterward they hired me."

"You're in his band?" Sarah asked.

"Yes, for about a year now. Once I heard Mason's voice, I just fell in love."

"A lot of women have," Lois mumbled.

Grandma pointed her fork at her daughter. "Don't start."

After that, everyone continued to eat in silence. The only noise in the room was the chatter of the little girls. When they were done, everyone carried their plates to the kitchen.

"Is it okay to smoke in here?" Layla asked Grandma.

"No, Lois would have a fit with the children around. You have to go outside to smoke."

Mason and Layla slipped out the patio doors to the backyard.

Bo took a helping of Kelsey's banana pudding because no one else was eating it. He carried his plate to the kitchen and knew time was up. He had to talk to his father. He walked to the patio doors and Kelsey was right behind him.

"You're not doing this without me," she said.

Mason sat in the swing and Layla sat beside him. Both were smoking, which was the last thing Mason needed to be doing, and blowing puffs of smoke into the air.

When Layla saw them, she got up and went back into the house, throwing her cigarette onto the grass as she went. Aunt Lois was going to love that.

Kelsey sat on a large car toy and Bo shoved his hands into his pockets, waiting for the words to come.

Kelsey took it out of his hands. "I'm sorry you have cancer and I'm sorry you're in pain."

"Thank you, Kel," Mason replied.

"I remember you singing in the mornings and I liked that. I knew you were home."

"I like singing to my kids, too, and I'm not expecting forgiveness. I just wanted to see you, both of you, to say how proud I am of you. Despite my behavior, insecurities and the many problems I heaped upon your mother, you turned out better people than I will ever be."

"Then why heap another one on her by bringing that woman today?" Bo couldn't keep the words inside.

"Because she gives me an injection if I'm in a lot of pain and I knew today would be stressful. I talked to your mother and she said it would be fine. But if it bothers you, we will leave."

"No. I just worry how it affects my mother."

"Your mother is not in love with me anymore, so you don't have to worry about that." He pushed to his feet and staggered. Bo grabbed his arm and Kelsey jumped up and grabbed the other one.

"Are you okay?" Bo asked.

"The pain is getting bad and I need to go home." He reached into his jacket and pulled out a large white envelope. "I wanted to give you this. It's not a long, sorrowful letter about how I'm sorry and excuses. There is no excuse for the way I lived my life. It's just something that needs to be opened when I pass. Since you're my son, I want you to do that."

Bo didn't hesitate in taking the letter. It seemed important to his father and it was the least he could do. With him and Kelsey on either side of Mason they walked into the house, where Layla joined them at the front door.

"What's wrong?" Grandma wanted to know.

"I'm a little tired, Mom, and I'm going back to the motel. Goodbye, everyone. Thanks for the beautiful dinner."

Bo and Kelsey walked him to the passenger side of the car and he got in. Mason was ghost white and his hands shook. "Just remember, a day didn't go by that I didn't think of the two of you."

Bo looked at Layla. "You might want to give him something for pain."

"The motel we're staying in is not far away and I'll wait until we get there. He usually goes to sleep."

Bo nodded.

"Goodbye, son, Kel," Mason muttered.

Bo closed the door and Layla drove away.

He stared at the car and Kelsey's left arm went around his waist. "That didn't go too bad, and for the life of me I can't dredge up any resentment. It's absolutely gone."

"I know." All the anger and bitterness had

disappeared. His dad was a shell of a man now, and needed their sympathy and support, and Bo would give him that until his father's last day.

"Let's go eat some more of that banana pudding," he said to lighten the atmosphere. "I'm in a daredevil mood."

Kelsey laughed, and arm in arm they went back into the house.

CHAPTER SEVENTEEN

IT WAS SEVEN O'CLOCK when Bo got back to his mom's house. After he and Kelsey went back in, it had been a whole different atmosphere. The tension that had gripped everyone was gone. Everyone was laughing and joking and carrying on.

Aunt Lois made them do the dishes and they had a line going, washing, drying and putting up. They talked as they worked and he got to know his cousins a little better, especially Andrea. Their next assignment was in Germany and she was excited to get to see her parents again.

Just as they were talking, Uncle Jim called and Grandma yanked the phone out of Lois's hands. He talked to everyone and Andrea got teary-eyed. She was pregnant and missed her parents. Grandma told Uncle Jim he needed to call his brother and he told her he already had. Uncle Jim was always a stand-up kind of guy.

He always had a beer with Grandpa Walt on Thanksgiving and afterward that's where he went. Grace's friend Frannie was there and also Miss Bertie, who lived down the road. It was a visit of laughing and telling stories, and it gave Bo a lift. But he was glad to go home because he had a big day tomorrow with Becky and Luci.

When he walked into the house, he saw his mother sitting in her chair with her feet propped up. He sat across from her.

"You look tired."

"I am a little. It was a big day." There was something in her voice that was different and he was trying to pinpoint what it was.

"Did Layla bother you?"

"Layla? Heavens, no. Her being so young did, but that's your father's life and doesn't concern me anymore."

"I think she's good for him," Bo said, looking at the situation through different eyes.

"Yeah, I think so, too. She's taking care of him and not many women that age would do that."

"Then why do you look so sad?"

She removed her feet from the stool and sat up. "Bo, I think you're old enough to hear what I have to say."

He was startled for a moment. *Old enough?* He'd been old enough for a long time. He sat patiently, though, waiting for whatever she needed him to hear.

"I told you I'm not in love with your father anymore and whatever he does doesn't concern me or affect me. I'm glad he's found someone and I'm deeply saddened that he's in pain and not going to live much longer.

"But—" she took a deep breath "—I've been seeing someone else, someone that I love deeply, and he was upset that I was spending Thanksgiving with my ex's family. I told him I had to go because of my children and he didn't quite understand that. He's such a nice man and I didn't want to hurt him. Now I'm worried I've ruined everything between us."

"Huh…" Words filled his mouth, unspoken. *Seeing someone else?*

He cleared his throat. "How is that possible? You never go anywhere. You work all the time. When did you find time to meet someone? Is it your boss?"

"Of course not. He's almost seventy and has grandchildren."

"Then who?"

His mom slipped her feet into her shoes

and grabbed her purse. "I'm not going to sleep until I see him. I'll be back later." She headed for the back door and Bo followed.

"Who is it? Mom, who are you seeing?"

She ignored him and got in her car and drove away.

He went to the refrigerator, grabbed a beer and downed a gulp. His mom was dating. He would've never guessed that in a million years. He walked into his bedroom and stared out the window at the Tullous house. The lights were on. Everyone was home, enjoying the holiday. Suddenly, the garage door went up and Craig backed his truck out and drove down the street.

As a cop, warning bells went off in his head. Could it be? Craig was the only man she saw outside work. They'd gotten very close since Craig's accident. There were the flowers in Craig's yard. Some of the same flowers as in his mom's. Could it be?

Bo set his beer on the dresser and went out the front door and across the street. When Becky opened the door, he walked right past her.

"I think my mom and your dad are seeing each other."

She brushed hair behind her ears. "I've had my suspicions for a while now."

"So they are?"

She shrugged. "I don't know."

He took a long breath to calm down. "I think it would be wonderful. Someone would always be there for her."

"Me, too. And my dad wouldn't be so lonely."

"I'm waiting up for her and she's going to tell me the truth."

"Don't push, Bo. If they're seeing each other, they'll tell us when they want to."

"Yeah," he mused and leaned toward her. "Sometimes I smell that scent even when you're not around."

"What scent?" she whispered.

"Mimosa Rain."

"Bo…"

He kissed the side of her face, his lips lingering for a moment. "See you tomorrow." He walked out, forcing himself not to look back.

Bo went home with a smile. They were getting along and that's what he wanted. He wanted to make up for everything and to feel her love again. He took a shower and waited up for his mother. At almost twelve she came through the back door, humming. She was in a better mood. "Oh, Bo, you scared me," she said as he got up from the sofa. "I thought you'd be in bed by now."

"I just wanted to make sure you were okay. You were kind of sad when you left. I guess you talked to the new man in your life."

"I should've never told you that. Now you're going to hound me to death."

"Yes, I am. Who is he?"

"I'll tell you when I'm ready. Now I'm going to bed." She turned on her heel and walked to her bedroom. He went to his, looked out the window and saw Craig drive into his garage. Oh, yes. His mom was in love with the neighbor.

THE NEXT MORNING Becky rushed around trying to get Luci ready, and trying to get herself ready. She put jeans, a pink polo and a pink hoodie on Luci. For herself, she decided on a red hoodie and put her hair up to show off some Christmas earrings.

Bo rang the doorbell about nine and Luci ran to answer it, shouting, "We gonna get a tree. A big tree."

They loaded up into Bo's truck.

"There's a Christmas tree farm between

Horseshoe and Temple. Are you game?" Bo asked. He was wearing jeans and a black sweatshirt, which reminded her of just how handsome he was.

"Sure. I thought we'd just go down to the Christmas tree lot, but that sounds much more fun."

Luci kept singing songs that they'd learned. Every now and then she'd stop and announce something. "Santa got reindeer."

"We know, baby. What do you want for Christmas?"

"I can't tell you."

Becky frowned. "Why not?"

"I don't know. I have to tell Santa."

Becky looked at Bo and he shrugged.

They turned off the highway onto a country dirt road and traveled about a mile until they came to the tree farm that grew miles and miles of Christmas trees. They were in Santa land for sure.

"Trees, Mommy."

"Look, Bo. They have a trailer pulled by a tractor to carry customers around to pick out their trees. This is going to be so much fun for Luci."

"Really?" He lifted an eyebrow at her.

"Okay, me too." She laughed.

There were other people waiting in line to get Christmas trees. The fall temperature was brisk and Becky pulled the hoodie over Luci's head so her ears wouldn't get cold. There were lots of children running around and Luci's eyes were glued to them. Bo held her and she wanted down. A little boy about her age was in front of them with his parents and two sisters.

Luci walked up to him. "My name is Luci. What's your name?"

"John," the little boy replied.

"We gonna get a Christmas tree," Luci told him.

"We are, too."

"She's having a conversation," Becky whispered to Bo.

"Yeah, she's getting braver."

A tractor trailer pulled up and the man shouted, "Two families."

They got on the trailer with John's family and the man drove them into the trees. Becky felt as if she was being swallowed by Christmas trees. Christmas music played and the kids clapped and sang along. John scooted over by Luci, and they giggled and laughed and it made Becky's heart happy. She took pictures with her phone, as did John's mother.

The man stopped the tractor. "When you find your tree, just holler."

It didn't take them long to find a tree, and the man cut it down and put it on the trailer. Luci's eyes were huge as she watched. When they got back to the office, Bo lifted it off the trailer and placed it in the back of his truck as if it was no more than a limb.

"Bye, John," Luci called as Bo put her in the car seat.

Luci chattered all the way home and Becky smiled at Bo. It was good to feel free from the pain and to share this Christmas moment with him. She didn't think beyond that.

She made turkey sandwiches for lunch and then they spent the afternoon putting up the tree. Her dad had already gotten all the decorations out of the attic and the living room was full of Christmas stuff.

Luci was super energized, telling her grandpa all about getting the tree and about John. Her dad just smiled. Becky sorted through the decorations and paused as she came across a box she remembered well. She knew what was inside and couldn't open it in front of everyone.

She carried it into her bedroom. Removing the lid, Becky stared down at ten crystal angels, angels her mother had given her for Christmas every year until her death. A tear rolled down her cheek as she pulled out an angel and looked at the inscription: *To my baby, Rebecca Diane. Love you, precious.* And then it had the date.

"Hey, what are you doing sitting in here by yourself?" Bo asked from the doorway.

She brushed the tear away quickly. "It's nothing. I'm just a little emotional when I see these angels."

He sat beside her. "Those are the ones your mom gave you."

She blinked through tears. "You remembered."

"I helped you to hang them on the tree, being very careful not to break one. I know how much they mean to you."

"I get so sad when I see them. And then I get mad. Why didn't she realize what was happening to her? Why did she ignore all the symptoms?"

Bo put his arm around her and pulled her close. She soaked up his strong presence, his protectiveness that she craved. "I guess she didn't think it was a big deal and it would go away. Isn't that what most women think?"

"No! Women today seek out treatment like

they should. If you want to live, you need to be conscious of what's going on with your body."

"Your dad said you cried for your mother when you had the miscarriage."

"I was seventeen years old and I needed my mother so badly. I…"

He stroked her hair. "Don't relive it. I will always be here now. Trust me. I'm not going far and the only thing I want is for you to smile and be happy."

"Bo…"

"Mommy? Mommy?"

He kissed her lips gently. "Let's go put some stuff on that tree."

Becky made hot chocolate and they decorated the tree. Luci put ornaments on a bottom branch, all in one spot and as close together as possible. Becky didn't change a thing. Luci didn't remember last Christmas, so this Christmas was extra special.

The day ended way too quickly, and Bo went home and the house was very quiet. But they'd made plans to go into town the next day and look at all the Christmas decorations the townspeople were putting up.

There was life after a devastating heartache.

THE NEXT MORNING Bo was at the house early and they decided to walk into town for the exercise. Becky tried to explain to Luci that it was a long way and she might get tired, so they would use the stroller. Luci refused.

"I not get tired."

Becky looked at Bo.

"Where's the stroller?"

"No! I walk."

So they started out with one stubborn little girl between them. They'd walked about two blocks when Luci said, "My feet are tired."

Bo swung her up and placed her on his shoulders. Luci giggled and Becky linked her arm through Bo's as they made the trek into town. The temperature was still in the fifties, but it didn't feel as chilly as the previous day.

They made it to the square and Becky could see the townspeople were busy putting up decorations. All the lampposts had big wreaths on them with red and green plaid bows. As did the courthouse doors. All the shops that surrounded the square looked festive with trees, wreaths, poinsettias or garland in the windows. It was definitely Christmas in Horseshoe, Texas.

A truck and trailer pulled up to the curb at

the courthouse and on the trailer was a huge Christmas tree.

"Look, Bo, they're going to put up the tree at the courthouse."

"I'll see if they need some help."

As they got closer they could see Cole, the sheriff, Bubba, a couple of Rebel brothers and some people Becky didn't know.

"Hey," Cole called. "Just what we need, another pair of strong hands."

Bo lifted Luci to the ground and she quickly clung to Becky, a little shy of all the people. Becky noticed Grandpa Walt and a dark-haired woman sitting on the courthouse steps and she walked over and introduced herself for she knew the woman was Cole's wife. Becky sat by Grace and they talked, and Becky took to her immediately. She was down-to-earth and easy to like. Luci still clung to Becky.

A little girl between two and three with dark hair came over to Grace, and Becky knew it was her daughter. Two little boys stood behind her. "Mommy, can she play with us?" She pointed to Luci.

"Ask her."

"Do you want to play with us?" the little girl asked Luci. That was all it took. Luci took off running with them across the lawn. She tripped and got back up and kept running. They ran to the benches and sat there. Two boys and two girls.

"That's Jericho's boys," Grandpa announced. "They're good kids. The older one is standing by his dad over there."

Soon Angie, the DA's wife, and Peyton, the sheriff's wife, showed up with boxes of lights to be put on the tree. It was a town affair as everyone helped. People stood watching and Becky kept an eye on Luci playing with the kids. She was having the time of her life. She caught Bo's eye and her heart filled with love. The day couldn't get much better.

The tree stood tall in the Horseshoe square, fully loaded with lights. On Christmas Day they would turn on the lights. Tradition varied from mayor to mayor, but lately the tradition was that the tree would be lit on Christmas Eve and stay lit until after the first of the year. On Christmas Eve they'd have hot chocolate or coffee and kolaches provided by the bakery.

Soon everyone dispersed to their respective jobs or homes. Bo and his family went upstairs in the courthouse to Cole's office.

Grace had said they were going to get their tree that afternoon. Luci was sad that the boys and Zoe had to go.

A tall, handsome young man and a woman walked up. Becky recognized him, as did Bo.

"Hey, Chase, what are you doing home? Shouldn't you be playing football?" Bo asked.

"I got lucky this year and got to spend Thanksgiving with my family and Jody."

Chase Rebel, the son of Elias Rebel, was well known around Horseshoe. He'd helped win the first state football championship for Horseshoe and was drafted into the NFL as a wide receiver, where he'd won a Super Bowl. Jody had been his high school girlfriend and was the sheriff's daughter. There was conflict at first. The sheriff hadn't approved of Chase, but now the future was theirs. Happy endings. Oh, how she loved happy endings.

They talked for a minute and then Chase asked, "Have you seen my dad? We're catching a plane in three hours and I wanted to say goodbye."

"I think he went over to the diner."

"Thanks. Good seeing y'all."

The couple walked over to the diner. "Don't they look happy?"

"You look happy." Bo's eyes looked into Becky's and warmth surged through her. Yes, she was happy for the first time in a very long time.

They had a late lunch at the diner. Later they milled around in some of the shops, especially the hardware store. They sold toys. It was a moment out of time for Bo. If he wanted a family, this was what it would be like, sharing these moments with them. He was a workaholic and most of his thoughts were centered on work and the safety of others, but now his focus was somewhere else. He wanted a life with Becky and to get that he would walk barefoot through hell.

In the store they found tricycles, bicycles, red wagons, trucks, cars and dolls. Luci got on the tricycle and tried to make it go. Bo helped her, but then her eyes caught a doll in a wedding dress and she ran to it.

"Mommy, it's a dress with a tail."

He didn't know what that meant, but obviously Becky did.

"Baby, it doesn't have a tail. It's just a wedding dress on a doll."

"Oh."

"What do you want for Christmas, little angel?" Bo asked. "Take your pick."

Luci didn't say anything.

"How about the tricycle or the doll?" They tried to get her to pick out something, but for some reason she was resisting.

"What do you want for Christmas?" Bo tried again.

"I'll tell Santa."

"Okay." And that was that. Luci had something she wanted, but they didn't know how to get it out of her.

In the late afternoon they walked home. Luci fell asleep on Bo's shoulder and Becky linked her arm through his. His happiness was building to a crescendo. He and Becky needed to talk and he planned to do that as soon as they got home. Luci would take a nap and he and Becky would have some time alone. He was hoping Craig wasn't there.

His hopes were dashed. Luci woke up as soon as they walked into the house and Craig was not only there, but Bo's mother was there, too. Luci crawled onto Craig's lap and told him about the Christmas tree and all the people and the kids she'd played with. On and on she talked.

"I'm glad y'all are here," his mother interrupted. "Craig and I would like to talk to you."

Bo glanced at Becky and she shrugged.

"Should I take Luci to her room?" Becky asked.

"No, no," Ava said. "I want her to hear this, too.

"I not sleeping," Luci announced.

Becky sat on the sofa and Bo sat beside her, waiting for what he knew was coming.

"Craig and I have been friends for a long time and, well, we wanted you to know that it turned into something more. We got married about six months ago."

"Huh…" Bo's words trailed away. He'd suspected they were seeing each other, but the marriage surprised him.

"Why would you keep it a secret?" Becky wanted to know. "We're happy for you." She turned to Bo. "Aren't we?"

"I couldn't be happier, Mom. Congratulations. Why did you keep it a secret?"

"Well, considering your relationship with Becky, we didn't want to stir up any problems. You and Becky are hardly ever here, so it worked out, but suddenly you're both home and we were unsure of what to do."

"Who got married?" Luci asked.

She was sitting on Craig's lap and he squeezed her tight. "Grandpa and Ava got married. She's now your grandma."

Luci clapped her hands. "Oh, boy, I don't have a grandma." She crawled out of Craig's lap and went to Ava. "Did you get a dress with a tail?"

His mother was stumped and it showed on her face.

Ava picked up Luci and looked at Becky over Luci's head, mouthing, "What's that?"

"It's a wedding dress with a train," Becky explained.

"Oh, sorry, no, sweetie. I just wore a dress."

"You need to get one with a tail. They're pretty."

Ava hugged Luci. "When you get married, we'll make sure you have a dress with a tail."

Luci clapped her hands again, and Bo got up and offered his hand to Craig. "Congratulations." And then he hugged his mother. "No more secrets, Mom. We're getting too old for this."

Everyone laughed and they decided to go out to celebrate. It was a happy occasion and Bo was happy for his mother. She deserved all the happiness in the world. He glanced at Becky and saw a whole lot of tomorrows in her eyes.

CHAPTER EIGHTEEN

THEY DIDN'T GET any alone time on Saturday, but Bo planned on Sunday being the day he and Becky would have some time to spend together.

It didn't work out quite as he'd hoped. His mom had called early to explain that they were going to announce their marriage in church, and then the pastor called and said the congregation wanted to give them a luncheon after the service in the Fellowship Hall. And she wanted her children present. So they spent most of the morning in church.

It was after two when they returned home, and Becky put Luci down for a nap. Kelsey stayed for a while and then went back to Austin. When Becky came out of Luci's room, Bo grabbed her hand and led her through the living room and out the door.

"We'll see y'all later," he shouted to Craig and his mother, who had perplexed looks on their faces.

"We need some time alone," he said as they walked across the street.

"I agree," Becky replied.

They went through the front door and Bo locked it. He gathered Becky into his arms and kissed her deeply. They were lost in all the emotions they'd experienced in the past few days. Before they could get lost in each other, his cell went off.

"Dammit!" He rested his forehead against hers. "I have to get it." He grabbed his phone out of his pocket with one arm around her. He wasn't letting go that easily.

It was the lieutenant. His heart sank. She would only call for one reason. He had to go. Dammit! "Goodnight," he responded.

"I need you back here as soon as possible. We have a situation."

"I'm on my way."

Becky groaned and pulled back. "No, Bo. Please, don't go now." She kissed his lips and it reminded him of the time eighteen years ago when she'd begged him to stay. Was he always going to make the same mistake?

He cupped her face. "I have to go. It's my job. Someone's life is in danger and I can't ignore that. I'll call you as soon as it's over."

She stepped back with a heavy sigh. "I

feel as if I'm seventeen years old and need-ing you to stay as much as you need to go. Is this going to be our lives?"

He kissed her forehead. "We'll talk later. I have to go."

Without another word, Bo marched out of the house, got into his truck and drove away, wondering if the past was destined to keep haunting him.

Becky walked across the street and forced herself not to cry. This was life. Real life with Bo and his real, dangerous job. She had to face that and deal with it in a manner much better than that seventeen-year-old had. While Luci slept she packed their things to go back to Austin. It was too late for Bo to return tonight, so she thought that was best.

Ava walked in as she was packing. "You're leaving?"

"Yes, Bo got a call and had to go."

"And you're upset?"

Becky sat on the bed with a turtleneck in her hands. "Honestly, yes. I've been avoid-ing thinking about what he does for a liv-ing. How he lives life on the edge, always facing danger."

"I always thought it was because of his fa-ther, that he needed to keep the adrenaline pumping so as not to think about his dad. That's just my opinion."

"He said the meeting with Mason was good at Thanksgiving."

"Yes, better than I had expected. Mason is terribly sick and Bo could see that and it kind of cooled all the rage inside him. I don't think he has it anymore, and that has something to do with you."

Becky laid the turtleneck in her carryall. "I don't know. We're so good together, but we have a lot of issues to get through. I love him and I guess I'm always going to love him. I just don't know how to live with what he does for a living."

Ava sat on the bed and put an arm around Becky. "If you love him, then you have to love what he does. It took me a while to get used to it—although I don't know if I'm really used to it. I just dread that one day I might get that call, but I try not to let it show because he helps a lot of people. He saves lives. I try to look at it that way. With the way the world is today, you and I are probably more likely to get shot than he is. And if we didn't have people like Bo, who would catch all those bad guys?"

Becky hugged Ava. "Thank you. I really

needed to hear that. And I'm really glad you're my stepmom. I'm so happy you and Dad have each other."

"I am, too. I've never been this happy in my whole life."

After that, Becky felt better. She packed up the car, waved goodbye and went back to her small condo. And waited.

The call came three hours later. "Hey, Bec, I'm back and everything is fine."

Her heart beat so fast she could barely speak. "Are you okay?"

"Sure. It was a basic takedown. Everything ended peacefully. You didn't have to worry."

"But I do worry and I'm trying to deal with the fact that one day you might not come home."

"Bec…"

"You have a very dangerous job and I don't know if I can live with that. I think we need to take a break to decide what we want."

"Break? We haven't even gotten started yet. Come on, Becky. I'm very good at what I do and I've been well trained. You have to trust me."

"It's not about trust. It's about you living life on the edge all the time."

"Do you want me to quit?"

"Yes. No. I just need some time to understand why I feel this way."

"How long?"

"Bo…" She paused. "I don't know. I've been pushing your job to the back of my mind so I didn't have to deal with it. I keep seeing that video of the man shooting at you. It's all in my head, but we've grown very close and I want to be sure about our future, especially for Luci."

"Can we talk about this in person?"

"I'm tired and going to bed, and I have a busy week ahead. I'm sure you do, too. Let's talk at the end of this week."

"Bec…"

"Every time I hear a siren I'll think it's you. I don't know if I can live like that."

"I thought when you loved someone, you loved them warts and all. And I do love you and I know you love me. You haven't said the words, but…"

She held the phone close to her ear and soaked up every word, and still she couldn't let go. "Just give me some time."

"Fine."

That final clipped word twisted her heart. She sat on the sofa and an errant tear ran down her cheek. She brushed it away quickly. She wasn't going to cry. This time she was going to deal with life head-on and make sure her choices were the right ones. For Bo and her. And for Luci.

Bo THREW HIMSELF into work. That was the only thing he knew to do. She had to come to the right conclusion on her own and he couldn't push her. There were a lot of thefts and robberies going on this time of the year, so he had plenty to do. And if he wasn't on the job, he was training and trying to keep his thoughts at bay. Giving her time wasn't an easy thing to do. After all, it was the holiday season and he wanted to be with her. His love was patient so he could wait.

"Hey, what's up with you?" Hutch asked, shoving his combat boots into his locker.

He and Hutch had become good friends, as all of his crew had, and he felt he could tell him anything. He told him about Becky and Luci. It wasn't like Bo to share personal stuff, but he needed to talk.

"And she wants you to quit your job?"

"My job scares her and I can understand that. I'm just trying to weigh my options here, because this time I'm not walking away."

Hutch sat by him on the bench. "Did you say Luci was that baby you saved years ago?"

"Yeah, small world, isn't it?" He talked on and on about Luci and couldn't believe his own ears. But Luci was special to him and always would be.

Finally, Bo got to his feet. "I better go so I can get here early in the morning. I'm trying to get on the lieutenant's good side."

"There isn't one," Hutch replied, picking up his carryall.

They laughed together as they walked out of the building.

Bo got into his truck and was tempted to call Becky. It was Saturday and it had been almost a full week. Why hadn't she called? He'd promised to give her time, though. He slipped his phone back into his pocket just as it rang.

He glanced at the caller ID, hoping it was Becky. It wasn't. It was Layla.

"Bo, this is Layla. Your dad just passed away."

He closed his eyes and pain ripped through him so hard he had to take a deep breath. "Why didn't you call me sooner?"

"He didn't want me to. But he did ask me to call you first so you could tell your mother and your sister."

"Thanks, and thanks for all you've done for him."

"I loved him and I would've done anything for him. I know you had your problems, but he always talked about you and Kelsey."

"Thank you. Where are the arrangements being made?"

"I have no idea. I asked Mason about that and he said it had been taken care of."

"By who?"

"I don't know, but he was very sure."

"Do you think it was my grandmother?"

"No, I'm almost positive about that. Mason never wanted her to worry about anything."

"I'll check into it and get back with you."

The next person he called was his mother. "Are you at a place where you can stop for a moment?"

"Yeah, I'm in my office at the grocery store, getting ready to go home to Craig."

"I'll call you when you get there."

"Why? Just tell me now. I've been through a lot, son, and I can handle anything, I promise you."

"Dad just passed away." There was silence on the line. "Mom..."

"I'm here. I'm just trying to accept this. They said he had longer and he didn't get that time. That makes me sad, especially since he was finally talking to his kids. I wanted that for y'all. Do you know who's taking care of the arrangements?"

"That's what I'm wondering. Layla said that Dad said it was all taken care of. You know anything about that?"

"No. We never talked about arrangements. I have no idea who would be paying for his funeral. We need to get this straight soon."

"I'm on it, but first I have to call Kelsey. Oh, no— Grandma! I don't want to have to tell Grandma. I'll just call Aunt Lois."

"Estelle's much stronger than you think."

"I'll call you later."

"Bo."

"What?"

"You called him Dad for the first time in a very long time."

He didn't say anything. He couldn't.

He sat in his truck for ages, trying to accept this final blow. It was over, all the anger, the resentment and the bitterness were over. Now there was nothing left but the regrets, and he could pave the streets of Horseshoe with those. If he had learned anything, he'd learned that he couldn't stitch together memories of his childhood and make it look picture-perfect. It wasn't. It wasn't even close.

Now he had to figure out who was paying for his father's funeral. He went back and forth through the family and thought maybe his uncle Jim had paid, but Jim was far away, and according to him, the brothers never talked that much.

Something his father had said crossed his mind. *It's just something that needs to be opened when I've passed.* The letter his father had given him could hold the answer. He hadn't thought much about it until now.

He fished a key out of his pocket and unlocked the glove compartment where he had put the letter. He pulled it out and ripped it open, unfolding a legal document. It was a life insurance policy on his father. The beneficiaries were Bo and Kelsey. There was a note attached at the very top, written by hand. *You might use a little of this to put me away. Bury me close to my dad in the Horseshoe Cemetery. Love, your father.*

The policy was for five hundred thousand

dollars. Bo was always steady and strong, but today his hands shook as he stared at the note and the policy. Forgiveness now was simple and easy, not because of the money, but because he'd opened his heart and accepted his dad for who he was. He'd taken the step and talked to him man-to-man, and now he would bury his father with forgiveness in his heart. There was nothing left.

He made arrangements to bury his dad on Tuesday and used his own money. He hadn't had time to deal with the insurance policy yet. There was a small family service at the church in Horseshoe. A lot of people he didn't know came, friends of his dad. Most of the town showed up because of his mom. They all knew her.

Bo had Maribel from the diner do the lunch afterward and Anamarie who used to run the bakery now had her own shop and made all the sweets. Today he would honor his father.

His grandmother had wanted Mason's gospel recordings to be played during the ceremony. His earthy, rich voice filled the small church and memories, like snapshots, floated through Bo's mind. There were those mornings in the bathroom when he would sing with his dad. When he was smaller, his dad would put him on the vanity and he would clap and pump his leg to his dad's voice. Kelsey couldn't carry a tune if her life depended on it and they would laugh at her. There had been a lot of laughter on those mornings, but then... Bo refused to think about the bad times. Today was a day to remember the good. As his dad's voice rang out, a pang of sadness pierced his heart and he wondered for a brief moment how he was supposed to get through the rest of this.

Grandma and Aunt Lois and her family sat in the front row. Bo, Kelsey, his mom and Craig were in the second row. Bo sat on the end in case his grandmother needed him. Someone touched his shoulder and he looked up to see Becky in a black dress and heels. They all scooted down to let her in.

As the pastor began to speak, she reached out and took his hand, and he now knew how he was going to get through this. The service was short, as was the drive to the cemetery. Only the family went to the graveside and he held on to Becky's hand, making sure she went with him. Bo worried about his grandma, but she was holding up really well. It was after two when they finished eating and he shook hands with everyone as they left.

"Do you need anything?" Cole asked.

"Just some time." And Bo realized that was true. He needed time to adjust to this new situation, just as Becky did. He understood it now.

He walked her to her car and held her hand all the way.

"Are you okay?" she asked.

"I'm not sure. I didn't expect it this soon and I have this good and evil warring inside me. I just wonder if that will ever end."

She wrapped her arms around his waist and held on to him for a little while, and that helped more than he could ever have imagined.

She drew back. "I'm sorry. I know this is hard for you."

"I'm supposed to be strong and fearless, so this should be easy for me, right? But it isn't." He told her about the insurance policy. "I don't want the money. It's like putting a Band-Aid on the past and I just can't accept it. I don't understand why he did that."

"Because he wanted to give you something, something he never gave you in life—security. But if you don't want the money, give it to a charity in his name. Or better yet, you could set up a scholarship fund at the Horseshoe high school for underprivileged children. Do something that makes you feel better about it."

"I don't know if I'll ever feel better."

"You will. It takes time, and I wish I could stay, but I have to pick up Luci."

She stood on tiptoes and kissed him. "We'll talk later."

Bo watched her drive away and then went back into the Fellowship Hall. Later, his grandmother asked if he would take her home and he did. She talked and talked about Mason when he was little and all the things that he'd done, and it was what Bo needed to hear.

As he listened to his grandmother, he realized something. He really hadn't known his father. He had memories of the singing and memories of him being in the house, but other than that there was no close connection and now there never would be. It really was over, and that's what was hurting the most.

BECKY WAS IN her pajamas, getting ready for bed. She already had Luci tucked in for the night with Pink and Purr. She flipped off the kitchen light and was about to unplug the little Christmas tree she and Luci had put up when there was a knock at the front door. She glanced at the clock and saw it was after ten. Who could that be?

She glanced through the peephole and saw a distraught, disheveled man. She opened the door. "Bo."

He walked past her to the sofa and plopped down. "I can't stay in my apartment alone. I have all these thoughts I don't understand. I hated that man most of my life, so now why do I have these feelings?"

"Because he was your father and you loved him in spite of his behavior."

"Maybe." Bo rested his head on the cushions and stretched out his legs. "Life is hell and I don't understand any of it." In a second he was sound asleep.

She wasn't even sure if he knew where he was. He wasn't drunk. He was just on emotion overload. She went upstairs and got a blanket and a pillow.

Covering him up, she kissed his cheek, but he didn't stir. She placed the pillow on the coffee table in case he needed it. He was trying to hate his dad, but he couldn't and she admired him for that. Staring at him, she knew she was never going to stop loving him and she had to come to terms with her own feelings about him.

When she woke up the next morning, Bo was gone, as she'd known he would be. Her phone buzzed.

"Hey, sorry for crashing at your place last night."

"No problem."

"Since I was off yesterday I'll be working straight through over the weekend."

"How are you?"

"Adjusting. Work takes my mind off of things."

She wanted to say so much, but she sensed he didn't want to talk and she let it go. "Well, call when you can."

She felt as if she was talking to a stranger. Where was the man who'd held her hand yesterday with such strength and seemed to need her? Or maybe she needed him, high-risk job or not.

That week she didn't hear from Bo so she decided to go home for the weekend. Luci wanted to see Grandpa and the tree. With her father's marriage she couldn't drop in just any time she wanted anymore. Things were changing and she didn't mind.

Becky liked Ava, who was perfect for her dad. When she'd found a moment to talk to Ava she asked about Bo, and Ava said he was very busy this time of year. That meant he was working himself to death to keep from thinking about his dad.

Later on Sunday afternoon she returned to Austin and the days passed quickly as they neared Christmas. Still Bo hadn't called. On the twenty-second she gave up waiting and picked up her phone to dial his number.

"Hey, Bec." His voice was as calm and pleasant as if she'd seen him yesterday.

"I don't want to bother you, but I wanted to let you know that Luci and I are going home for Christmas. I have to work a half a day on the twenty-third and then we're leaving for Horseshoe."

"Yeah, Christmas. I'd almost forgotten about it."

"Bo, Luci expects you to be there." *And so do I.*

"I put in for time off, but the lieutenant hasn't okayed it yet. Bec..."

"If you want this relationship to work," she broke in, "you will be there and not let anything keep us apart this holiday season."

She threw her phone into her purse. Would he bail on them this Christmas?

BO WALKED INTO the lieutenant's office. Becky was right; he needed to do something about their lives. But lately he'd been grappling with his dad's death and the insurance money, and in his mind it stood out like a sore thumb that had been beaten by a sledgehammer. Or an open wound that he couldn't ignore. He had to decide what to do with the money.

Kelsey said it was his call. Neither one of them wanted it. Money didn't erase the past or make anything better. They both had good jobs and made good salaries. They didn't need it. But evidently, his father had thought it would make up for the past. And deep down Bo knew that wasn't possible—not like this. He had to get his act together before he lost the most important person in the world—Becky.

"What is it, Goodnight?" The lieutenant's eyes were on the computer screen and not him.

"You haven't okayed my time off for Christmas."

"There are a lot of guys who want off for Christmas."

"Does that mean I'm not getting it?"

She didn't reply, just tapped a few keys on the computer and it angered him. He put in a lot of hours and hardly ever took a vacation. He deserved time off.

"Let me make this easy for you. I'll be leaving SWAT at the end of the year."

She finally looked up at him. "What?"

"I'm seeing someone who doesn't like my job and I happen to love her more than SWAT. And this Christmas I'm spending time with her, one way or another."

She leaned back in her chair, her jaw one stubborn line. "You've trained a lot of years for this job and you're one of the best. You can't throw away your pension and everything just like that!" She snapped her fingers.

"I can. It's my decision."

Her eyes narrowed on him. "Are you pushing me against the wall to get your way?"

"I would never do that. But I haven't had a vacation in over two years, just the two weeks you imposed on me."

They stared at each other in silence. Bo wasn't backing down. He meant every word he'd said.

"Okay. Take the time off and we'll talk again when you get back. I won't mention this to the commander. I know your life has been stressful lately with your father's death."

"Yes, it has, but I'm serious about quitting SWAT. I'll let you know for sure when I get back." He walked out, feeling as if a weight had been lifted off his shoulders. He could now breathe and sort out the rest of his life.

He worked late that night, and went home and fell into a deep sleep. On the twenty-third he was at work early and they got a call from police for help. Some man had stormed his way into his ex's house and was holding her hostage with their two kids. Another custodial battle over kids at Christmas, which never ended easily.

Neighbors had called the cops. It turned into a three-hour standoff as they tried to talk him out of the house. It didn't work and they had to go in and take him. It had been a long morning, and Bo was looking forward to time off and seeing Becky and Luci.

He sent her a quick text: Meet you in Horseshoe on Christmas Eve.

They cleaned the Hummer and made sure everything was back in place for the next call. Even though he was a sergeant, he worked alongside his crew. Maybe it would be a slow day and he could concentrate on going home. He was ready.

The lieutenant came into the room. "Load up. We've got a serious situation. Shots have been reported at the Women's Center. I'm taking the lead on this one."

The Women's Center? That was where Becky worked. Panic gripped him until he realized that she had only been working until noon. He let out a long breath. Thank God she wasn't there.

CHAPTER NINETEEN

AT TWO O'CLOCK Becky walked the last patient into the waiting room. The day had run longer than they'd planned. A lady had come in with a swollen breast and Dr. Eames had decided to go ahead and do a mammogram. She'd known it was probably cancer and wanted to know right away so something could be done after the first of the year. That was why Becky loved working with Dr. Eames. She always did what was best for the patient.

Carla, the receptionist, and Leesha were ready to go home for the holidays—their purses were on the counter.

"Do you think we can leave?" Carla asked. "There's no one else scheduled."

Before Becky could answer, the door opened and Kathy Purcell came in, red in the face, as if she'd been running. "I need to see Dr. Eames. Is she still here?"

"I'll check," Becky said. She knew Dr.

Eames was still there, but she wanted to make sure the doctor had time. She and her husband were catching a flight in three hours for Miami.

Becky knocked on the doctor's door and stuck her head around. "Kathy Purcell is here and wants to see you. She's really nervous and agitated."

"Send her in. I have a few minutes. Tell Carla and Leesha they can go home. Happy holidays to everyone."

Just then screams and two gunshots rang out. She and Dr. Eames ran to the waiting area to find a man holding a gun. Kathy lay on the floor, bleeding from her chest. Bile rose in Becky's throat and for a moment she was paralyzed with fear.

"Who's Dr. Eames?" the man snapped in an angry voice, waving a gun.

Dr. Eames stepped forward. "That would be me. Is there something I can help you with?"

"You aborted my son."

"Excuse me?"

"My wife comes in here all the time and you talked her into an abortion because she didn't want the kid. You did it." He waved the gun at Dr. Eames. "You killed my son and now I'm going to kill you." He pulled the trigger before anyone could move, and Dr. Eames staggered and fell backward to the floor, blood oozing from her chest.

"What are you doing? You're insane!" Becky pulled her medical jacket off and knelt by Dr. Eames, trying to stop the bleeding.

The man yanked her up by an arm.

"Let me go," she shouted, pulling away from him.

He smacked her across the side of her face with the gun. Sharp pain crippled her, the room spun and she prayed she wouldn't pass out. Blood trickled down her face and she made an effort to brush it away, but her hand didn't seem to work. She drew a ragged breath.

"They...they need medical attention."

He laughed a laugh that slid down her skin like a poisonous snake. He grabbed her around the neck and yanked her close to his body. He smelled of cigarettes and liquor. "You do one more thing and I'll put a bullet in your head."

Fear wrapped around her heart and she had this feeling she was going to die here today. She thought of Bo. He would come.

That's what he did for a living, and on this day she was very grateful for that.

Out of the corner of her eye she saw Leesha's head pop up from behind the desk. She and Carla were hunkered down behind it. They needed help. Becky wondered if anyone had heard the shots because no one was coming to their aid.

The center had three doors, one into the hospital, the big glass front doors and the back door. The door into the hospital was the closest. It was usually closed, but today, for some reason it was open. That was the way out. They had to go for help. She looked into Leesha's frightened eyes and glanced toward the open doorway. She did that twice and Leesha finally looked toward the door, getting the message. Becky had to distract the guy.

"Listen, Mr. Purcell, we don't do abortions here. We did not abort your son. Your wife had a miscarriage."

His arm tightened around her neck and he almost lifted her off her feet. "Shut up. Shut up! My wife's a liar and your boss is a killer and she's paying for that."

"Listen—"

At that moment Leesha made a run for

the door. She'd been a track runner in high school and she made it, but not before the man raised the gun and fired three times. He missed. Becky's ears rang from the gunshots, but she could see Leesha hightailing it down the hallway. Now they would get help and she hoped it was in time.

The man dragged her toward the door and slammed it shut, locking it.

"Mr. Purcell, please, they need medical attention."

"Do you think I care? She killed my son."

"If anyone killed your son, it was you. You beat your wife so badly she lost the baby."

His hand tightened around her neck and she could barely breathe. "Shut up! That's not true."

Sirens blared and she could see policemen running outside. The cops were here! Now maybe this nightmare would be over. First he had to let go of her and she had a feeling he wasn't going to do that.

SPEED DROVE THE Hummer just as close as he could get to the scene. Police were everywhere and had the perimeter marked off. The lieutenant talked to the sergeant handling the scene.

"Mr. Purcell thinks his wife had an abortion here and is very angry. He shot his wife and Dr. Eames. They're both lying on the floor and need serious medical attention. He's holding Dr. Eames's PA with a gun to her head. He won't hesitate to use it and we can't figure a way to get in there to get him without hurting Ms. Tullous. He won't pick up the phone. We need to get those people out of there as soon as possible."

Ms. Tullous! Becky was in there! Fear slammed into Bo's gut and almost knocked him off his feet. What was she doing here? Oh, man! No! No! He couldn't let on that he knew Becky. The lieutenant would send him back to the station.

The lieutenant used a bullhorn. "Mr. Purcell, come out with your hands up or we're coming in for you. This is your last chance."

"You come in and I'll kill her," he shouted back. "I want a car out front. Now!"

The hospital was in sort of a lopsided U-shape, and the lieutenant looked across the street to another three-story medical building. Then she looked at Bo. "See if you can get on the top of that building and get a clear shot. Hutch, you go with him. Speed and Preacher, take the back door. James and

Cruz, take the hospital entrance going into the clinic. Patel, stay here with me."

Someone with the hospital led Bo and Hutch to the top of the building. He didn't actually lead, they ran. They went up the stairs to the roof, which housed air conditioners and exhaust fans and such for the big hospital. Once they were there they scrutinized the space and the view to see if Bo could get a clear shot at Mr. Purcell. The roof was enclosed with about a three-foot brick wall all the way around, and there was a ledge looking right out over to the clinic. Bo placed his rifle on the ledge, then knelt on one knee to look through the scope.

"Doesn't that girl you're dating work here?" Hutch asked, sighting his rifle.

"Yeah, that's her the shooter is holding."

"Oh, man, the lieutenant doesn't know, does she?"

"No. And neither do you."

"You're very calm."

"This is what I'm trained to do. If I lose my cool, someone will die." Inside, his stomach burned, but his nerves were steady and he tried not to think about anything else.

"Do you have a visual?" the lieutenant asked through their earpieces.

"Yes, ma'am," Bo replied. "I can see right into the clinic. The perp has a gun pointed at Ms. Tullous's head. She's…she's bleeding from the head."

"Can you get a shot?"

"Not like this." *Don't think. Don't think. Don't think.* "Patel, I need specifics. Wind velocity. Distance."

Hutch laid an iPad in front of him. "Patel sent this." It gave him the information he needed and the layout of the clinic. Three entryways. He had to figure this out fast.

Hutch pointed to the iPad. "James and Cruz are here. Preacher and Speed are here."

Bo spoke into the mic. "Preacher and Speed, stay to the far right of the door. And make sure there's no one back there."

"Done," they replied.

"Is it a go?" the lieutenant asked.

"I need a distraction so he'll move the gun away from Ms. Tullous's head. Your call, Lieutenant."

"I'll take the shot," Hutch whispered to Bo.

"No one's taking the shot but me." Bo made that very clear.

"Okay, Sergeant, Cruz is going to make a noise at the door that goes into the hospital, and hopefully the perp will point the gun at the door. Give Cruz the okay when you're ready."

Bo looked through the scope and tried not to let Becky's bloody face get to him. He had them in the crosshairs and now he had to be as fast as the perp. Becky's body covered the man's chest so there was no shot there. His plan was to shoot the gun out of Purcell's hand. And if that didn't work Bo would get him in the arm. One way or the other, the man was going down.

Bo took a long breath, steadied himself and concentrated totally on what he saw in the scope. The big exhaust fans hummed behind him, but he shut them out. His rifle was secure on the ledge. His nerves were steady. He was ready. "Speed and Preacher, when you hear the shot, breach the office. Copy, James and Cruz. Ready, Cruz?"

"Ready," they echoed.

"Go."

As soon as he said the words Cruz did something because the man swung his arm to the right, toward the door, and Bo had a clear visual of the gun. He pulled the trigger. Glass shattered, the gun went flying and SWAT breached the office in a split second.

The man was down and Becky crumpled to the floor.

He handed his gun to Hutch and took off running down the stairs. The sound of his combat boots slapping against the floor echoed down the empty hallways. The hospital was on lockdown, but all he could think was that he had to get to Becky.

As he reached the bottom floor he saw a team of doctors and nurses rolling Dr. Eames and the other woman into the ER. Where was Becky?

He ran down the hall to the clinic.

"Bo! Bo!"

He saw Becky running toward him with two nurses behind her. She collapsed into his arms and he held her for a brief second. He removed her face from his chest. "Bec, Bec…are you okay?" He felt her arms, her shoulders, and saw the big black-and-blue knot on her head.

She was trembling and he held her a little closer.

"I love you. You're my whole life and I realized that the moment I saw you in the crosshairs. I'm sorry I've been so conflicted lately. I love you more than life itself. I haven't loved anyone else like that.

Just you, Becky." He was rambling but he couldn't seem to stop. He just wanted to hold her forever.

"Bo—" she murmured and fainted in his arms. Two nurses stood behind Becky with a stretcher. He motioned for them to bring it forward and then he picked her up and laid her on it. He looked at her face, and didn't see any burns from the gun blast.

"Bo," she murmured, coming around.

"Shh, we'll talk later." He tried to keep her calm.

"Did... Are you the one who shot the gun...out of his hand?"

"Yes."

"I knew you would get us out of there." After saying that, she closed her eyes again.

They rolled her into an ER cubicle and a doctor immediately checked her over. A nurse started an IV and Bo stepped back and let them do their jobs. But he didn't go far.

Becky stirred when they stuck the needle in her arm. "Please, Bo, check on Dr. Eames and Kathy. And Luci... Bo."

He put a finger over her lips. "Relax and let the doctors take care of you. I will take care of everything else."

From there it was chaos as reporters and

people tried to get in to get information. SWAT had to help the cops keep everyone away. Dr. Eames and Kathy were in surgery, and Bo stayed close to Becky as they worked on her.

The doctor examined her and still Bo wouldn't leave the room. There were bruises on her left arm and shoulder. The doctor checked her eyes and head.

"Do you remember being hit?" the doctor asked.

"Yes. He had a gun and raised it toward me while I was trying to help Dr. Eames. I jerked away, but not fast enough."

"I think it was fast enough," the doctor replied. "If you had gotten the full brunt of the gun it would look much worse. Right now it looks superficial, severe bruising along your skin and hairline. I don't think your skull is involved, but we'll do an MRI to make sure."

That was the best news he'd heard all day and he began to relax. They took her for an MRI and he went with her. He wasn't leaving her for one moment.

"Bo," she called. "Luci…"

"I'll take care of it."

She reached for his hand. "I love you," she

said as they pushed her away. And that was all that mattered. She still loved him.

The lieutenant walked toward him and held out her hand. He shook it. "Good work today. Perfect shot, as always. I would sure hate to lose you, but it's your call." She glanced toward the room they were pushing Becky into. "I'm assuming you know Ms. Tullous."

"Yes, ma'am. I've loved her since she was sixteen years old. I walked away from her when I was eighteen, but I'm not going to do that ever again."

A young woman walked up, interrupting the lieutenant's response. "I was looking for Becky and the nurse told me to talk to you." She spoke to Bo. "Tell her not to worry about Luci. My mom keeps her and she can stay there as long as she needs to."

"I'll pick Luci up as soon as I can get out of here. I'm hoping they'll release Becky, as well, but we'll have to wait to see what the test shows. I will pick up Luci, though. She won't be too happy without her mommy."

"Okay. Now I'm going home. I'm still a little shaky."

"You were very brave women," the lieutenant said.

"I've given a statement to the police and like I said, I'm going home. I'll look in on Dr. Eames and Kathy before I go."

She walked away and the lieutenant turned to him. "Take until after the first of the year, Sergeant, then we'll talk. Maybe you'll have your life sorted out by then."

"You're giving me that much time off?"

"You've been through a tremendous ordeal today and I believe you deserve it. Besides, Ms. Tullous is going to need a lot of TLC."

"Thank you."

She glanced at his head. "And you might want to remove your helmet."

His hand immediately went to the helmet and yanked it off. A smile curled its way through his chest to his lips and it released a lot of tension. He also removed his Kevlar vest, gun belt and duty belt.

The lieutenant held out her hands and he handed everything to her. "They'll be at the station when you need them. See you after the first. Now I have to inform Hutch he's working the holiday."

Bo sank to the floor and pulled out his phone. He had to let Craig know what had happened and it wasn't going to be an easy call. He called his mother first.

"Mom, where are you?"

"At home with Craig. We're about to have supper and then I'm going back to the store. Why?"

"I have something to tell you and I want you to remain calm."

"You're hurt, aren't you? Did you get shot? How are you?" She kept firing questions.

"Mom, stop! It's not about me. It's about Becky."

"What?"

"Put the phone on Speaker so Craig can hear. I don't want to have to say this twice."

"Okay."

"Craig, are you there?"

"Yes, what's going on?"

"There was a shooting at the Women's Center this afternoon. Two people were shot and Becky was held as hostage. She's okay, but he hit her in the head with the gun. They're running tests on her now. As soon as the doctor releases her I'm bringing her home. She's okay. She just needs some time to get over this, and I trust both of you want that for her, too."

"Oh, my poor baby. I'm coming to Austin."

"No, Craig. She wouldn't want you on the

roads. Just wait and be patient. I'm taking care of everything and we'll be home before you know it."

"I just want to see my baby."

Bo looked up and saw the stretcher coming toward him. He met it and put the phone to Becky's ear. "Say hi to your dad. He wants to know if you're okay."

Bo took the phone back when she'd hung up. "How did it go?"

"I'm sleepy. I think they gave me something in the IV."

They pushed her into a room in the ER and Bo sat by her bed looking at the bruise on her forehead.

"You have to get Luci."

"Stop worrying. I have it covered." He smoothed the wet, bloody hair away from her forehead. "You look beautiful."

She smiled at him and the world finally righted itself. "You're such a liar."

The doctor came in. "It's more or less a superficial wound. No concussion, no breaks in the skull, just a bad bruise that's going to hurt for a while."

"I want to go home. I have a three-year-old I have to pick up."

"Since it's Christmas, I'm going to allow

it. Just remember, you have to take it easy for the next few days. Relax and let everyone else do the work. If you get nauseous, have a bad headache or dizziness or loss of sight, come back to the ER immediately."

Within minutes they were out of the hospital. Bo brought Becky's car around to the ER entrance and picked her up. From there they went to get Luci and there was a lot of explaining to do. They told her mommy had had an accident. Then there were a lot more questions from Luci, who didn't want her mommy to be sick. They stopped to pick up Pink and Purr and then they were off to Horseshoe. It was a good thing Becky had the car already packed with everything they would need for the next few days.

They made it to Horseshoe in record time and Becky slept all the way on the passenger side. Luci slept, too. Bo touched Becky's arm as he turned on to Liberty Street.

She sat up straight. "That was fast."

"How do you feel?"

"Achy."

Before the car could come to a complete stop, Craig yanked opened the door to get to his daughter. "Oh, sweetheart! Let's get you into the house so you can get some rest."

Luci was sound asleep and didn't even wake up when Bo carried her into the house and put her into bed.

"I'll put her nightclothes on," his mother said. "Craig is really shaken up and doesn't want to leave Becky."

"It'll be fine, Mom." Bo went outside to get Pink and Purr out of the car. Then he carried Becky's suitcases and a bag of gifts into the house. Craig and his mom were still helping Becky and Luci. Bo took a long breath and sat on the sofa.

What a day! Becky was okay and she would get better. He buried his face in his hands at the thought and wondered how he could have shut her out the last couple of weeks.

That damn money! It had screwed up his mind, but now he knew what he wanted and had always known. His mind was on track and there was nothing on this earth that could separate him from Becky again. He leaned his head back on the cushions and was grateful that they had escaped a bad one today.

Craig and his mom came into the living room. "They're both asleep," his mom said.

"Becky is very sleepy," Craig noted with concern in his voice.

"They gave her something at the hospital so she could rest." Bo got to his feet and went down the hall to check on them. They were both out and safe. He then went to his mom's house to get out of his SWAT clothes and take a shower. Dressed in gray jogging pants and a long-sleeved black T-shirt, he went back across the street. His mom and Craig were sitting at the kitchen table.

"Go to bed and get some sleep. I'm on duty," he told them.

"I don't think I can sleep," Craig replied.

"Tomorrow is Christmas Eve and I expect both of you to be in a happy mood for Luci and Becky. No sad faces. Becky is going to be fine and I'll be right here to make sure that she is."

Craig got to his feet and held out his hand to Bo. "Thank you. Becky said you shot the gun out of the man's hand. I don't know how you did that, but I'm so grateful my daughter's alive."

"You're welcome," Bo said. "Now let's all get some rest."

He retrieved a pillow and a blanket from the hall closet and made himself comfortable on the sofa, which was hard to do because the sofa was smaller than he was. But he'd sleep on the floor, if he had to, to stay close to Becky.

BECKY WOKE UP to pain. One side of her head throbbed and she sat up to ease it. After a moment, she got up to check on Luci. Her baby was sleeping peacefully. The house was in darkness except for the night-light in Luci's room. Bo must have gone home. No, she said to herself. He wouldn't do that. He was here somewhere. She made her way down the hall and saw him sleeping on the sofa.

He jumped up immediately. "What are you doing? You shouldn't be up."

"I couldn't find you."

He took her hand. "Come on, sleeping beauty, you need your rest." Becky didn't feel like sleeping. She sat on the side of the bed and Bo sat beside her.

"Why do things like this happen?" she asked, almost to herself. "The man was drinking. I could smell it on him and he was shaking the whole time. I was trembling, too. It was like a nightmare come true."

Bo put his arm around her. "Don't think about it."

"But I do. Why is there so much evil in this world?"

"I don't know, but I see it every day in my work."

She looked at him in the moonlight. "I

don't mind your job so much anymore. Just like that—" she snapped her fingers "—as the gun pressed into my skull, I prayed you would come because I knew that was your job—to rescue people and I really needed you to rescue us. In that moment I realized what a great job you do for the community and everyone. We all need more men and women like you."

"Bec—"

"We're idiots, Bo. Selfish and insensitive idiots."

"I think you're being a little hard on us."

"It's true. I had all these good feelings inside about what was happening between us. We had found a way to communicate and love each other again. We tossed forgiveness around like an ingredient in a salad, but we made it work.

"Then I saw that video of a guy shooting at you and I hit a brick wall, not wanting to deal with that part of your life. Then your dad died and he gave you that large sum of money and you hit a brick wall because you couldn't deal with it.

"You shut me out, not wanting to talk. That hurt. All that angst didn't mean anything when it comes down to life or death.

Only one thing matters—how we feel about each other. That's what makes life work, not all that other stuff, just how we feel."

"I love you, bruises and all," he said softly. "And, yes, we forgot the most important part of being a couple."

She rested her head on his shoulder. "I love you, Bo Goodnight, warts and all."

"And now you have to go to bed."

"I don't want to be alone tonight." She raised her head and kissed his lips, and he returned the kiss eagerly.

"Mommy. Mommy."

"I'll get her," Bo said, kissing her one more time before he left the room.

"Hey, little angel, what's wrong?" she heard Bo say.

"I want my mommy."

Bo brought Luci to Becky and she crawled into bed with her baby in her arms. She was safe and loved. When Luci fell asleep, Bo took her back to her bed.

As Bo made to crawl in beside Becky his phone rang. He talked for a few minutes and then placed it on the nightstand. "Good news. Dr. Eames and Kathy Purcell are out of surgery and resting comfortably. The surgeons had to do a lot of repair work, but they are expected to make a full recovery."

"Oh, Bo. That's wonderful." The terror in her eased as she said a silent prayer for her friends.

"Yes, it is, and now it's time for you to get some rest." He crawled in beside her and said, "No fooling around tonight, beautiful lady."

She giggled like Luci and laid her head on his chest, feeling his strength, his warmth, and that they were all she would ever need. Sleep tugged at her, but they had to talk.

"Luci still won't tell me what she wants for Christmas and I don't have a big gift for her. I bought some books, puzzles, coloring books, crayons and clothes. Those are from you because you have to make her wear them. But she will not say what she wants for Christmas. She told Santa and I asked him what she'd said, but with so many kids he couldn't remember."

"I'll go in the morning to the hardware store and get the tricycle and maybe the bride doll. She'll be excited to get the tricycle. I think she has Christmas mixed up with a birthday wish. But we'll see on Christmas morning."

She snuggled closer and fell into a deep sleep, knowing she would always be safe, loved and happy with him.

THE NEXT MORNING Bo hurried to the hardware store to pick up the tricycle and doll, but they were both gone. He called Becky on the way to Temple to tell her he would find something similar. But first, he stopped and got a haircut. His hair and beard were getting scraggly again and he wanted this Christmas to be perfect.

The mall was packed with last-minute shoppers, but he waded shoulder to shoulder with them through the stores until he finally found a pink tricycle. They had sold out of the other colors. When he looked at the price tag of the pink one, he knew why. It was fancy, with a horn and lights.

He called Becky to see if that was what she wanted. As he was talking to her, he glanced at a row of dolls and saw a bride one. He pulled it out, looked at it and explained it to Becky. "It even has a tail, as Luci calls it. Oh, wow!"

"What is it?" Becky asked.

"Do dolls usually cost this much?" He told her the price.

"No. It must be a first edition or something."

"It's what she wants. I'm buying it."

"Go for it," she replied with a laugh.

While he was waiting to get checked out, he saw a red wagon. He bought it, too. It was Christmas. He took all the items to his mom's house. Kelsey had made it home.

He carried the items in and asked, "Can you wrap these?"

"You want me to wrap all that? It'll take over a hundred yards of paper."

"Have fun."

"Bo—"

He went to his room, took a shower, shaved and got dressed for Christmas Eve. When he came out of his room, Kelsey was trying to wrap the gifts. "You have a business degree and you can't figure out how to put paper around a tricycle?"

"Shut up."

He helped her finish and then made his way across the street to Becky. He was surprised to see her dressed in jeans, a red turtleneck and boots.

"You look gorgeous." He kissed her.

"With the good news about Dr. Eames and

Kathy, I've decided we're going to the lighting of the tree."

"Are you sure? You're supposed to rest."

"I want to go for Luci. I don't want her to miss it."

"Then we'll go, but we're not staying long."

At four o'clock that afternoon they made their way to Horseshoe Square. People were everywhere, milling around, talking, laughing and enjoying the holiday season. There was a table for coffee and hot chocolate and kolaches and cookies. They stood with Cole, Grace and Zoe. The whole Rebel family was there with their children. Bo shook hands with all of them. People had heard what happened to Becky and they stopped to ask how she was. It was one big family.

The mayor gave a speech and a group of first-grade students sang Christmas carols. Then the mayor flipped the switch to light the tree to a round of applause. It stood like a beacon in the night. All the children got to put an ornament on it. Bo held Luci up to put her ornament on as high as she could. Cole did the same with Zoe. Then everyone sang "Jingle Bells" and *Merry Christmas* echoed around the square. It was a fun night.

The next morning they woke up at five so they could get everything under the tree before Luci woke up. Bo hurried across the street to shower and change and to grab the presents. When all the gifts were under the tree, there was barely room to walk.

Kelsey trudged in before six. "Did I tell y'all I hate mornings?" She sank into a chair, staring at the gifts. "Is this all for Luci?"

"No, there's a present or two for you under there," her mother said, walking into the room.

"Mommy, Mommy, Mommy." Luci interrupted the scintillating conversation. Before they could move, she charged into the living room, her hair in disarray around her face. She came to a complete stop, her mouth forming a big O. "Santa came."

Becky picked her up. "Yes, he did. He came while you were sleeping. Merry Christmas, baby." Becky sat on the floor with Luci in her lap, and Bo placed gifts in front of them.

"Is this for me?"

"Yes," Becky said. "Open your gifts."

Luci tore into them like a whirlwind, paper flying everywhere. She jumped up and down and screamed when she saw the doll with the long veil. She put all her toys in the wagon and pulled it around, but her face wasn't as happy as it had been earlier.

"Something's wrong," Bo whispered to Becky.

"Baby, is something wrong?"

Luci shook her head. "I didn't get my wish."

"What wish?"

"My Christmas wish."

"Tell Mommy what it is."

Luci shook her head and went back to playing with her toys.

Becky and Bo sat on the sofa and the grown-ups opened their gifts. Bo waited until the last to give Becky his present. Then he got down on one knee and opened a velvet ring box. "Rebecca Diane Tullous, will you marry me?"

Before Becky could utter a word, Luci gave an ear-splitting scream and jumped over the wrapping paper to get to Bo. She fell face-first into the paper, scrambled up and flew into his arms saying, "Yes, we say yes!"

Laughter filled the room.

Bo pushed her back a little bit. "Is that your Christmas wish?"

Luci nodded. "I wished for you to be my daddy."

Bo looked at Becky and she brushed away a tear.

Luci looked at her mother. "We say yes, don't we, Mommy?"

Craig put his hands around Luci's waist and plucked her away from Bo. "Let's go outside for a bit and give Bo and Becky a little time alone."

"No, Grandpa. I want to stay and…"

"Craig, do you know its fifty-two degrees outside?" Kelsey asked.

Bo's mom shoved a blanket into Kelsey's hands and draped another around Luci. Then they made their way out the French doors.

Bo eased up onto the sofa. "Do you want to do this again?"

"No." She threw her arms around his neck. "My answer is yes. Yes! And if you don't put that ring on my finger soon, I'm going to freak out."

He removed the ring from its box and slid it on to her ring finger.

"It's beautiful. I love it."

"I'm so sorry for all that I put you through, but I will love you forever from this day forward. And I will always put you first."

Her hands shook and she took a deep breath. "And I will love you until my last breath. I'm sorry I was so stubborn through all those years, but I think my interest in Luci was about you. The nurses kept saying how wonderful you were and that somehow drew me to the little baby."

He sealed their love with a long, deep kiss. Whatever happened in the future they would handle it together as a team.

Bo rested his forehead against Becky's and saw Luci with her face and hands pressed against the glass door. "Look at the French doors," he whispered to Becky.

"I guess we better let them back in, because one little person is just as happy as we are. Who would've ever thought that's what she wanted for Christmas?"

He kissed her lips. "I kind of like that Christmas wish."

"Me, too."

Bo got up to open the door and glanced back at Becky. "If you're feeling okay, I thought we might go tell my grandmother this afternoon. She says she's been waiting for this from the day I was born."

"I would love to do that." Becky tried to sidestep wrapping paper and some of it got attached to her house shoes. She tried to shake it away and started giggling. "I'm so happy I can't even walk."

Bo laughed with her and it felt so good compared to the terror of yesterday. Now they would forge the future they had wanted since they were teenagers, and he couldn't be happier.

EPILOGUE

One year later...

Bo pushed the remote control on his truck's visor and the garage door of their brand-new home went up. Parking next to Becky's SUV he took a moment to reflect on the last year. It had passed quickly, but everything had fallen into place once they'd declared their love for each other.

They'd gotten married in the middle of January in a small church in Horseshoe. The bruise on Becky's face had almost healed by then. What marks remained, she covered with her hair.

Dr. Eames was able to return to work six months later. Kathy's injuries were more extensive, since she'd been shot twice, but she was lucky the bullets hadn't hit any vital organs. Once she was able to go home she and her mother had moved to a small town in Colorado to be near Kathy's brother and family.

Becky didn't go back to work until three months later. That gave her time to heal and look for a house for them, and she'd found one near the police station and the hospital that was perfect, complete with a big backyard for Luci.

He'd adopted Luci and his name was now on her amended birth certificate. He and Becky had talked about the future and what they wanted. Bo wanted to get his twenty years in and not lose his pension, and he wanted to stay in SWAT. Becky agreed wholeheartedly. Becky chose to continue working for the clinic and Bo was okay with that. The hospital had installed extra safety measures to ensure everyone's safety. Becky was back working with Dr. Eames, but she'd shortened her hours so she could be there for Luci. Their precious little girl had started school in August and had flourished being with other children.

The money issue had been settled easily. They talked with Kelsey about what they wanted to do with it and came up with a good solution. They had invested the money in a scholarship fund for Horseshoe kids who otherwise wouldn't have the resources to go to college. They had named it the Ava Goodnight Scholarship. She had objected strongly and wanted it to be in her kids' names. He and Kelsey wanted in it their mother's and she'd finally given in. And they'd given Layla ten thousand dollars so she could get by until she found a job. Everything had worked out. Bo was glad not to have that money hanging over his head. It had gone for something good to help the kids in the community.

He opened the garage door to the house and two things hit him at once—a delicious scent and the screeching of Luci.

"Daddy! Daddy's home!" She leaped into his arms. She'd grown the past year and was now at the same level of other children her age. She'd gained eight pounds and was the size of an average four-year-old. Becky was letting Luci's hair grow and it was now in a ponytail tied with a purple ribbon. Luci was off the color pink. She'd expanded her choices to all colors of the rainbow.

He kissed her cheek. "How was your day, little angel?"

"Good. I'm learning my letters." She wiggled down and went to the coffee table where she had alphabet blocks scattered everywhere. She picked up the letter B.

"Know what this is, Daddy?"

"B."

"When my teacher asks me for a word that starts with a B, I say Bo and Becky, my parents. Cool, huh?"

He kissed her nose. "You're cool."

Becky slipped her arms around his waist, and he turned and gathered her close. She wore shorts and a tank top, and she looked exactly as she had all those years ago from his bedroom window. From that day on she had owned his heart, but life and his dysfunctional family had intervened and had cost him dearly. But that was the past and they had put it behind them.

He stroked her hair away from her face and looked into her gorgeous blue eyes. This was the best part of his day, coming home to her, coming home to family. He had never had that before and he felt immensely blessed.

Standing on tiptoes, she kissed him and he ran his hands through her long hair. "I love your hair like this."

"I know and that's why I'm letting it grow.

Just for you." She smiled and the tiredness of the day washed away.

"Supper's ready."

They ate supper and Luci jabbered on about school. They'd waited forever for her to talk and now they couldn't shut her up.

He did the dishes while Becky gave Luci a bath and put her to bed. They both read her a story and had cuddle time and kisses and hugs before they walked out of the room. Arm in arm they went into the living room.

Bo sat on the sofa and Becky stood, grinning from ear to ear.

"What's up? You've been smiling all evening."

"I know. I can barely stand it." She danced from one foot to the other.

"If it makes you that excited, it must be something big."

"It is. It is." She hurried down the hallway and came back with a small white box. With a super-sized grin, she handed it to him.

"You bought me a gift?"

She shook her head. "No. I've had it for a very long time and this is the day you get to open it."

Her excitement was contagious and he

knew that whatever was in the box was going to change his life forever. Gingerly, he lifted the lid and pushed the tissue aside to reveal a tiny onesie. On the front was printed, *I Love My Daddy*. He remembered her saying something about buying it to let him know about their first child, the one they'd lost.

"Does this mean…huh…what I think it means?"

"I missed my period and I took a pregnancy test. It was positive. We're pregnant!" She raised her arms in a victory sign and danced from one foot to the other.

He grabbed her and pulled her onto his lap. "Wow! That was fast. We agreed to start trying, but I never dreamed it would be this quick."

"I think we're very good in the reproduction department." She rested her head under his chin. "But I'm so scared."

"Why?"

"I lost the first one and I'm afraid it will happen again." She touched the onesie still in his hand.

He kissed her forehead. "No. I'll be here this time and that's not going to happen. We'll do this together." He drew breath in deeply. "My heart is racing right now and I have a hard time finding words. This is one of the biggest moments of my life. A baby. Our baby." His throat went dry and he thought of the miracle that had been given to him after everything that had happened.

She touched the onesie again. "This isn't for the new baby. It belonged to our first child and always will. I just wanted you to see it. That pain in my chest is gone now, but that baby will always live deep in my heart."

He cupped her face and kissed her. "Do you know how much I love you?"

"As much as I love you," she replied, tears glistening in her eyes.

He kissed her again and they cuddled together. "We've been through hell, Bec, and we've made it through."

"Yes."

"I remember when Lucas was born. Cole was so nervous and about six shades of white. I can understand now. I'm feeling nervousness and happiness all at the same time, and I'm so grateful for everything that has been given to me." He looked deep into her eyes. "I love you and our life and our children and always will."

Tears rolled down her cheeks. "I love you, too."

And those were the words that cemented their lives forever.

* * * * *

Get 4 FREE REWARDS!

We'll send you 2 FREE Books plus 2 FREE Mystery Gifts.

Love Inspired books feature uplifting stories where faith helps guide you through life's challenges and discover the promise of a new beginning.

FREE
Value Over
$20

THE 2020 CHRISTMAS ROMANCE COLLECTION!

NEW YORK TIMES BESTSELLING AUTHOR

RaeAnne THAYNE

Christmas at Holiday House

MAISEY YATES

brenda novak
A California Christmas

'Tis the season for romance!
You're sure to fall in love with these tenderhearted love stories from some of your favorite bestselling authors!

YES! Please send me the first shipment of **The 2020 Christmas Romance Collection**. This collection begins with 1 FREE TRADE SIZE BOOK and 2 FREE gifts in the first shipment (approx. retail value of the gifts is $7.99 each). Along with my free book, I'll also get 2 additional mass-market paperback books. If I do not cancel, I will continue to receive three books a month for four additional months. My first four shipments will be billed at the discount price of $19.98 U.S./$25.98 CAN., plus $1.99 U.S./$3.99 CAN. for shipping and handling*. My fifth and final shipment will be billed at the discount price of $18.98 U.S./$23.98 CAN., plus $1.99 U.S./$3.99 CAN. for shipping and handling*. I understand that accepting the free books and gifts places me under no obligation to buy anything. I can always return a shipment and cancel at any time. My free books and gifts are mine to keep no matter what I decide.

☐ 260 HCN 5449   ☐ 460 HCN 5449

Name (please print)

Address   Apt. #

City   State/Province   Zip/Postal Code

Mail to the **Harlequin Reader Service**:
IN U.S.A.: P.O. Box 1341, Buffalo, NY. 14240-8531
IN CANADA: P.O. Box 603, Fort Erie, Ontario L2A 5X3

*Terms and prices subject to change without notice. Prices do not include sales taxes which will be charged (if applicable) based on your state or country of residence. Offer not valid in Quebec. All orders subject to approval. Credit or debit balances in a customer's account(s) may be offset by any other outstanding balance owed by or to the customer. Please allow 3 to 4 weeks for delivery. Offer available while quantities last. © 2020 Harlequin Enterprises ULC.

Your Privacy—Your information is being collected by Harlequin Enterprises ULC, operating as Harlequin Reader Service. To see how we collect and use this information visit https://corporate.harlequin.com/privacy-notice. From time to time we may also exchange your personal information with reputable third parties. If you wish to opt out of this sharing of your personal information, please visit www.readerservice.com/consumerschoice or call 1-800-873-8635. Notice to California Residents—Under California law, you have specific rights to control and access your data. For more information visit https://corporate.harlequin.com/california-privacy.

XMASR20

THE 2020 LOVE INSPIRED CHRISTMAS COLLECTION

Buy 3 and get 1 FREE!

This collection is guaranteed to provide you with many hours of cozy reading pleasure with uplifting romances that celebrate the joy of love at Christmas.

YES! Please send me **The 2020 Love Inspired Christmas Collection** in Larger Print. This collection begins with ONE FREE book and 2 FREE gifts (approx. retail value of the gifts is $7.99 each) in the first shipment. Along with my FREE book, I'll get another 3 Larger Print books! If I do not cancel, I will continue to receive four books a month for four more months. I'll pay just $20.97 U.S./$23.97 CAN., plus $1.99 U.S./$4.99 CAN. for shipping and handling per shipment.* I understand that accepting the free books and gifts places me under no obligation to buy anything. I can always return a shipment and cancel at any time. My free books and gifts are mine to keep no matter what I decide.

☐ 299 HCN 5494   ☐ 499 HCN 5494

Name (please print)

Address   Apt. #

City   State/Province   Zip/Postal Code

Mail to the **Harlequin Reader Service:**
IN U.S.A.: P.O. Box 1341, Buffalo, NY. 14240-8531
IN CANADA: P.O. Box 603, Fort Erie, Ontario L2A 5X3

Visit
ReaderService.com
Today!

As a valued member of the Harlequin Reader Service, you'll find these benefits and more at ReaderService.com:

- Try 2 free books from any series
- Access risk-free special offers
- View your account history & manage payments
- Browse the latest Bonus Bucks catalog

Don't miss out!

If you want to stay up-to-date on the latest at the Harlequin Reader Service and enjoy more content, make sure you've signed up for our monthly News & Notes email newsletter. Sign up online at ReaderService.com or by calling Customer Service at 1-800-873-8635.